Recent Titles by Christopher Nicole from Severn House

The Russian Sagas

THE SEEDS OF POWER
THE MASTERS
THE RED TIDE
THE RED GODS
THE SCARLET GENERATION
DEATH OF A TYRANT

The Arms of War Series

THE TRADE
SHADOWS IN THE SUN
GUNS IN THE DESSERT
PRELUDE TO WAR

TO ALL ETERNITY
THE QUEST
BE NOT AFRAID
THE SEARCH

RANSOM ISLAND

RANSOM ISLAND

Christopher Nicole

This first world edition published in Great Britain 2001 by
SEVERN HOUSE PUBLISHERS LTD of
9–15 High Street, Sutton, Surrey SM1 1DF.
This first world edition published in the USA 2002 by
SEVERN HOUSE PUBLISHERS INC of
595 Madison Avenue, New York, N.Y. 10022.

Copyright © 2001 by Christopher Nicole.

British Library Cataloguing in Publication Data

Nicole, Christopher, 1930–
    Ransom island
    1. Terrorism – Channel Islands – Guernsey – Fiction
    2. Suspense fiction
    I. Title
    823.9'14 [F]

ISBN 0-7278-5754-1

Typeset by Palimpsest Book Production Ltd.,
Polmont, Stirlingshire, Scotland.
Printed and bound in Great Britain by
MPG Books Ltd., Bodmin, Cornwall.

A man that studieth revenge keeps his own wounds green.

Francis Bacon

Prologue

The sergeant flicked his radio, attached to the collar of his lightweight black assault suit. 'One mile,' he said. The five men knew what they had to do: spread out, two crossing the road to the other side. In the darkness, with balaclava hoods over their heads, they were all but invisible. The landscape was empty – silent save for the whisper of the gentle breeze. Dust stirred; the few trees hardly swayed.

Then the silence was ended by the sound of engines. The sergeant checked his assault rifle with a click; his men followed suit. The two cars came round the corner, one close behind the other. They were travelling fairly fast, behind dipped headlights; but they had used this road often enough in the past.

The lead car was within a hundred feet of the black-clad men's position when a shot rang out, followed immediately by two more. The soldiers were using infra-red sights. The first bullet tore into the right-hand front tyre, causing the vehicle to swerve violently. The next two slammed into the engine, cutting into the metal. The car swung half round and seemed about to turn over, then settled back, only to teeter again as the second car slammed into it, despite having braked hard.

Now there was an entire fusillade of shots, all directed at the lead car. Two men, trying to get out, were hit and went down. The driver died behind the wheel. Three men were getting out of the second car, looking left and right, dazed by both the impact of the crash and the suddenness of the assault, uncertain where their enemies were.

'Up, up!' shouted the sergeant, in Arabic. 'Hands up, or die!'

The men hesitated, then dropped their weapons.

The sergeant ran forward, accompanied by his men. A fourth man was just getting out of the rear of the car.

The sergeant presented his rifle at his chest. 'You,' he said, 'are under arrest.'

Visitors

In early summer, La Villiaze airport on the Channel Island of Guernsey was as busy as usual. It was not a major airport, with only the one runway, but for all its reputation as an offshore banking centre and tax haven, Guernsey still relied heavily on its tourist trade. At this time of the year planes were landing or taking off every few minutes, while as always, since the sea warmed at a different rate from the air, the threat of fog portended total disruption, with hundreds of would-be visitors trapped at Gatwick, or Southampton, or Exeter, or Stansted – not to mention the continental links – and hundreds more were trapped in the small and inadequate terminal building.

This morning there was only a threat, so far; but Sophie Gallagher found herself growing impatient, and wandered across to the British Airways desk.

'Your Gatwick flight is late,' she remarked.

The uniformed clerk looked up with some pleasure: Sophie Gallagher was always worth looking at, with her yellow hair cut short to expose her somewhat pert features and her solid figure encased in a dark-blue trouser suit with a white shirt.

'Only a few minutes,' he said. 'We missed our slot.'

'BA missed its slot at Gatwick?' She was incredulous.

'Seems some of the passengers couldn't be found at take-off time. Bunch of Arabs.'

Sophie sighed. 'My clients.'

'Is that a fact? Whoever would've thought a bunch of Arabs would be coming to Guernsey for their holidays!'

'I have an idea they're actually coming to see if the banks in which they keep their money really exist,' Sophie suggested.

The tannoy crackled.

'Here they are now,' the clerk said.

Sophie picked up her card and returned to the exit from the Customs Hall. This involved a lengthy wait, and after a few minutes she was joined by one of the officers.

'I'm told this is your lot,' he said.

'Twenty of them, I believe,' Sophie said.

'Are they all right?'

'Eh?'

'Well . . . Arabs, you know. Shall we do them for drugs, concealed weapons . . . ?'

'Mini atom bombs?' she suggested. 'I have no idea, Phil. My business is to deliver them to the Guernsey Island Hotel. But . . . as they are booked in to the Guernsey Island, I would suggest they're fairly well-heeled.'

'Hm.' He withdrew, and a few moments later the passengers started filing through.

The Arabs were not the first out; Sophie wondered if they *were* being detained and their baggage searched. She was actually quite intrigued. Her minibus was very popular with hotels that had tour parties, and even more with the tour parties themselves; but she had never driven a posse of Arabs before. From Saudi Arabia, the handout had said. Those had to be amongst the wealthiest people in the world; but at any level lower than sheikh they didn't seem to travel abroad a lot.

She wondered if they would be wearing burnouses . . . was there such a word? But the emerging passengers did not seem to be either excited or alarmed by, or even very interested in, their travelling companions.

'Ah, you are the DriveRite representative?'

Sophie started. She had allowed herself to be distracted, while still displaying the *Saudi Group* card. Now she found

4

herself looking at a tall, very distinguished-looking man, with
aquiline features and a short, carefully trimmed beard. He
wore a dark-grey business suit with a quiet tie and a carnation
in his buttonhole.

Behind him were his party, equally well dressed and all
bearded.

'Oh, yes,' she said. 'Mr . . .'

'Al-Rakim,' he said.

'Oh, yes,' she said again. 'No problems?'

'Should there have been problems?'

'Oh, no,' she said. 'None.'

Why was she so suddenly breathless?

'You are to take us to the hotel,' al-Rakim remarked.

'Absolutely. Yes. My vehicle is outside. Your luggage . . . ?'

'We have it with us.'

Each man was carrying an identical small suitcase.

'I see. Well . . . if you'll follow me.'

She smiled, almost apologetically, at the girl behind the
Europcar desk, and walked through the automatic doors into
the afternoon sunlight, indicating the waiting minibus. The
door being open, the Arabs dutifully climbed the step and
filed inside. They were a remarkably silent lot; but then,
as she didn't know anything about Arabs, perhaps they
always were.

Al-Rakim sat in the front beside her. 'This is a very small
island,' he remarked.

'Yes. About twenty-nine square miles,' she said, starting
the engine and sliding into the traffic moving away from the
airport building forecourt.

'So, how many people live here?'

'Say sixty thousand.'

'That many? In twenty-nine square miles?'

'And it'll get around to doubling over the next few months,
as the season gets under way. I know lots of people say we're
overcrowded. I suppose we are. But people like living here.
It's a beautiful island . . .'

5

Now she swung on to the Forest Road, driving towards the capital town of St Peter Port.

'And there are other advantages,' al-Rakim suggested. 'Taxes, eh?'

'That helps.'

'There are no personal taxes in Saudi,' he said.

'Because of the oil, eh? Oh, there are taxes here, but we keep them low.'

'And you are British, eh?'

'In a manner of speaking.'

'Eh?' Again he was surprised. 'I was told you are British.'

'Well, we're members of the Great Britain group,' Sophie conceded. 'The British government handles all our foreign affairs, but we have total independence within the island.'

'Yet you are important to Britain,' he pressed.

Sophie giggled. 'I suppose a lot of British people keep their spare cash here. But then, so do a lot of Europeans.' She glanced at him. 'Even a few Arabs.'

'Of course.' He changed the subject. 'We would like to sightsee. You will take us sightseeing?'

'Ah . . . I'll have to check our diary. When did you have in mind?'

'Tomorrow morning.'

'Well, we'll see what we can do.'

She swung through the broad gates of the hotel, stopping outside the entrance lobby. 'Here we are.'

'Very impressive,' al-Rakim remarked, not entirely convincingly. Sophie supposed they had much grander hotels in Riyadh.

Her passengers filed off the minibus as silently as they had boarded, and porters hurried forward to assist them.

'Tomorrow,' al-Rakim said.

'I'll check and let them know at reception if I can make it. Bye.'

She waited while they entered the hotel and were checked in. Then she went in herself to sign the chit.

'Should be an interesting week,' the receptionist remarked. 'They have a list as long as my arm of food they don't eat, and food they do; and all minibars must be removed from their rooms.'

'They're only staying a week?' Sophie asked.

'That's their booking. Seems a long way to come for just a week, don't you think?'

'It's probably part of an "if today's Thursday it must be Holland" type tour. Seems they want me to drive them about tomorrow. I'll just check that out and let you know if I'm available.'

The receptionist grinned. 'Made a hit, eh?'

'I reckon they've never been driven by a woman before. Back in a mo.'

Sophie returned to the minibus, used the company radio.

'Tomorrow?' said the despatcher. 'Looks OK. Let me have a time, though. And don't forget this evening.'

'What about this evening?'

'You're picking up a party in Hauteville for a drive round the island. Eight sharp.'

'Oh, sh . . . oot. All right.' Damn and blast, she thought, and went back inside. 'Seems I can make it tomorrow,' she said. 'I wonder if you'd find out when they want to be picked up and phone it through.'

'Will do. Sophie, queen of the desert, eh?'

Sophie made a face and, returning to the minibus, looked at her watch: a quarter to three. At least she had the time for a bath and a lie-down.

She used her mobile. 'Hi. You free?'

'Briefly,' James Candish said. They had been partners for two years. James, an assistant harbourmaster, was becoming increasingly interested in marriage; he was in his early thirties and thinking of a family. Sophie, in her late twenties, wasn't sure she was ready for that commitment. It was not, in any event, a serious question as yet – they enjoyed each other's company too much.

'Just to say I'm working this evening,' Sophie said. 'Eight till ten type thing.'

'Fuck it,' he said. 'And I'm going to be late in.'

'Why?'

'There's some bloody big yacht due in this afternoon. It's coming up from the south-west, and we'll have to make sure it anchors in the right place. We're going to put it in Havelet Bay and hope the weather stays settled. Actually, it doesn't look too good.'

'You mean she's too big for the harbour?'

'If we want to use it for anything else. She's a hundred metres overall. That's well over three hundred feet. Oh, we'll squeeze her in if we have to. But she's better anchored off. Bunch of bloody Arabs.'

'What did you say?' Sophie asked.

'She belongs to some oil-rich sheikh. Ali ibn Kasim al-Fuad. I don't know if he's on board, mind. But her crew is mainly Arab.'

'Now that is odd,' Sophie said.

'What?'

'My pick-up this afternoon was an Arab group.'

'So?'

'Well, isn't it odd? I've never picked up an Arab group before. I don't ever remember an Arab group in Guernsey before. And now all of a sudden we have both my group and an Arab yacht arriving on the same day. I thought the Med was the happy hunting ground of wealthy Arabs.'

'Well, if they're shifting up here it won't do the island's economy any harm,' James said. 'What are your plans for dinner? Like I said, I'm not going to be in till past seven, I shouldn't think.'

'And I'm out at half past, so I'll have eaten. I'll leave yours in the oven. See if you can stay awake until ten.'

Ships that pass in the night, she thought, as she drove out of the hotel grounds. Ships! Arab ships. But as James had said, the island had to benefit from an influx of big spenders.

8

*   *   *

'I have her,' said the harbour watch.

James Candish picked up his binoculars and climbed the steps on to the top of the office building to look out past the pier at the southern reaches of the Little Russel Channel that separated Guernsey from its satellites of Herm and Jethou. He was a tall, lanky man with the slim hips and wide shoulders of someone who enjoyed his sport; his features were strong rather than handsome, his dark hair was cut short. He levelled the glasses at the large motor yacht that was just coming into sight round St Martin's Point. She was a real ocean-going job, the short of ship that could probably cross the Atlantic, to and fro, without refuelling. She even had her blue-jacketed crew lined up on the foredeck as if she were a warship.

'I assume she has adequate charts?' he said into his mobile.

'So she says,' the watch replied. 'I've given her the cross references for a safe anchorage.'

'How safe is it? Isn't there a front coming up? A big one?'

'Yes, there is. But not until tomorrow night. She'll be gone by then, I should think.'

'Suppose she isn't?'

'Then I suppose we'll have to squeeze her in. But only until the storm is past, mind.'

Jim returned downstairs. 'I think I'll go out and have a look at this super gin palace,' he told his boss.

The harbourmaster grinned. 'If she really is an Arab ship, you won't find much gin, I shouldn't think.'

James joined the Customs officer on the harbour launch, and they moved out through the pierheads as the big yacht approached, her diesels a low rumble across the evening. She came into position just inside and to the south of the bulk of Castle Cornet, the ancient fortress that dominated the harbour, and her anchor was let go. Her companion ladder was dropped and secured as the launch came alongside, while James noted that, wealthy Arab or not, her owner had his ship registered in Panama; the red-and-white quartered flag drooping lazily from the stern. Her name was *Gloriosa*.

He followed the Customs officer up the ladder. At the top two sailors and an officer waited for them. As they were all swarthy, James assumed they were Arabs; but the officer at least spoke perfect English.

'If you will come up to the bridge, gentlemen?'

They followed him up ladders, passing several other crewmen on the way. There was no sign of any passengers.

'Gentlemen.' The captain waited on the bridge, wearing a white uniform like his officer. Unlike his officer, however, he had a ruddy complexion and spoke with an American accent: 'John Honeylee, at your service.'

'Douglas Orr,' the Customs officer said. 'Assistant Harbourmaster James Candish.'

Honeylee shook hands. 'Come through.'

He led them into the chartroom-cum-office just behind the bridge, James pausing for a moment to glance enviously at the elaborate navigational equipment. He owned a twenty-two-foot sloop in which he and Sophie raced and occasionally weekended in Sark, but had always dreamed of something bigger and more sophisticated. Not that there was any possibility of his ever having something like this.

'Please sit down.' The captain indicated the leather armchairs bolted to the deck, and he himself sat behind his desk.

'Formalities.' Orr handed over the various forms, and Honeylee passed them to the waiting officer, who sat down and began filling them out.

'Do you require a crew list?' Honeylee asked.

'No, that's not necessary. How many do you have?'

'Forty-one.' Honeylee smiled at the Guernseymen's expressions. 'A large percentage are stewards and cooks. Sheikh al-Fuad is very interested in food.'

'But not wine,' James suggested.

'No, Mr Candish. Not wine.'

'So I assume you have no bonded stores?'

'None.'

'And your passengers are . . . ?'

'We have eight passengers at the moment.'

'The sheikh and his family?'

'No, no. These are friends of the sheikh, to whom he has lent the yacht for this cruise.'

'Very good. Do they have any pets? Animals?'

'One of the ladies has a little dog.'

'Ah. You understand that it is not allowed ashore.'

'I understand.' Another quick smile. 'But the lady is, I assume.'

'Of course. Without dog.'

'I will explain it to her.'

'Thank you. Now, I must ask you this: have you any drugs?'

'We have a doctor. I am sure he has drugs.'

'I meant illegal drugs, for the use of either your crew or your passengers.'

'My crew do not use illegal drugs, Mr Orr. I really cannot answer for my passengers.'

'I'm afraid you will have to, sir. Listed drugs without prescription are illegal in Guernsey. Possession can lead to a fine, or imprisonment, or even, supposing they are discovered in sufficient quantity and it was proved that you, or your passengers, were attempting to sell them, the confiscation of the ship.'

The captain gave one of his bleak smiles. 'My passengers do not need to peddle drugs, Mr Orr.'

'I still think you should mention it to them, sir. It would be best for all if, when they come ashore, they leave any illegal substances behind.'

'I will mention it to them.'

'Now, lastly, firearms?'

Honeylee nodded. 'Of course. This is a valuable ship.'

'What, exactly?'

11

Honeylee nodded to the officer, who got up and unlocked a fitted bulkhead cupboard at the rear of the cabin. Here were four rifles and two shotguns, as well as two automatic pistols; all the weapons were carefully arranged, clipped to the inner board.

'Quite an arsenal,' James remarked. 'What make are those rifles?'

'They are Minimis.'

'Fully automatic?'

'Their use as such is optional; but in addition to the normal box of twenty-five they can be belt fed and then are almost machine guns.'

'And you really need those?'

'Hopefully not in Guernsey, Mr Candish; but in the Mediterranean – well, it pays to be safe.'

'I will have to ask you for the key during your visit,' James said.

Honeylee raised his eyebrows.

'Those weapons are illegal in Guernsey,' James explained.

'They are licensed.'

'Not in Guernsey, sir. I'm sorry. I will take the key, and you may collect it when you are ready to sail.'

Honeylee hesitated, then shrugged. 'As you wish.'

'How long were you planning to stay, sir?' Orr asked.

'Until my passengers are bored, and wish to move on. I do not suppose it will be very long.'

'Touché,' James remarked, as the launch took them back into the harbour. 'One supposes they'll be bored in twenty-four hours.'

'Let's hope so,' Orr remarked.

'Aren't you happy with our visitors?'

'I'm never happy with ships carrying enough weaponry to start a small war, and pets, *and* drugs.'

'You reckon?'

'I'd put money on it. Well, they've been warned.'

James grinned. 'What are you going to do? Search the ladies as they come ashore?'

'Just keep an eye on things. And alert the police to do the same.'

They had just come up to the pierheads. James looked back at the yacht. 'You'd better do it pronto. I think they're aiming for a night on the town.'

Orr also looked back, to watch the yacht's launch being swung out and lowered. 'Come on,' he said to his coxswain. 'Let's move it.'

Sophie felt better for her hot bath. She wished she could have a drink, but that would have to wait until she had finished driving her tourists about.

She ate a TV dinner, put another in the oven for James, and heard him clumping up the stairs.

'So how was *your* day?'

He kissed her, poured himself a short Scotch.

'Lucky for some,' she commented.

He sat down, stretched out his legs. 'That yacht is really something. I didn't get to see much of it, but I'd bet there's probably a swimming pool tucked away below decks.'

'Green, green, green.'

'You bet. I mean, how do some people get to have that kind of money? I'm damned sure the old sheikh didn't work for it. And he's not even on it – just a bunch of friends out for a jolly. Some jolly!'

'And lots of beautiful birds to keep them company?'

'I wasn't permitted to find out; but one of them has a pet poodle or something. Dougie Orr is having kittens in case she decides to bring it ashore.'

'What'll he do?'

'He'll have to slap it in quarantine. And with people of this calibre, that will probably cause a diplomatic incident.'

'Well, like I said, your dinner's in the oven, and I should be back around ten thirty.'

She hurried off, collected her passengers, and drove them round the island. They were a jolly, middle-aged, bantering crowd, amused by everything she had to tell them. It was a splendid evening, still fully light, as they were coming up to the longest day, as she swung the minibus down the twisting, scenic route of Le Val de Terres to emerge on to the Havelet seafront.

'Wow!' someone remarked behind her. 'What is that?'

'I believe it belongs to an Arab sheikh,' Sophie said.

'Looks like a million dollars.'

'I think you're short of a zero or two,' Sophie suggested, driving slowly through the crowds of people who had gathered to look at the big yacht.

She turned up the steep, narrow hill into Hauteville, dropped her passengers at their hotel, and then on an impulse made the one-way circuit to turn back down to the front. It was quite dark now, and the yacht was a blaze of light as it rode to the tide. Sophie drove slowly along the esplanade, past the shops and banks on her left, the crowded visitors' marina to her right. There was a lot of traffic, and even more people, drifting to and fro across the road. The lights changed from green to red as she reached the foot of the pier steps, and she braked and waited, looking left and right, as she knew it was going to be a good minute before she could move again . . . and found herself gazing at al-Rakim, standing on the marina side of the road, speaking with a man wearing the white uniform of a ship's officer.

Al-Rakim saw Sophie looking at him, and immediately turned his back, while the officer, also immediately, walked away from him. The lights changed and, releasing the brake, Sophie allowed the minibus to slide forward. Then she turned up St Julian's Avenue towards her flat, situated just off the Grange.

Why was she perturbed? Why should al-Rakim not be talking to someone? Save that he had said this was his first visit to Guernsey, and therefore he did not *know* anyone.

14

Anyone who lived here. Therefore the officer had to be off a ship, and the only ship in tonight was the yacht. Therefore . . .

Suddenly she knew she was being paranoiac. There was no earthly reason why there should be anything suspicious about al-Rakim talking with an officer from the yacht. So they were both Arabs – what was wrong with that? Indeed, it made more sense than if he had been talking with a Guernseyman.

It was just that there had been so much talk in the last few weeks about Arab revenge for that kidnapping of a terrorist leader by the SAS. But how could it possibly be anything to do with Guernsey? Of all the countries in the world, Guernsey – the whole Channel Islands – had to be about the most terrorist-free.

She parked the minibus, went upstairs to the flat, let herself in. The remains of James's dinner were, predictably, scattered about the table and, equally predictably, even though it was only just past eleven owing to her detour, James himself was fast asleep, on his back, snoring faintly.

We could just as well be married, she thought, as she got in beside him.

'What is the problem?' Salim spoke English even though, as he moved away from the people waiting to cross at the light and stood at the edge of the dock looking down at the moored yachts, he did not suppose he could be overheard. But to speak Arabic might, if he *was* overheard, attract attention.

Al-Rakim moved back to stand at his side. 'That minibus. It was the same as we used this afternoon. And the driver looked directly at me.'

'Is that important?'

'Only that she saw me speaking with you.'

'But surely she cannot know who I am?'

'She can guess who you are, because of the uniform. You should not have worn it.'

'It is not important. So this woman knows you for an Arab tourist. In this context I am also an Arab tourist.'

'It is very bad luck that she should happen along like that. She told me there are sixty thousand people living on this island. Sixty thousand! And it had to be her drive by.'

'It is still not important. Who is she, the chief of police? She is a bus-driver. But . . . sixty thousand? That is what she said?'

'Does this frighten you?' al-Rakim asked.

'Not at all. It makes them the more vulnerable. Now, you have the positions marked?'

'On the map. I still have to identify them. But I shall start on this tomorrow.' Al-Rakim gave a somewhat sour grin. 'This woman will show me.'

'Eh?'

'She is taking us on a tour of the island. I will tell her what I wish to see.'

'Be careful you do not make her suspicious.'

'You have just said she is not important.'

'In the context of you and me meeting, no. But the sighting of these positions . . . they must be integrated with others of tourist interest.'

'That will not be a problem.'

'Good. How long will you need?'

'Tomorrow. When can you let us have the weapons?'

'Not until we are ready to strike. But it will be simple. There is a front coming up: strong winds and big seas. We will represent that it is too dangerous for us to remain anchored offshore, and they will have to allow us into the harbour. We will lie alongside. Tomorrow night, al-Rakim. Find out everything you need to know by then, and have your people ready. Tomorrow night.'

He faded into the darkness.

'This fellow ibn Hassan,' said Colonel Gracey.

General Peart leaned back in his chair, stroking his moustache, as he was wont to do. 'Not some more threats?'

'No, no, sir.' Gracey was young, enthusiastic, efficient and ambitious. He also slightly worried Peart. Chaps like this were all very well, and even desirable, when there was a war on. In peacetime one was never sure what the beggars were going to be up to next.

'Threats like those are never to be taken too seriously,' Peart pointed out.

Gracey cleared his throat. He knew his superior did not altogether trust his judgement, but for his part he entirely distrusted Peart's confident assumption that everything would always turn out the way he, and therefore the British government and army, felt that it should. 'As you instructed, sir, before bringing him to trial at The Hague, we have been following various lines of investigation, seeking additional evidence that could be used against him.'

'Very good. And what have you found out?'

'Something we did not know before. That he has a half-brother.'

'Well, that's fairly common in the Arab world, isn't it? All those wives.' Peart, who had only ever had the one, rolled his eyes.

'Yes, sir. The point is, this half-brother – his name is Ali ibn Kasim al-Fuad – is a multimillionaire.'

'Quite a few of these Arab chappies are,' Peart pointed out. 'All that oil.'

'Quite so, sir. However, I think, in all the circumstances, that it would pay us to keep an eye on this fellow.'

'Oh, quite. Absolutely. Do we know where he is now?'

'No, sir, we do not. However, we do know where his yacht is.'

'His yacht?'

'He has a yacht, sir. An ocean-going vessel that rather makes the old *Britannia* look like a tramp steamer.'

'Does it, indeed? And where is this yacht now? Not steaming up the Thames, I hope.'

'No, sir. It is presently anchored in the roads off Guernsey.'

'Guernsey?'

'It is an island, sir. In the Channel. But it happens to be British.'

'I know where Guernsey is, Gracey. I honeymooned there. And I can tell you that if this sheikh fellow is anchored there, it is the best possible place for him to be. There is absolutely nothing – I repeat, nothing – on the island of Guernsey that is of the least interest or importance to anyone in Great Britain, or anyone else in the world.'

'Except, perhaps, to the people living there,' Gracey suggested.

The Yacht

'So, you think I'm paranoid,' Sophie said, breaking her egg with quite unnecessary violence.

James poured coffee. 'No, I do not think you are paranoid,' he said. 'Just . . . well . . .'

'Paranoid.'

'I think you have a racist thing about Arabs.'

'I do not,' she said angrily.

'How many do you actually know?'

'Well . . . twenty, for a start.' She could not help laughing. 'I'm taking them driving this morning.'

'Right. Well, take your mobile, and if they start raping you, give me a call.'

'What will you do?' She was genuinely interested.

'Tell them to behave themselves,' he suggested.

'You are a bastard,' she remarked.

But actually, she reflected as her party left the hotel lobby and filed into the minibus, she had never in her life had such a well-behaved bunch. It was a warm June morning, yet every man wore blazer, grey flannel trousers, white shirt buttoned to the neck, and a tie. The ties were matching, indicating that they were perhaps all members of the same cricket club.

Did they play cricket in Saudi? Sharjah, certainly.

Each man also wore a fresh red carnation in his buttonhole.

'A beautiful day.' Al-Rakim sat beside her in the front, as before.

'The forecast is for rain later, and strong winds,' she remarked.

'Ah. Is this a serious matter?'

'It's only a nuisance, here on shore. It'll be pretty uncomfortable for that big yacht out in Havelet Bay.'

'No doubt the authorities would allow her to shelter, if the sea got very rough.'

She was tempted to make a reference to last night, but decided against it; he probably hadn't seen her, anyway. 'I'm sure they would. Now, I thought we'd take a drive around the coast, look at the sea, and the beaches, and the rocks . . .'

'We are more interested in your infrastructure. With a view to investment, you understand.'

'Do you know, Mr al-Rakim, I have never been absolutely sure what infrastructure means. What exactly did you wish to look at?'

'Well, for instance, how many electricity generating plants do you have?'

'Just the one.'

'Is that so. One plant does for the entire island.'

Sophie engaged gear and drove out of the hotel grounds. 'Like I said, it's a small island, Mr al-Rakim. Actually, we get our electricity from France, but it is distributed from the one plant.'

'We should like to see this power station,' al-Rakim said.

'No problem. It's actually in St Sampson's – that's our port in the north. That's on our drive round the island. I'm not sure they'll allow you inside, though. Unless you apply for permission.'

'We just wish to look at the outside. You are certain that this one generating plant provides power for the entire island?'

'Yes,' Sophie said, taking the road to the coast.

'Then, if this plant were to cease to function, the island would be entirely cut off from the outside world?'

Sophie giggled. 'Happens regularly. No, I'm joking. But

20

it has happened in the past. Can you imagine what it does to the finance industry? They blow their minds.'

'I can understand that. But surely they have back-up generators? What about the airport? That must have a back-up system for its traffic control, in the event of a mains failure.'

'I don't really know about that,' Sophie said. 'I suppose they do have an emergency generator. But I shouldn't think any of the finance houses do.'

'But they can still telephone out, can they not? I presume they all have mobiles?'

'Have you tried to run a finance system by telephone, without a computerised back-up? All you can really do is shout help.'

'I see. Yes. However, I would still like to see the central telephone exchange.'

'Ah . . . right. I can show you that. It's just a building, mind.'

'Of course. Now let me see . . . where does the Governor General live?'

'We don't have a governor general.'

'But you are a province of Great Britain. All provinces of Great Britain have a governor general.'

'We are not a province of Great Britain.'

'Did you not say, yesterday . . . ?'

'I said we were a part of the Great Britain Group. The British Isles. We are actually a bailiwick.'

'Bailiwick? I do not know this word.'

'Well, in its simplest form, it means a place ruled by a bailiff. Ours is a more complicated situation.'

'Tell me about it.'

'Well . . . it's a bit of a history lesson, really. Have you ever heard of William the Conqueror?'

'Certainly.'

'Well, the Channel Islands were part of the Duchy of Normandy before William the Conqueror invaded England.

So they were his personal possessions, you might say. Then they became rather forgotten, and while the English government went through several changes to arrive at its present form, and Normandy was eventually reclaimed by the French, the islands just existed as they had always done, personal possessions of the English crown. Down to not so very long ago, the society was virtually feudal. So like I said, yesterday, we are independent, within our own shores, while the British government handles our overseas relations.'

'Then you are saying you are ruled by the Queen.'

'Well . . . I suppose we all are, figuratively speaking. She has her own representative here in Guernsey. But like the Queen herself, he doesn't have any political power. In so far as anyone does, that's our Bailiff. He runs the government – we call them the States – and he's our chief justice, as well, and – well, he's the big wheel.'

'I understand. I would like to see where he lives.'

'It's just a house, you know. Not a palace.'

'Nevertheless, you will show it to me, please.'

'If that's what you want; but I have no idea where he lives. I would have to look it up in a phone book, and then in Perry's guide map. The Lieutenant Governor, now – he lives in a sort of palace.'

'You will show us this also, please?'

'Surely.'

'I presume these houses, or palaces, are guarded?'

'Good heavens, no,' Sophie said. 'We don't have things like armed guards in Guernsey.'

They emerged on to the front, overlooking the Little Russel. The tide was flowing swiftly to the north, but the sea itself was calm.

'You said there is supposed to be bad weather coming,' al-Rakim remarked, 'but I do not see it.'

'It'll be here,' Shirley promised him. 'See those wisps of cloud in the sky? That's wind.'

'Ah.' He seemed pleased, which she thought odd, if he was a friend of the yacht captain.

She swung north towards St Sampson's.

'So,' he said, 'this Bailiff – he is the effective governor of the island.'

'I wouldn't put it quite like that.'

'But, for example, he commands your armed services.'

'We don't have any armed services.'

'I have been told this,' al-Rakim agreed. 'But I find it hard to believe. What would you do if you were invaded?'

'Who's going to invade Guernsey?'

'It is a hypothetical question. In the Middle East, there is always a risk of being invaded by someone.'

'Well, this isn't the Middle East, thank God.'

'But suppose it did happen? What would you do?'

'Well, I suppose we would telephone or radio England, and they'd send over warships and troops.'

'But they could not possibly get here for some hours.'

'Well, like you said, it is a hypothetical question.' She turned on to Bulwer Avenue, still close to the sea, but now it was hidden by the huge storage tanks.

'What are those?' al-Rakim asked.

'Our fuel supplies. Oil and gas storage.'

'All together in one place. How very convenient.'

'Could be dangerous, if you ask me.'

'But I am sure they are well guarded?'

'Not so far as I know. We're lucky here in Guernsey: we don't have people running around blowing things up. I suppose you do, in the Middle East.'

'Sadly, that is so. But tell me, Miss Gallagher, you must have *some* means of keeping order here. What about a police force?'

'Oh, we have a police force; but it's not actually there to keep order, except maybe on the front on a Friday night. It copes mainly with traffic offences.'

'But, surely *they* have arms?'

'Do you know, that's something else I don't really know about; but they must have, because they use the rifle range.'

'Ah! You have a rifle range. For the use of the police.'

'And the Elizabeth College cadets.'

'Explain, please?'

'Our local public school. It has a cadet force, and they use the range as well.'

'Ah. Yes. So they have guns.'

'Some.'

'And where do they keep these guns? At their homes?'

'Good Lord, no. The guns are kept under lock and key at the College.'

'Very wise. Can you show me this college?'

'Surely. It's in town.'

'And the police station?'

'If you wish to see it. There's the electricity station.'

She had driven round the harbour and was crossing what was still known as The Bridge, a busy street whose name dated back a couple of hundred years to a time when it really had been a bridge, linking the two halves of the then separate islands of Guernsey and The Vale.

'Slowly, please,' al-Rakim requested. 'How does one get in?'

'The entrance is down that side street there. But as I said, I don't think they'll let you in just to sightsee.'

'Very good. Now, Miss Gallagher, let us look at the rest of this beautiful island of yours.'

'Here comes the rain,' said the harbourmaster. 'Have you seen the latest forecast, James?'

'Yes. It doesn't sound too good. Sixty-mile-an-hour winds from the south-west.'

'I was thinking of your friend out there.'

'Have we room?'

'Not out at the White Rock, and that's for sure. He'll have to come right in, and go alongside the Cambridge Pier.'

'Shoot,' James said. 'I wonder what he draws. Anyway, it'll only be practical at high water. That is . . .' He looked at the tables pinned to the wall above his desk. '. . . between four and five this afternoon.'

It was just noon.

'And he'll have to take the ground overnight,' the harbour-master pointed out. 'You think they have any idea of how to do that?'

'I shouldn't think so. We'll have to show them.' He telephoned the harbour watch.

'Have you had any communication from *Gloriosa*?'

'Nothing yet, James. Her people came ashore this morning, and they're just heading back. Some of them, anyway. I can see their launch. I think maybe the passengers elected to lunch ashore rather than get wet.'

'Well, she can't stay where she is with a southerly blow coming. You'd better call her, Brian, and tell her we can berth her in the harbour until the blow is past.'

'Oh, yes? Where?'

'The skipper says she can go inside the Cambridge berth.'

'But . . .'

'I know. She'll have to take the ground. She'll be better off doing that than riding a gale in the midst of all those rocks.'

'Do you think they can handle it?'

'I'm going to find out. Let me have a harbour launch at the outer steps in fifteen minutes, will you?'

'You'll get wet,' Brian remarked.

James called Customs. 'Oh, hello, Dougie. I thought I should let you know that we're going to have to bring that Arab yacht into the harbour. It's going to be a foul night.'

'Damn and blast and shit,' Dougie remarked. 'What about that bloody dog?'

'They'll just have to keep it below decks. The ship is big enough. I'm going out to them now. I'll read them the Riot Act. Unless you want to come along and do it yourself.'

'In this rain? I'm sure you'll manage.'

25

James made a face and replaced the phone. Then he pulled on his oilskins and boots, adjusted the cover for his cap.

'And the best of luck,' the harbourmaster said.

The rain was now falling quite hard, but as yet there was little wind; the sea remained calm, but there was a heavy swell coming round St Martin's Point. The small launch rose and fell but shipped no water as it passed through the pierheads, Brian looking down on them with a sympathetic smile. They rounded the southern pier and approached the yacht; *Gloriosa* was rolling in the swell, but as yet only slightly.

'Ahoy!' James bellowed. 'Harbour Office. Permission to come aboard.'

Three men hurried to the top of the ladder, waited while the launch nosed up to it. James timed his move to coincide with the top of the swell, and stepped on to the platform.

'Half an hour,' he told the coxswain, and went up the ladder. 'Captain Honeylee aboard?'

'On the bridge, sir,' said the English-speaking officer.

James gazed at him. Was this the chap Sophie thought she had seen speaking to her tour leader? He didn't suppose he could ask him.

He followed the officer forward to the ladder to the bridge, and checked as one of the saloon doors opened and a woman came out. To James's surprise she was brown-haired and fair-skinned, dressed in very tight-fitting pants and blouse, which indicated a full figure, and had bold features.

She was also carrying a small dog of the terrier variety.

'Have you come to arrest me, or my dog?' she enquired, her voice a low contralto, her English perfect.

'I hope neither. James Candish, Assistant Harbourmaster.'

'My name is Jeannette,' she said, and set the dog on the deck. He immediately scuttled to the scuppers; as the yacht had bulwarks, there was no risk of his going overboard. 'When is this rolling going to stop?'

'For you, hopefully, very soon. You'll excuse me.'

He followed the officer up the steps. 'I assume she is not a member of the crew,' he suggested.

'No, she is not,' was the short answer.

Honeylee was waiting on the bridge. 'I don't care much for our position,' he remarked.

'Nor do we,' James agreed. 'We're preparing a berth for you in the harbour.'

'That's good of you, old man. How soon can we move?'

'I'm afraid not for another three or four hours. It's the tide, you see. To get you alongside we'll need the top of the tide.'

Honeylee frowned. 'Your whole harbour dries?'

'No, no. Only the inner half. But the outer berths are reserved for our ferries to the mainland, and to France.'

'But if you put us on a drying berth . . .'

'You'll dry out at half-tide. Don't worry; we'll make sure you don't fall over or anything like that. I assume your hull is fairly flat-bottomed?'

'Yes. But she has never taken the ground before.'

'Just about all ships using our harbours, whether here or St Sampson's, dry out at low tide,' James said. 'Like I said, we know how to cope.'

'I don't like it,' Honeylee said.

'Listen: you'll be absolutely safe. Out here, you won't be, with the wind and sea coming up from the south.'

'I see. Very well, we must place ourselves in your hands, Mr Candish. Tell me what we must do.'

'Just prepare to move, at four o'clock this afternoon. I'll come out again then, with a pilot, and we'll take you in.'

'Thank you. You understand this is a new experience for me.'

'I do. Oh, there's one thing more.' He stood at the sloping bridge windows, looking down on to the foredeck, where the tightly clad Jeannette was walking, somewhat uncertainly in the roll, with her dog. 'Once you're alongside, the dog must stay below.'

'You're saying it can't use the deck?'

'Not alongside. You must have facilities below. I mean, what happens in a seaway? It can't come on deck then, surely.'

'Miss Aldridge won't like it.'

'She'll have to like it. Is she important?'

'Very. It's her party. She's a close friend of the sheikh's, and these are her friends.'

'I get the message,' James said. 'But I'm afraid she'll just have to put up with it.'

'Yeah, well, I'll have a word with her. What time did you say you'd be back?'

'Four o'clock. The tide will be right then.'

James slid down the ladder and then took the accommodation ladder back to the harbour launch, which came back alongside the platform for him.

Honeylee leaned on the bridge wing to watch him go. Salim joined him.

'Any problem?'

'None at all.' Honeylee grinned. 'They couldn't be more co-operative.' He went down the ladder to the foredeck. 'We're going in,' he told Jeannette Aldridge. 'Just as we planned.'

'Great. When?'

'Four o'clock this afternoon. But the harbour people want your dog locked up. Seems if he's on deck he's breaking the quarantine laws.'

'Fucking stupid people,' she growled. 'He's had all his shots.'

'Well, they have their laws, I guess.' He grinned. 'Never mind, ma'am. This time tomorrow you can make your own laws.'

Even in oilskins James was thoroughly wet by the time he regained the harbour. He had a brief sandwich-and-coffee lunch in the cafeteria along the dock from the office, returning just before two. Sophie had been on the Ansafone.

28

He called her at the flat. 'It's a good afternoon for being in bed,' she remarked.

The wind was getting up, now, and the rain was still driving down. 'Lucky for some. You mean you're off duty this afternoon?'

'So who wants to go driving in the rain? Or boating. What time will you be in?'

'It may be a little late.'

'Not again.'

'I'm afraid so. We have this bloody yacht on our hands. She can't stay where she is in a southerly gale. Quite apart from being damned uncomfortable if she were to drag her anchor, she'd be on the rocks in no time. So we're bringing her in at high tide. Four o'clock.'

'That's not late.'

'It may take a little while. The crew have no experience of big tidal waters. Not only do we have to get her in, but we have to show them how to moor her up so that she sits snug against the dock when she settles. I have a suspicion that someone is going to have to stay with them until she does settle, to reassure them she's safe. That'll be after six going on seven.'

'Shoot,' she commented. 'Then there'll be a few drinks to make everybody happy . . .'

'No way,' he said. 'She's Arab, remember? Dry as a bone, alcohol-wise.'

'Oh, yes,' she agreed. 'Arab!'

'How did you get on with yours, this morning?'

'Very well. They even gave me a great big tip.'

'So what's the reservation? I can tell there is one, from your voice.'

'Well . . . they really are the oddest people. I showed them all the west coast beaches – you know, Grand Rocques, and Cobo, and Vazon, and Rocquaine – and they really were no more than politely interested. What they wanted to see was the centres of what they called our infrastructure: the

29

electricity-generating plant, the police station, the telephone exchange, Government House . . . I suppose you'll accuse me of being paranoid again, but . . .'

'What?'

'I don't know. It sounded more like the list of places to be bombed in an attack than an ordinary sightseeing trip. They even wanted to be shown where the Bailiff lives.'

'It does sound odd,' he agreed.

'And now, that ship . . .'

'She can't be part of anything sinister. Or if she is, her plans have been totally disrupted by this weather. If she planned to stay anchored off . . .'

'Did she?'

'Well, that was where she was put . . .'

'On a temporary basis. She's an ocean-going yacht, James. That means she has an ocean-going crew. Didn't you tell me she has dream controls and instruments? That has to include a weatherfax. She has to have known there was weather coming when she put in here. But she meekly allows herself to be anchored offshore in an exposed bay, from the south-west. Don't you think her officers knew that you'd have to take her into the harbour when the weather arrived?'

James stroked his chin.

'And then, my al-Rakim meeting up with the officer last night? Don't you think they could have been co-ordinating plans?'

'Plans to do what?'

'Well . . . to blow up things.'

'With what in mind?'

'Well . . . something to do with this terrorist chief who's being held in London.'

'Tell me how blowing up something in Guernsey – even the main generating plant – can possibly help this chap in London? And how could they hope to get away with it? They'd have the entire Royal Navy breathing down their necks, not to mention the air force, the moment they tried to leave.'

'Oh . . . brrr. I still think we should *do* something.'

'What?'

'Well . . . Jack Harding.'

'Eh?'

'Well, he's a friend, isn't he? You play tennis with him. He's a member of the yacht club. *And* he's a member of the States. Why don't you mention it to him?'

'He'd laugh.'

'Let him laugh. But make him listen.'

'With what in mind?'

'Well . . . he's on the Police Committee, isn't he? What about putting a police patrol on the dock where this yacht is going to be berthed, to make sure no one leaves her? Or goes on board,' she added, thinking of her tour party.

'He couldn't do that.'

'Why not?'

'Well . . . look, these people have broken no laws. They're very wealthy tourists who are probably buying up half St Peter Port right this moment. There is no way we can put them under some kind of preventive restraint without proof that they're up to no good. Even if we did have proof, I'm not sure we'd be entitled to do anything about it until after they'd actually committed a crime.'

'You mean until after the electricity-generating plant has been blown up.'

'Oh, for heaven's sake, Sophie. Listen: I'll be back about seven thirty.' He hung up. When Sophie got a bee in her bonnet she was very difficult to restrain. What was worse, when she became agitated, he also became agitated.

There was nothing these people could possibly do to upset the even tenor of Guernsey life. One immediately thought of something like a gigantic robbery, of banks or jewellery stores; but that was Guernsey's great asset: it was virtually impossible to get off in a hurry – certainly by yacht, which might make twenty knots. As he had told Sophie, they'd have the Navy and the RAF round their necks before they could reach Ushant. So . . . but suppose she was right. Suppose she *could* be right.

He tried to do some paperwork, but found himself looking again and again at his watch as the afternoon drifted by. Harbourmaster Harrison came in.

'Grim, out there. I reckon we're just going to get that ship inside in time. The seas are starting to build.'

'Hm,' James said, portraying massive calm. 'Maybe I'd better go out now; otherwise I might not make it.'

'That's not a bad idea. Who're you taking?'

'Clarrie Goodman. I'll just wake him up.'

He called the pilots. 'Seas are getting up, Clarrie. I've an idea we'd better get out there now.'

'Good thinking,' Goodman said. 'Ten minutes?'

'I'm on my way.'

'I'll make sure that berth is clear and ready,' Harrison said. 'But there won't be water for another hour.'

'I'll bear that in mind.' James called the watch. 'Will you get on to the yacht and tell them the pilot and I are on our way. We can't bring them in yet, but we want to be sure of getting aboard without being swamped.'

'Will do, James.'

James put on his oilskins and boots and went down on to the dock. The rain was driving now, propelled by the wind, which he reckoned was a good thirty knots. Outside the harbour mouth whitecaps were beginning to show.

He waited at the top of the steps as Goodman and another pilot rowed out to the pilot boat and clambered aboard.

'Excuse me, please.'

James turned to look at the young woman who stood at his elbow. She was definitely of Middle Eastern extraction, he reckoned. So were the four people standing behind her, wrapped up in raincoats and an odd assortment of hats, looking very damp.

'Can I help you?'

'We are from the yacht,' the woman explained. 'We have been shopping.'

That was apparent from the large number of paper bags they were carrying.

'We are supposed to be returning, now; but the launch is not here. Is there some means of contacting the ship, and asking why they have not come for us?'

'We can reach the ship by radio,' James said; 'but the reason the launch has not come in for you is that the ship herself is coming in.'

'Coming in here?' asked one of the men.

'That's right. We are berthing her in the harbour while this storm lasts. She'll be alongside about half past four. So, if you'd like to get yourselves a cup of tea in that cafeteria over there, you'll be aboard in another hour or so.'

'I see.' The woman watched the pilot cutter nosing its way in to the steps. 'But you are going out to her?'

James nodded. 'We're going to con her in.'

'Then can we not come with you, now?'

'I don't think it would be a good idea,' James said. 'This boat isn't really big enough for seven people, and it's going to be a rough ride. Believe me, you'll be better off here.'

She looked as if she would have argued, but the pilot boat was alongside, and James left them to go down the steps. Even in the harbour there was now a swell, and the little launch was rising and falling, but James stepped aboard without difficulty, and Clarke, the other pilot, backed off before turning for the harbour mouth.

It was a truly bleak afternoon. To the west the houses, shops, banks and restaurants of St Peter Port were already showing lights, although technically it was broad daylight; but the clouds were low and dark. The mass of the town, rising up the hillside above the harbour, sheltered it from the worst of the south-westerly wind, but even so the halyards on the yachts in the marina were clacking against their masts; the

33

marina itself was just becoming functional, as the rising tide began to seep over the sill that kept a permanent depth of six feet within the basin. Out in the pool, the yachts waiting for entry – and on a June evening there were quite a few – were bobbing and heaving against the lay-by pontoons.

Against the outer pier the mass of a big hydrofoil of the Condor Line was more sedate; she was in for the night – even had there been a passage scheduled, she would not go out in a gale.

'I'll bet those Arabs are going to be glad to be inside,' Goodman remarked.

'I won't argue with that,' James said.

Now they were in the pierheads, and the watch was giving them a wave. Then they were out in the Russel. Even in three hours the seas had increased considerably. Fortunately the pilot boat had a small wheelhouse, in which the three men huddled as the rain poured down and spray clouded over the bows with every dip; the clearview screen whirred constantly.

The big yacht was now rolling heavily, although she was bows-on to the seas, which meant that she was also rising and falling, her anchor chain coming clear before being immersed again. As before, there were several men on deck waiting for them. James wondered how the dog was getting on, and had a sudden idea. If it was possible to have a look below, he might find something – he had no idea what. But if he didn't find anything, that should allay Sophie's fears.

With great expertise, Clarke nosed the pilot boat alongside the platform. James as usual attempted to time his step to the movement of both ships, but this time didn't get it quite right. The yacht was going down, so that green water surged over the platform and up to his knees, getting into his boots.

'Damn and blast,' he muttered, as he squelched up the steps.

Behind him, Goodman was more accurate, and made it drily.

'Welcome aboard, Mr Candish,' Salim said. 'It is setting up to be a nasty night.'

'You can say that again.' James got into the shelter of the superstructure and pulled off his boots to empty out the water. His socks were cold and soggy, but he'd have to put up with that.

He followed Salim up the ladder, Goodman at his heels. Honeylee and another officer were on the bridge, along with two crewmen. All were looking somewhat anxious.

'This came up a bit quick,' the captain remarked.

'It always does, around these parts,' James said, and looked down at where Clarke was circling with the pilot boat before returning to the harbour.

'You are very wet,' Honeylee observed. 'Would you like a change of clothing?'

'I'll manage,' James said, but he and Goodman stripped off their oilskins and hung them in the locker. 'Another half an hour and I reckon we can get under way. You'll have to go straight into your berth; there's not really enough room to turn.'

'I understand. I assume there will be help waiting?'

'That's correct. On the other hand, with the wind where it is, it'll be pushing you against the dock, so that should make it easier.' He wandered about the bridge, looking at the equipment, which included a Navigator so finely tuned that it showed the movement of the ship even at anchor.

It was a matter of timing, now, if he was going to carry out his plan.

'Coffee,' Honeylee said, and the steward presented a tray. 'This is Arabian coffee. Very strong.'

James sipped, shuddered, and hastily added sugar. Goodman seemed more used to it. James finished the cup, looked at his watch. They'd be moving in about ten minutes.

'Excuse me, Captain,' he said. 'Do you mind if I use the loo?'

'The loo?'

'The toilet. I need to have a leak.'

'Oh, of course. Use mine. It is on the deck below. The first cabin. Ibrahim will show you.'

'Thank you.' James followed the steward down the ladder and through a bulkhead door into a warm, well-lit corridor, lined with jalousied doors; at the far end there was a ladder leading downwards. There was no sound above the hum of the generator.

The steward opened the first door on the left and showed James into a large, well-appointed stateroom; it was in fact a double, the first half an office-cum-sitting room, with the sleeping cabin behind it. The sitting room contained a television set as well as a computer.

The steward stood at the inner doorway, indicating the bathroom.

'Thanks a million,' James said. 'Look, I'm going to be a little while. Don't hang about.'

He wasn't sure whether or not the man understood him, but he bowed and left the cabin. James did use the loo – he wanted no distractions – then he returned to the sitting room and cautiously opened the door again. The corridor was empty. He took off his seaboots, and his wet socks, left them just inside the door, then went into the corridor and made his way to the aft ladder, which was, in fact, a staircase that led down to a very luxuriously appointed dining saloon. This was presently empty, and the table was as yet unlaid; the galley crew were obviously waiting to be snugly alongside before getting ready for dinner.

The galley was just forward of the dining saloon, directly beneath the officers' quarters; the double swing doors were closed, but James could hear the clatter of crockery and the chatter of voices. Hastily he went down the ladder, crossed the dining room to the aft door, and opened it.

Instantly there was a yap, and he found himself facing the terrier, which was bristling at the intrusion. Hastily James closed the door behind himself, before anyone in the galley could hear the dog and come to investigate.

'Good boy,' he said. 'If you don't shut up, I am going to wring your neck.'

The dog, if he couldn't understand the words, certainly understood the tone, and backed across the carpet, teeth bared and growling.

And it was a carpet, James realised – Persian, he guessed, and worth a fortune. But then, so were most of the other appointments in the room, from the leather-upholstered arm-chairs and settee to the elaborate bar in the far corner, behind which was a multicoloured array of bottles, to the paintings on the bulkheads, to the huge television screen against the far wall, presently blank.

How the other half live, he thought, crossing the floor to the inner doorway. The terrier continued to growl but made no move towards him.

James opened the door, and stepped through, closing it behind him. He was now in a lobby, from which a spiral staircase led downwards. And . . . he frowned as he listened. The hum of the generator continued to be muted, and now he could hear other sounds, as of . . . There were several people below him, he was sure. Yet he was now in the passenger half of the ship. Honeylee had said he had eight passengers. One was the woman who owned the dog, and five of the others were ashore. So what the hell was going on?

Carefully he descended the staircase, which ended in a lower lobby. Off this a corridor led aft, between more staterooms. That was definitely passenger accommodation. Forward . . . the door was closed. He moved against it, then put his ear to it, listening – but could hear nothing.

Then the dog yapped again. James turned back to it, and found himself looking at the woman, Jeannette Aldridge, who was looking at him from behind a levelled automatic pistol.

The Victim

James gulped. He had never before in his life had a gun pointed at him.

'You are the harbourmaster,' Jeanette remarked.

'I am an assistant harbourmaster, ma'am. Is that gun loaded?'

'I would not be pointing it at you if it weren't,' she said.

'Well, would you mind pointing it somewhere else? It could go off.'

'It will go off, if I choose to fire it. What are you doing here?'

'Well, ma'am, I needed to go to the toilet. And the skipper said to use his, which I did; and then . . . I suppose I got lost when I left his cabin.'

He paused more in hope than in optimism.

Her lip curled. 'And you are a harbourmaster? Even an assistant harbourmaster. You have been to sea.'

James sighed. 'Twelve years in the Navy, ma'am.'

'So you do not get lost on board ships. You have been snooping. Turn round, raise your arms and place your hands on the bulkhead.'

James obeyed, and inhaled her perfume as she came closer. A moment later her hand slid over his back and shoulder, down to his buttocks, and then came round in front, sliding up from his crotch to his chest. At any other time he might have enjoyed what she was doing. He also supposed that, had he been a James Bond type, he would have chosen this moment to turn suddenly and take the gun away from her. Actually, he had always supposed he *was* the James Bond type, but he didn't fancy taking on the gun – with which he had no doubt at all she had practised – at such close range. Far better to talk his way out of a situation that had to be even more awkward for her than for him.

'I feel I should point out that harbourmasters do not normally carry guns,' he said.

'If you *are* a harbourmaster,' she remarked, and stepped away from him. 'You may turn round,' she said. 'Go up the stairs. Slowly.'

James obeyed, the terrier apparently trying to trip him up. He was trying to think as hard as he could. He had undoubtedly uncovered something sinister. His business now was to talk himself out of this and get ashore.

He re-entered the saloon, the woman – and the gun – close behind him.

'Sit.'

He obeyed, choosing a straight chair next to the grand piano. All the chairs in the lounge were bolted to the deck, as he would have expected; but there was always the chance that a more violent than usual roll might throw her off balance, although she clearly had her sealegs.

'Now tell me what you were really doing,' she said. 'I wish the truth.'

The gun continued to point unwaveringly at his stomach.

'Well, ma'am, I have to confess that I have never been on board a ship like this before. I do a bit of sailing myself, but this . . .'

'I am sure Captain Honeylee would have given you a guided tour if you had asked him.'

'It came over me suddenly, after I had been to the toilet.'

'And you felt it necessary to take off your boots and socks.'

'Well, they got wet, you see, when I was coming aboard. Now, if you'll permit me . . .' He stood up. 'I'll just go get them and return to the bridge, or my companion will be getting worried.'

'Sit down!' Her voice was like the crack of a whip.

James sat down.

'I should point out,' he said, 'that threatening someone with a gun is against the law here in Guernsey. As is carrying a gun at all, especially if it is unlicensed. So, ma'am, if you would like to avoid a lot of trouble . . .'

'Shut up,' she said, and moved across the lounge to where a telephone hung on the wall. She picked this up. 'Come down,' she said. 'No, this is an emergency. Bring Hamath with you.' She replaced the phone.

'I hope you're not thinking of doing anything stupid,' James said, trying to control both his voice and his thoughts. This sort of thing was totally outside his experience.

'Just keep quiet.'

She sat down herself, in a leather armchair, opposite him. The little dog, which had been staring at James throughout their conversation, settled at her feet, still staring.

Outside, the wind was now starting to whine, and the movement was increasing with every moment. While the time . . . There was a large clock on one of the bulkheads, and this was showing twenty past four. It was just about time to move. So what were they going to do? Because once they got inside the harbour they were at the mercy of the Guernsey authorities.

Or were they? He had the evidence of his ears that there were a lot more than eight passengers on board this ship. He had the assertion of his senses that they were probably all armed, probably with the Minimi assault rifles, weapons so powerful they made the Kalashnikov seem like a toy. He had the certain knowledge that there were twenty Arabs ashore, who had spent the day pin-pointing all the essential sites on the island.

And he had called Sophie paranoid!

The door opened, and Honeylee came in, followed by

an Arab man, wearing uniform but without insignia. As he was carrying a little black bag, James guessed he was the ship's doctor.

'What the hell . . . ?' Honeylee enquired, as he took in both James and the gun.

'He has been snooping,' Jeannette said.

'Oh, Jesus Christ!' the captain commented. 'To pull a gun . . .'

'I felt it was necessary.'

'Shit!' He gave James what he presumably thought was an ingratiating smile. 'This is all a mistake, you understand, Mr Candish. The lady is just a little bit nervous. And you didn't really have any business down here. If you'd come back up to the bridge, we're just about ready to move.'

'Of course,' James said, and stood up again. 'But she really shouldn't go around pointing guns at people.'

'I'll see that she doesn't do it again,' Honeylee said. 'Now . . .'

'Oh, shut up,' Jeannette said. 'Are you a total fool? Don't you know the moment we go alongside he will report to the police?'

'Report what?' Honeylee asked. 'About the gun? I'm sure we can sort this out.'

'I'm sure,' James agreed.

'You fool,' Jeannette said. 'He knows, Honeylee. He knows all about the boys downstairs.'

Honeylee looked at James, who did his best to look innocent.

'Shit,' the captain said again.

'He can't leave this ship. At least, not able to talk,' Jeannette said.

'I beg your pardon,' James said.

'Shit,' Honeylee said a third time. 'You have put us in a damned difficult position, Mr Candish.' He turned back to Jeannette. 'You realise we are about to up anchor and go into the harbour. His mate is on the bridge waiting to con

41

us. We can't get in without him. And he is going to ask what's happening if Candish doesn't show up.'

'Absolutely,' James said. 'I don't know what you're up to, but in the circumstances your best bet is to make a clean breast of it to the authorities.'

'Shut up,' Jeannette said again. 'I have thought what we must do. It all, as you have said, must be above board and acceptable to the authorities. What time is X-hour?'

Honeylee hesitated, glancing at James but then deciding there was no further point in concealment. 'Twenty-three thirty tonight.'

'Very good. Mr Candish will have a fit. Hamash, you will give him a sedative to calm him down, and this sedative will knock him out. It will be strong enough to keep him out until after midnight. Then you will radio for an ambulance to be waiting for us when we go alongside. He will be transferred to the ambulance, with the utmost care and sympathy, and removed to hospital, unconscious and unable to do us any harm.'

'But when he wakes up . . .'

'By the time he wakes up, the island will be in our hands, you say.'

'That's true,' Honeylee said thoughtfully. 'Heck, it might work . . .'

James realised he had to make a run for it – now – bolstered by the fact that Jeannette had made it plain that she dared not shoot him. He leapt from his chair and ran for the door leading to the steps.

'Stop him!' Jeannette shouted.

The dog barked.

The doctor was standing in front of the door, but James was the larger man. He grasped the doctor's tunic to hurl him to one side, and was struck a paralysing blow on the back of the neck. He fell to his knees, and Honeylee hit him again. Now he was on the deck, only half-conscious, trying desperately to push himself up . . . Then he felt the prick of a needle.

42

*　　*　　*

It might have been pouring with rain and blowing a gale in Guernsey, but the weather had not yet reached England. Sophie was lying in bed and watching a pre-Wimbledon tennis tournament when the phone rang.

'Sophie? Bill Harrison here.'

'Oh, Captain Harrison. Don't tell me: James has got himself stuck on board that yacht.'

'Ah . . . it's a little more serious than that, Sophie.'

Sophie sat up. 'What? What do you mean?'

'The people on the yacht have called for an ambulance. The ship is on her way in now, but it seems there's been some kind of an accident.'

'An accident?' She realised she was shouting, and made herself speak more calmly. 'To James?'

'It does seem so, yes. They assure us it's not life-threatening . . .'

'But they've sent for an ambulance. So it must be serious.'

'He may have broken something. Anyway, they're coming through the pierheads now, so we'll know in a few minutes.'

'I'm coming down,' Sophie said. She put down the phone, got out of bed, dragged on pants and a shirt, thrust her feet into docksiders, and ran down the stairs. They each had their own car – hers was a small Renault – and a few minutes later she was turning into the car park beside the Cambridge berth, and running across the roadway, regardless of the driving rain that had her soaked through in a moment.

The *Gloriosa* was still not berthed, as she was moving very slowly in the strong wind; she carried a lot of top hamper and was inclined to drift to leeward. There were several people on the dock waiting for her: longshoremen to handle her mooring warps as well as some men and women Sophie assumed were her passengers. There were also quite a few sailors on the yacht's deck, and a cluster of heads on the bridge; but she could not identify any of them.

'Sophie!'

'Oh, Captain Harrison.' She retreated into the comparative shelter of the nearest building. 'Have you heard anything more?'

'No, and I think we shouldn't bother them again until she's moored up.'

Sophie bit her lip as she watched the yacht, now manoeuvered into position, slowly edging her way towards the berth, while the warps were thrown and made fast to the bollards on the dock, to allow them to be winched in. The heavy fenders were already in position, and a few moments later she was securely alongside, while extra warps were carried out to hold her firm as she went down to the sand.

By now the ambulance was coming down the road, turning on to the dock, siren wailing. A gangplank was run out from the yacht, but at this stage of the tide – approaching full – her deck was some feet above the dock, and there was a considerable slope on the plank.

'Permission to come aboard,' Harrison shouted.

'Please do.' Honeylee slid down the ladders from the bridge. 'Some operation.'

'You're snug now,' Harrison said, leading Sophie up the plank and on to the deck. 'Where is the casualty?'

'Below. I'll have him brought up.'

'I'd prefer to have the ambulance men do it,' Harrison said, and signalled the waiting medics.

'As you wish.' Honeylee looked at Sophie.

'This is Sophie Gallagher. She's Mr Candish's . . . ah . . .' he wasn't sure how the Arabs, or even an American working for the Arabs, viewed the laissez-faire morals obtaining in the West.

'He's my partner,' Sophie said.

'Oh, indeed. You must be very worried,' Honeylee said.

'Is he badly hurt?'

'I don't think he's really hurt at all,' Honeylee said. 'Physically. But we had to give him a strong sedative.'

'Why?'

'He just went berserk. Started smashing things and attacking people. We had to restrain him.'

Sophie looked at Harrison. Neither of them could imagine James, normally the most laid back of men, ever behaving like that.

'I'd like to see him,' Sophie said.

'Of course. Mr Salim, will you take Miss Gallagher below?'

The officer from the dock the previous night! Sophie found herself beginning to tremble. With what?

A bulkhead door was opened and she was shown into utter luxury. A carpeted corridor, then a door was opened to admit her to the main saloon. Here there were several people, and James. He lay on his back on a settee, absolutely still, mouth slightly open.

'Oh, my God!' she cried. 'He's not . . .'

'No, no, miss,' said a short, dark man. 'He is just sedated.'

'But . . .' Dropping to her knees beside James, Sophie made sure he was actually breathing.

'He attacked me,' a woman said.

Sophie looked up. 'James attacked *you*?'

'He said he was going to strangle Lulu.'

Sophie realised the woman was holding a small terrier in her arms. 'I'm sure there was some mistake.'

'I can assure you there was no mistake,' Jeannette said coldly. 'I thought I was going to be raped.'

'By James? As well as having your dog strangled? You're making it up.'

Jeannette stared at her, then looked at the doctor.

'I'm afraid it is quite true, Miss Gallagher,' Hamath said. 'Miss Aldridge rang the bell for assistance, and when I came in, she was fighting for her life. That I why I felt it necessary to give Mr Candish a sedative.'

The two medics were now bending over James, one taking his pulse, the other lifting an eyelid. 'You must have given him some dose, doctor,' one of them said.

'Possibly it was stronger than necessary,' Hamath agreed; 'but I had to make a very quick decision. Quite apart from what had happened to Miss Aldridge, we were about to dock the ship under extreme weather conditions. We simply could not afford to have a madman running about the vessel in those circumstances.'

'A madman!' Sophie shouted.

'That is what he was – yes, Miss Gallagher.'

Harrison caught Sophie's arm as she seemed about to hit him.

'Well, the sooner we get him up to the hospital the better,' the medic said. They had already wheeled in the trolley. Now they wrapped James in blankets and a waterproof before carefully lifting him on to the stretcher and strapping him into place.

'He *is* going to be all right?' Sophie begged.

'I should think so,' the medic said. 'But it may take a little time to bring him round. It would help if you would tell us exactly what you gave him, doctor.'

'I will write out the formula.' Hamath sat at the desk in the corner of the lounge. 'Would you like me to come with you?'

'No, I don't think that will be necessary. Once our people know what they're working with, they should be able to sort things out. Let's go, George.'

They wheeled the trolley to the door, where several sailors were waiting to help them lift it over the sill and on to the deck.

Only then did Sophie realise that the lounge had become quite crowded, with the people from the dock having come aboard, and with various other people asking questions – as most of the talk was in Arabic or some foreign language, she didn't understand any of it.

'We'd better get ashore,' Harrison said.

'Yes.' Sophie glared at Jeannette, then went to the door. On the deck she encountered Goodman, just coming down from the bridge. 'Clarrie! Tell me what happened, really.'

'I don't know anything more than you, Sophie,' Goodman said. 'James went below to use the loo and didn't come back. It was time for us to make a move, and I was just wondering what to do, when there was a hell of a hullabaloo from below. It seems James had had some kind of fit and run amok. Well, they said they had him under control, and we had to use the tide while we could, so I had them radio for an ambulance and brought the ship in.'

'Do you believe James had a fit?'

'Well . . .' Goodman looked embarrassed. 'Their doctor . . .'

'I wouldn't trust him further than I could throw him,' Sophie snapped.

'Sssh,' Harrison begged. They were still standing on the deck of the yacht, surrounded by sailors, several of whom seemed able to speak English. 'Let's get ashore.'

He hurried her down the gangplank, where they encountered a newspaper reporter. 'They won't allow me on board, Bill,' he complained. 'Will you tell me what happened? We saw a man being removed by ambulance . . .'

'James Candish, Pete. He fell and hurt himself. Nothing more dramatic than that.'

Pete Smith was understandably disappointed. Somewhat short and a trifle overweight, he regarded himself as Guernsey's number one newshound. 'Oh. Right. Well . . .'

Sophie held Harrison's arm and half-pushed him to one side. 'Captain, what are we going to do?'

'Well, I suppose that depends on what sort of a report is made by Captain Honeylee. Or that woman. If they charge James with assault . . .'

'You don't believe that story, do you?'

'Well . . . something must have happened; otherwise they wouldn't have had to sedate him.'

47

'Of course something happened. He went nosing about the ship, looking where he shouldn't, and they caught him out.'

'Now, Sophie, really. Nosing about the ship? Why should he do that? And why should they take offence if he did?'

'There's something odd about that ship, Captain.'

'She's a beautiful job, I'll grant you that.'

'I meant sinister. I think we should call the police and have them mount a guard on her.'

'We can't do that. No one on board her has broken any law. Anyway, what would the guard be for?'

'Oh . . . look, I'm freezing. Can we go to your office?'

'I think you should go home and change those wet clothes. Are you planning to go up to the hospital?'

'Yes, I am. But I'm more worried about the ship.'

'You're a little upset,' Harrison said. 'Look, go home and change; then go up to the hospital and have James tell you what really happened. That'll answer all your questions. Right?'

Sophie hesitated, then nodded. 'I suppose you're right, Captain. May I call you after I hear what James has to say?'

'Please do. I'll be in the office till six.'

Sophie drove back to the flat in a seethe, not helped when she sneezed several times. If, on top of everything else, she'd caught a cold . . . Be rational, she told herself. Not paranoiac. But how could she not be paranoiac? If there was one thing on earth she would stake her last penny on, it would be against the possibility of James ever having some kind of fit. As for attacking that woman, threatening her dog . . . James loved animals, especially dogs.

Something had happened on board that ship – something that had caused the crew to render James unconscious. Something to do with the Arabs staying at the Guernsey Island Hotel? That was simply a gut feeling . . . and the sight of al-Rakim talking on the dock with Mate Salim from the yacht. But what had happened to James made no sense. When he woke up, he'd be able to tell them exactly what had happened. And then . . . She hurried upstairs, had a hot shower and a cup of coffee, and then hurried out again, suitably wrapped up this time, to go to the Princess Elizabeth Hospital. 'James Candish,' she told reception. 'He was brought in a couple of hours ago.'

'Oh, yes,' the nurse said, peering into her computer. 'Intensive Room Seven. Are you a relative?'

'We live together.'

'Ah. Does Mr Candish have any relatives in Guernsey?'

'No. He's from England.' Alarm bells were ringing again. 'Why, is something the matter?'

'I think Dr Murrain would like a word.' She punched various keys. 'Miss Gallagher is in Reception, doctor. Mr Candish's, ah . . . flatmate.' She gave Sophie a bright smile. 'He'll be right down.'

Sophie paced up and down. Again, something was going on about which she didn't know. Dr Murrain was a young man with horn-rimmed spectacles. He bustled in.

'Miss Gallagher?'

'What's happening?' Sophie asked.

'Ah . . . I suppose you could say the problem is that nothing is happening.'

'What do you mean? Is James . . . ?'

'Mr Candish is all right, at the moment, Miss Gallagher. But he's been rather heavily sedated. One could describe it as an overdose.'

'An overdose? An overdose of what?'

'Well, going by the prescription given our people by the doctor on the ship, and my own tests, it comes down rather heavily on pentathol and morphine. That's not really a very good mixture. I'm not sure it isn't illegal.'

'Oh, my God! You mean . . .'

'I said, he is all right, Miss Gallagher. But his pulse is weak, and I have him on a ventilator, just in case. Hopefully, there will be no lasting ill effect, but I'm afraid he may have to stay in for a day or two.'

'Shoot!' Sophie said. 'Those people . . .'

'What people?'

'The people on the yacht.'

'Ah.' He led her to an upholstered bench in a corner of the large room as some more people came in, and sat beside her. 'What exactly did happen on board the yacht? The medics were a little vague.'

'Oh . . . they said he'd had some kind of fit, and attacked one of the passengers. So they had to put him under sedation.'

'They seem to have overreacted. I understand they're Arabs.'

'Well, the crew, certainly.'

'Yes. I suppose their methods are somewhat different from ours.'

'Do you think James had a fit?'

'I really can't say.'

'But . . . they said he attacked this woman and her beastly dog. Wouldn't there be marks?'

'If she and the animal defended themselves, certainly.'

'She said they did, while she called for help.'

'Then there would be marks. I must confess I didn't look for any, not being in possession of all the facts. But . . . you wish me to find marks?'

'Of course I do not. Because there aren't any.'

'What are you trying to say?'

'That she's lying. That they're all lying.'

Dr Murrain put up his hand as if he would have scratched his head, then lowered it again. 'Then what do you think happened?'

'I don't know. I'm trying to find out. I only know that James did not attack that woman. You can prove that.'

'I cannot do that, Miss Gallagher. You have asked me to see if there are marks on his wrists or face from a woman having resisted his attack. You do understand that if I examine him and find no marks, this will not prove that he did *not* attack the woman, while if I *do* find such marks, it will prove that he did.'

'Well,' Sophie said, 'you are going to examine him anyway, aren't you?'

'I feel obliged to, after what you have told me.'

'May I come with you?'

He frowned. 'Don't you trust me?'

'I just want to see him, doctor.'

He hesitated. 'Oh, very well. You realise – well, he's not conscious, you know.'

'I do know. I just want to see him.'

She followed the doctor into a small ward on the ground floor, with four beds, all unoccupied save for the one in which James lay, linked up to several machines and with gauges behind his head. A nurse stood by the bed, and Sophie joined her, to look down at the unconscious man. He appeared perfectly normal, except that his face was partially obscured by the ventilator tubes. 'How is he?' she asked.

The nurse looked at Murrain, and received a nod. 'Improving all the time. He has a strong constitution.'

It was Sophie's turn to look at Murrain, as he bent over James's body, examining his wrists and forearms, before peering at his face in turn. 'Well?' she asked.

'There are no marks consistent with his having been scratched or hit or violently resisted. However . . . there is a severe bruise on the back of the neck. Caused by a hand rather than an instrument, I would say.'

'Well?'

'So, someone hit him. I would say it was more probably a man than a woman, unless she were an absolute expert at karate. I am bound to say that doesn't look too good, from the point of view of a defence to a charge of assault.'

'You are saying that you think James is guilty of assault.'

'I am not saying anything, Miss Gallagher, other than that,

51

whatever he was doing, someone found it necessary to lay him out.'

'That blow would have laid him out?'

'I think there were two blows,' Murrain said. 'Either one would certainly have caused temporary incapacity.'

'Yet they still found it necessary to overdose him with sedatives? Don't you think you need to do something about that?'

'I'm a doctor, not a detective, Miss Gallagher. Don't you think your best course is to wait for Mr Candish to wake up, and ask him what happened?'

'He *is* going to wake up?'

'Of course he is.'

'When?'

'I would say . . . in a few hours' time. Before tomorrow morning.'

'When he will still have to stay in hospital for several days?'

'When he will have to remain under observation for twenty-fours hours,' Murrain said, patiently, but obviously thinking, how in the name of God did I get involved with this woman?

'But you will admit the circumstances of his being here at all are suspicious.'

'They are a result of different medical practice from ours, Miss Gallagher. Now you really must excuse me; I do have other patients. However, if you are really worried, you may spend the night here if you wish. You may use one of these beds.' He gave a quick smile. 'I won't promise you won't be interrupted. This is an emergency ward.'

He left the room. And Sophie looked at the nurse.

'*Would* you like to spend the night?'

'I have things to do,' Sophie said. 'You'll be with him, won't you?'

'Someone will be with him,' the nurse promised.

*   *   *

52

Sophie sat behind the wheel of her car in the car park, listening to the rain pattering on the roof. Things to do? What things? As James did not appear to be in any danger, wasn't the sensible thing to do what Harrison and Murrain had both recommended: go home to bed and wait until tomorrow morning, when James would be able to tell her exactly what had happened? That is what the police would tell her as well. If she went to them. But how could she go to them? What could she tell them that would not get her laughed at? Only James had half-believed her. Had that persuaded him to go investigating the ship, once he was back on board, and led to this? But who was going to believe her about that?

Facts – she had to have facts. So what did she have? Think, she told herself. Fact number one: two months ago the SAS had located the desert hideout of Hassan the terrorist, raided it, and arrested him after a shoot-out in which several people had been killed. That had caused a storm of international comment and condemnation, but it had absolutely nothing to do with Guernsey. Fact number two: a party of Arabs had checked in at the Guernsey Island Hotel. That they said they were from Saudi Arabia had no importance. They could be from any Middle Eastern country. But that in itself also had nothing to do with Guernsey, save that if it was getting itself on the tourist map for wealthy Arabs, that had to be a good thing. Fact number three: on the same day that the Saudis had arrived, there had appeared a huge yacht owned by a very wealthy sheikh. That again had to be good for Guernsey tourism. That the two groups had arrived on the same day could be coincidence. Fact number four: the leader of her group had met and talked with an officer from the yacht last night. If *that* was coincidence – that the two men had somehow known each other, and just happened to bump into each other on the Guernsey waterfront within hours of their arrival – then one really had to believe in miracles. But only she had seen them, and she had told only James about it.

Was anyone going to believe her now, when everyone was already thinking she was being paranoid?

Even James had thought that. But James had, obviously, thought about it, and thus tried to do something, find out something, which had ended with him being knocked unconscious and shot full of drugs. So full of drugs that he was going to be out until well after midnight. So, back to square one. She had no facts to present to anyone, until James woke up to confirm her story. So . . .

Her hands closed on the wheel, so tightly that her nails bit into her palms. The people on the yacht would know that James was going to wake up, sometime before tomorrow morning but, as they had measured the overdose, not until after midnight. They also knew that when he woke up he might well have the information that could have the yacht impounded pending investigation. Therefore whatever they were planning, whatever reason they had for being here, had to be completed, and they to be away again, by just after midnight.

Save that they couldn't be away again just after midnight. They would already be on the ground, and they would not float again before half past four tomorrow morning. She looked at her watch. Half past six. They were stuck where they were for the next ten hours.

Perhaps, being Arabs, they didn't understand enough about tides to know that. In which case the laugh was on them. Or was it?

She drove home, telephoned Bill Harrison.

'He's just come in,' Doris Harrison said. 'I'll call him.'

'Sophie,' Bill said. 'How's James?'

'In a stable condition. But he's out for several hours.'

'But he's going to be all right?'

'So they say. Captain, I wanted to ask you two things: has there been any complaint about his behaviour on board the yacht?'

'No complaint has been made to me.'

54

'What about the police?'

'I shouldn't think so. I can see the yacht from my office window, and certainly up to the time I left there had been no police on the dock, as one would have expected if there had been a complaint to them.'

'Don't you find that odd?'

'Now, Sophie, isn't it likely they just thought better of what might have turned out to be an international incident?'

'OK,' she said. 'I'm being paranoid. Everyone's agreed on that.'

'Sophie . . .'

'Just a joke,' she said. 'My other question is: what was the reaction of this Captain Honeylee when he was told his ship would have to take the ground for ten hours tonight?'

'Well . . . I wasn't actually there. You'd have to ask James . . . or Clarrie Goodman. But as I understand it, he was just happy to be in and snugly alongside. It's blowing a real hoohah out there.'

'I can hear it. Thanks anyway, Captain.'

She replaced the phone, gazed at it for several seconds. It was tempting to call Goodman, but she didn't think she would get any further there. Honeylee had clearly not objected to having his ship take the ground. Therefore he had never intended to go anywhere before tomorrow morning. Therefore . . .

But by tomorrow morning, James would be awake and telling his story. She felt her brain was going round in ever-decreasing circles.

Thus whatever the Arabs were planning, it did not depend upon their being able to depart again by midnight, or just after. And as James had pointed out, whatever they were planning, escape in a relatively slow means of transport was simply not on, in such close proximity to the Navy and the RAF. Therefore they were not planning anything, and that woman had been telling the truth when she had claimed James had gone berserk – but if she believed that, she might as well go to the loony bin and clamour for admittance – or whatever they were planning had nothing to do with getting away from Guernsey. Which was crazy.

But it very obviously *did* have to do with the group at the Guernsey Island, or why would al-Rakim have met up with Salim?

Seven o'clock. Sophie put on her coat.

The Guernsey Island Hotel car park was both large and somewhat rambling, several different parks adjoining each other. Sophie was therefore able to leave her car completely out of sight of the hotel, and walk back to the lobby, where she pulled off her soaking headscarf and fluffed out her hair.

'Sophie,' said the woman behind the desk. 'Don't tell me people want to go driving on a night like this?' She glanced down her list. 'There's no record of it.'

'No, no, Bertie,' Sophie said. 'I'm not working. Is the Arab contingent at home?'

Bertie looked over her shoulder at the empty pigeonholes. 'Looks like it. They're probably dining. They're all going out tonight.'

'Going out? Where?'

'I have no idea. But they've arranged for five hire cars to be delivered at nine o'clock.'

'Can they do that? Have they got driving licences?'

'English ones, yes.'

'I'll bet they're forged.'

'Oh really, Sophie. And even if they are forged, it's nothing to do with me. They looked genuine. Mr Roller saw them himself. He arranged the cars. What's eating you about them, anyway?'

Sophie thought as fast as she could. If they really were going out, it would be safest to wait until they had gone. But once they had gone, the ball could be rolling: she *couldn't* wait. 'They invited me to have a drink with them.'

'You really have made a hit, haven't you? It'll be orange juice and coffee, I'm afraid.'

'I'm driving, anyway. I'll go up.'

'Like I said, they're probably in the dining room. Let me give them a buzz and tell them you're in reception.' She picked up the house phone.

'No,' Sophie said. 'Please.'

Bertie replaced the phone, frowning.

'I'd rather wait for them upstairs,' Sophie said, aware that she was flushing.

'Where?'

'Well . . . if you'd give me a pass key for al-Rakim's room, I'll wait for him there.'

'I can't let you into a client's room without his say-so, Sophie.'

'I don't want anyone to know I'm here,' Sophie explained. 'With an Arab, you know. Several Arabs.'

'Twenty,' Bertie said, absently.

'Exactly. Just let me wait in his room. For heaven's sake, Bertie, you know I'm not going to steal anything.'

Bertie stared at her in consternation. 'I'd lose my job,' she muttered.

'No, you won't. Al-Rakim is expecting me. I'll make sure there won't be any trouble.'

Bertie chewed her lip. 'Does . . . James know about this?'

'So have you never cheated a bit?'

Bertie bridled. 'Never.'

'Well, there's a first time for everything.'

'I hope you know what you're doing,' Bertie said; but she picked up a key ring and checked through it before extracting one. 'Arabs!' She gave a little shudder.

'You won't say anything about this to anyone?' Sophie asked.

'Well, of course I will not. And the same goes for you. But . . . please don't shout for help.'

Sophie winked.

What am I *doing*? she asked herself, as she rode up in the lift. Well, for one thing, she had entirely changed the nature of her friendship with Bertie. Although hopefully not to that extent. If everything went according to plan, and she was back downstairs in a few minutes, all she had to do was tell Bertie she had lost her nerve. They'd have a giggle over that.

Then what was she hoping to find? There had to be something – something suspicious, something she could offer to the police to support her theory.

The lift stopped, and the door opened. Sophie took several deep breaths before stepping into the corridor, which was thankfully empty. She hurried along to al-Rakim's room, hesitated again before the door, then drew a deep breath, inserted the key, and opened it.

The light was on! Sophie checked, nearly slammed the door and fled. Then she realised that the room was, actually, empty. She stepped inside, closed the door behind herself, inhaled various scents, most of them pleasant. The bed was made up, al-Rakim's suitcase was on the rack, open; he did not appear to have unpacked to any great extent.

Sophie drew a deep breath, then riffled through the clothes, all very European, and all very ordinary. There was nothing to which anyone could have taken the least objection, not even a camera, much less a gun, or a radio . . . Had she really expected to find a gun or a radio?

She moved to the wardrobe, but this was empty, as were the drawers. She tried the dressing table, but there was nothing in the drawers there either. Then she tried the table, which doubled as a desk. It had two drawers, but these contained only hotel bumf. She stood in the middle of the room, fists clenched. She had drawn a complete blank, and made a fool of herself with Bertie.

Then she looked at the waste-paper basket beside the table. It was empty save for a few slivers of paper. She stooped and took them out, spread them on the table. It had originally been one sheet of paper, she reckoned, torn into several strips. Carefully she laid them together, stared at the words and figures: the writing was in Arabic, but the figures were international.

[One word] – 23.30
[Two words] – 24.00 – 2
[Two words] – 00.30 – 4
[Two words] – 00.30 – 3
[One word] – 01.00 [one word] – 10
[Two words] – 24.00 – 20
[Several words]
[Two words] – 01.00 – 6
[Three words] – 01.00 – 4
[More words in Arabic]

Sophie stared at the words and numbers in total consternation. Her brain was working on two levels. One was mentally totting up the numbers, which had to be men – she made it forty-nine, and there were only twenty here in the hotel. That meant twenty-nine off the ship, and they would have to leave a crew on board . . . so just how many people did they have? At the second level she was trying to assimilate what she was reading, what she was being told by the timings on the paper. Eleven thirty had to be the time they would rendezvous on the dock. The two midnights had to be places close at hand, in town and close to the ship, probably the watch house and . . . the police station, of course. Then within the next hour all the other required positions – which she had so meticulously shown them this morning.

These people actually intended to take over Guernsey. But how could even fifty armed and determined men take over an island of sixty thousand inhabitants?

Very easily, in the short term, because Guernsey was totally defenceless. It relied on the armed might of Great Britain only sixty-odd miles away, and if the chips were really down, the armed might of France much closer than that. But if they were determined enough, and from what she had heard and read of Arab terrorists they usually were, they could hold the island long enough to . . . make demands, which had to be to do with the captured terrorist leader.

It was going to happen, unless they could be stopped. Now she knew why they had laid James out until after midnight at the earliest: after midnight it would not matter what he had found out, what he could tell the authorities. Only she could do that in time.

She crammed the slivers of paper into her pocket, moved to the door, and heard voices in the corridor.

The Police

S ophie stood with her ear against the door, heart pounding.
The voices were definitely speaking a totally foreign language, and they were coming closer. She left the door and ran
to the window, opened it and looked out – at pouring rain and
the trees being whipped by the wind. Even if she had had a
head for heights she didn't think she could go out there, five
storeys up, and hope to reach the ground, except by falling.

She closed the window. The voices were almost at the door.
She opted for the wardrobe, as there was nothing in it, stepped
inside and, closing the door, tried to control her breathing.

The bedroom door opened, and she thought three men came
in, from the different level of voices. And one of them was
asking a question. Perhaps some of her scent had lingered.
Perhaps he had noticed that there must recently have been an
influx of fresh air into the bedroom – through double-glazed
windows?

There was more discussion; then the door opened and
closed again. One of the men had left. To do what? In
any event there were still two left. So how was she to
get out? She simply had to get out, and get to someone who would be able to do something. Jack Harding!
He'd know what to do . . . She wished she knew him
better.

The wardrobe door opened.

'Miss Gallagher?' Al-Rakim seemed genuinely surprised.
For a moment Sophie could think of nothing to say.

'I knew someone had been in the room,' al-Rakim said.

'I was even reasonably sure she was still here. I knew it was a she, you see, because of her perfume. But you . . . ?'

Sophie was pulling herself together. 'I'm terribly sorry,' she said. 'I came to the wrong room. And when I heard you coming, I guess I got scared. And tried to hide.'

'Ah,' he said.

'So, if you'll excuse me, I'll leave.'

She stepped out of the wardrobe, past al-Rakim, and faced the other man. Like al-Rakim, he was flawlessly dressed and maintained a calm expression; but his eyes frightened her.

'Whose room were you intending to go to?' al-Rakim asked.

'Ah . . . I have a friend in the hotel. She's on this floor.'

'I see. Take off your jacket, please.'

'My . . . I will not.'

'Would you like Hamid to do it for you?'

'Listen: if I were to scream . . .'

'Hamid would probably hit you, at the very least.'

Sophie glanced at Hamid, and swallowed. Then she took off her blazer. At least they were polite about . . . what? She had no idea. She had never been in a position like this before.

'Thank you.' Al-Rakim held out his hand, and she gave him the garment. He began going through the pockets.

'You have no right to do that,' she snapped.

'I think I have every right,' he said. 'You are in my room, uninvited. I must assume you have stolen something. Ah . . .' from her left-hand side pocket he took the pass key. 'My number. Where did you get this?'

'I . . . I stole it, from Reception,' Sophie said.

'Thinking it was the number of your friend's room.'

'Yes,' Sophie said.

'Do you not know that lying is abhorrent to Allah? No, I suppose you do not. What have we here?' He was feeling in the right-hand pocket and extracting the slivers of torn paper. He held one up to the light.

Hamid made a remark.

Al-Rakim nodded. 'Hamid says he told me it was dangerous just to throw these into the trash. Now I agree with him.
But I really did not expect to be burgled. What did you intend
to do with these pieces of paper, Miss Gallagher?'

Sophie sighed; she did not suppose continuing to lie would
get her very far. 'Show them to someone who would be able
to do something about them. About you.'

'I see. You understand this places me in a difficult position.
I have no wish to harm you. If everyone is sensible, no one
will be harmed. But I cannot let you leave the hotel.'

'Until after midnight,' Sophie said.

'That is correct. After midnight, anything you might say,
or do, will be irrelevant.' He threw the scraps of paper on
to the table, and spoke to Hamid. Then smiled. 'I have
told Hamid to burn those, and he says he would far rather
burn you.'

Sophie drew a sharp breath and stepped backward.

'Perhaps later,' al-Rakim said.

Sophie heard the scraping of a match and smelt the
scorching paper.

'But I am interested to know why you came here, and
for what you were looking. You could not have known you
would find the itinerary.'

'I just knew that something was wrong,' Sophie said. 'I
wanted to see what I could find.'

'And if I had not been so careless with the itinerary, you
would have found nothing. What would you have done then?'

Sophie shrugged. 'Gone home, I suppose.'

'You must be regretting finding that paper. Now, I am
going to finish searching you. I hope you do not object?'

'I do object,' Sophie said. 'If you lay a finger on me, I will
charge you with indecent assault.'

'Ah, but to whom will you present your charge? Turn
round.'

She hesitated, biting her lip. But she was really absolutely
in their power. She turned round and faced Hamid, who was

burning the last piece of paper. He grinned at her, sweeping the ashes into the waste-paper basket.

Then she felt al-Rakim's hands on her shoulders, moving down her back into her armpits. Oh, Lord, she thought, and tensed her muscles as his fingers plucked at the catch for her brassiere, then moved round the front to touch her breasts. She made herself keep still as they moved down her stomach to slide down to her groin, then round to her buttocks. She felt she was going to scream, drew a deep breath . . . and the door opened.

It was another Arab – she supposed the man who had been earlier sent on some job. But his appearance distracted both al-Rakim and Hamid. Al-Rakim was in any event bending over Sophie's bottom. Now, as he straightened, she kicked behind her as hard as she could. He gave an exclamation of alarm, and Sophie ran for the door. Hamid, on the far side of the room, lunged at her, but missed. The third man was smaller than the other two, and Sophie's appearance, followed by her shoulder charge, took him entirely by surprise. He fell against the door, and she was through, into the hallway.

She could see the lifts, but now two doors opened between her and that route, and four more of the Arabs appeared. Sophie swung round and ran the other way, before the men in the bedroom could get out. At the far end of the corridor there was an emergency exit, which led on to a flight of stone steps leading both up and down. Sophie ran down, panting, for two flights, then opened the door, stepped on to the third-floor corridor – and saw, to her utter relief, two couples standing outside their bedroom doors and chatting.

She went towards them, mind churning. She could not involve them; it would take too long to explain what was happening. But they provided cover, even if they looked at her with some curiosity; she was definitely untidy at the least.

She smiled at them and called the lift. It arrived just as one of the Arabs appeared at the far end of the corridor, having come down the main staircase. She stepped inside and pressed

'Ground'. They would surely know where she was going, but equally surely the lift would exit into a crowded lobby.

The lift halted; the doors opened. There were several people waiting to ascend, and the lobby was, as Sophie had hoped, quite crowded with people leaving the dining room and deciding what to do with their evening. There were also several of the Arabs, but not al-Rakim, she noted. And they could do nothing about her at the moment.

She pushed her way through the throng and reached Reception.

'Sophie?' Bertie gazed at her in consternation. 'You look a sight.'

'Listen,' Sophie said: 'call the police.'

'Call the . . .' Bertie's eyes rolled, and she looked past Sophie.

Sophie turned, and faced al-Rakim, who was with, obviously, an under-manager.

'Oh, thank God,' she said. 'Listen . . .'

'This is the woman,' al-Rakim said.

'You . . .'

'Mr al-Rakim says he found you in his room, madam,' the under-manager said. 'Is this true?'

'Well . . .' Sophie hesitated.

'Is this yours?' The under-manager held up Sophie's blazer.

'Why, yes, it is. But . . .'

'This has just been given to me by Mr al-Rakim. He say you took it off in his room.'

'Yes, well . . .'

'Which seems to prove that you were there. Alberta, call the police.'

Bertie gulped, and began punching numbers.

'The police,' Sophie said. 'Thank God.'

'I think you need to understand that this is a serious matter,' the under-manager said. 'How did you get into the room, anyway?'

Sophie could almost hear Bertie gulp from behind her. But she couldn't let her friend down. 'The door was open.'

The under-manager looked at al-Rakim, who shrugged. 'It is possible. We do not lock our doors in my country. There is no theft.'

'No theft?' The under-manager was clearly disbelieving.

Al-Rakim smiled. 'There is no theft, because anyone caught stealing has their right hand chopped off.' Now he smiled at Sophie, who involuntarily took a step backwards.

By now the scene at the desk was attracting the attention of the clientele. 'I think we had better go into the office,' the under-manager said. He opened the door and Sophie went in. Al-Rakim obviously felt he was in command of the situation; but when she told her story . . . what story? She realised.

Rakim had accompanied the under-manager into the office, and closed the door.

'I would like to speak to you alone,' Sophie said.

'The police will be here in a little while. I think it would be best if you spoke to them.'

'Oh, for God's sake,' Sophie shouted. 'I'm not a thief! I'm Sophie Gallagher. I drive the bus for DriveRite. I am in and out of this hotel, and most of the other hotels, all day and every day. Ask Bertie . . . Alberta. It just happens that this man is a terrorist, and is planning . . .' she hesitated. To tell this oaf that al-Rakim intended to take over Guernsey might be a mistake. He simply wouldn't believe her.

But would the police?

'Are you a terrorist, Mr al-Rakim?' asked the under-manager.

'Do I look like a terrorist?' al-Rakim commented. 'This woman is demented. She is also trying to confuse the issue. She was in my room, attempting to steal, when I interrupted her.'

'That's not true,' Sophie snapped. 'That . . .' She bit her lip, because the under-manager definitely didn't believe her.

66

There was a knock on the door. 'The police are here, Mr Roller.'

'Ah, show them in, please.' Roller stood up as a police sergeant and a constable, both in uniform, entered the office.

'Oh, Derek,' Sophie said. 'Am I glad to see you.'

The sergeant peered at her; he was a good friend of James. 'Sophie? What on earth is happening?'

'Do you know this young lady, Sergeant?' Roller asked.

'Of course I do, sir. Everyone knows Sophie Gallagher.'

'I see. This is Mr al-Rakim, who is a guest in the hotel. When he went upstairs after dinner tonight, he found Miss Gallagher in his room.'

Derek's eyes were round. 'Sophie?'

'Look, I can explain,' Sophie said. 'I'd like to see you alone.'

'This is ridiculous,' al-Rakim protested. 'These people are obviously good friends. Sergeant, I wish to prefer charges against this woman.'

'What charges?'

'Of entering my bedroom illegally, with intent to steal.'

'Were you in this gentleman's room, Sophie?'

'Well, yes, I was. But I can explain.'

'She will tell you, Sergeant, that she was looking for evidence that I and my associates are terrorists. I'm afraid she seems to have a fixed idea about this. Well, you are welcome to search all of our rooms, all of our belongings, all of us. I do not know what you would expect to find to identify us as terrorists. Guns, perhaps? Bombs?'

Derek looked at Sophie, doubtfully.

'They are going to get bombs, and guns, Derek,' Sophie said urgently. 'Off the yacht in the harbour.'

Derek looked more doubtful yet.

'Haven't you heard about James?' Sophie asked, desperately.

'I heard he'd had some kind of an accident on board the yacht,' Derek said.

67

'Accident, hell,' Sophie said. 'They hit him and virtually OD'd him on a cocktail of drugs, laid him out cold.'

'This woman has a most inflamed imagination,' al-Rakim remarked.

'Ah . . . why should they wish to do that, Sophie?' Derek asked.

'Because he found out what they are up to.'

'Which is?'

Sophie drew a long breath. 'They're going to take over the island at midnight. Tonight. That's less than three hours away.'

Derek looked at al-Rakim, who smiled. 'As I said, Sergeant. I think she must be the one on drugs.'

'You must admit this is a little far-fetched, Sophie,' Derek suggested.

'Far-fetched or not, it is what is happening,' Sophie insisted. 'This man and his friends came here to link up with that yacht, and . . .' she hesitated.

'Take over the island,' Derek said. 'How many people would you say there are on that ship?'

'I have no idea, but not less than sixty.'

'Sixty men. And your party, sir?'

'There are twenty of us,' al-Rakim said.

'So that makes eighty. Hm.'

'To take over an island of sixty thousand inhabitants,' al-Rakim said.

'Yes . . .'

'It's not difficult,' Sophie shouted. 'They know all the key places. For God's sake, I *showed* them all the key places.'

'Haven't we heard enough of this nonsense?' al-Rakim asked. 'I am formally charging this young woman with entering my bedroom, illegally, and with intent to steal. What do you intend to do about it?'

'Well, sir, if you are making a charge, I will take Miss Gallagher down to the station, certainly. You will have to make a statement; but that can wait until tomorrow.'

'And she will be locked up until tomorrow?'

'Oh, I don't think we can do that, sir. She will be formally charged, and then released on police bail.'

'But that is ridiculous. You mean you are just going to let her go?'

'We know where to find her, sir.'

'If that is how you handle crime in this country, I have to accept it. Under protest.'

'In his country, they'd cut off her hand,' Roller put in.

'Well, sir,' Derek said, with an attempt at humour, 'you wouldn't want us to do that, now would you? She has such pretty hands.'

After retrieving her blazer, Derek escorted Sophie out to the waiting police car, watched by a crowd of curious hotel guests. The constable held his raincoat over her head as she got into the back, beside the sergeant. Behind them the five hire cars were already waiting.

'Would you like to tell me just what you are up to?' Derek asked.

'Just what I told you. I know those men are terrorists. I know they are here to take over the island. I know . . .'

'Sophie,' Derek said patiently, 'even supposing taking over the island was a practical possibility . . .'

'It *is*, simply because nobody believes they can do it.'

'OK, OK, supposing they can and they do . . . what are they going to do with it? With everybody in it? I mean, it just doesn't make sense.'

'They are going to hold us to ransom,' Sophie said.

'Oh, come now.'

'Why won't you believe me?' She was close to tears. 'You'd believe James.'

'Well . . . James isn't here, is he?'

'No, he's not. He's in hospital, drugged to the eyeballs.'

'Can you prove that?'

'All you have to do is telephone the PEH.'

'I meant, can you prove he's drugged to the eyeballs?'

69

'The doctor who attended him can. Chap called Murrain.'

'Hm,' Derek commented.

'Listen,' Sophie said: 'you saw those five cars waiting at the hotel. They're for the Arabs.'

'So?'

'I will bet you my last penny they are going to use those cars to drive on to the dock at about half past eleven tonight, pick up their weapons, and then disperse to take over their objectives.'

'Oh really, Sophie.'

'If you were to go back to the Guernsey Island, Derek, and stop them using those cars, you could nip the whole thing in the bud.'

'What possible reason could I give for preventing them using cars they have legitimately hired?'

'Well . . . you could check their driving licences. I'm certain they're forged.'

'You get more far-fetched with every moment, Sophie.'

Sophie gave up, for the time being. The police car swung into station parking, and she hurried through the rain to the charge desk. 'You're not going to start fingerprinting me and photographing me and all that stuff,' she said.

'I think we can leave that until tomorrow, and see just what sort of a deposition your friend Rakim comes up with,' Derek said. 'But what I want you to promise me is that you will go straight home and go to bed and stay there.'

'You mean you're going to do nothing? By tomorrow . . .'

'So you say.'

'And you don't believe me.'

'Frankly, no.'

'Well, look – won't you at least put a man on the dock, to keep an eye on that yacht?'

'I'll see if we can sort something out.'

'And meanwhile al-Rakim and his friends are free to get on with their plans. You never did search their rooms.'

Derek sighed. 'If they have any plans. On a night like

this, I would suppose they are aiming to go to bed. Do you really suppose we would find anything if we did search their rooms?'

Her turn to sigh: 'No, I don't suppose you would. It's that yacht you need to search.'

'And that isn't practical, without a warrant, and frankly, even if it wasn't the worst night of the year to get a jurat out of bed, we have no grounds for asking for a warrant.' He held up a finger. 'Save for your suspicious nature.' He looked at his watch. 'Ten o'clock. Now, Sophie, you go home to your flat, have a stiff drink, and go to bed. Things will look brighter in the morning.'

'Am I allowed to go to the hospital and see James?'

'Certainly, but if you intend to drive, skip the stiff drink.'

'My car's at the Guernsey Island. I'll pick it up in the morning.'

'Good thinking. I'll have you dropped home.'

She went to the door, turned. 'Ten o'clock,' she said. 'That means there's less than two hours left before those people start moving.'

'Sophie!'

She hurried out into the rain.

So what now? she wondered, as she climbed the stairs to the flat, and began stripping off soaking clothing. No one wanted to know. No one believed it was possible. Save for James, and James was out for at least another two hours. After which . . .

She *couldn't* just go to bed and wake up tomorrow with Guernsey in the hands of a terrorist organisation. She *had* to do something – find someone who would believe her. And it was now ten fifteen.

She had a hot shower, partly to warm herself up and partly to give herself time to think. Her thoughts immediately went to people like the Bailiff, who was presumably on the hit list; but she had never met the Bailiff, and she did not suppose his reaction would be any more positive than that of someone like Derek Doofield. The same went for the Chief of Police. She

71

needed someone who could influence them into believing her. And who might believe her themselves!

And she could think of no one . . . save Jack Harding.

She wrapped herself in a towel and looked up the number in the book. Harding, as she recalled, was a bachelor. He was not a man she actually liked, although James seemed to rank him highly, as 'one of the boys'. She had never been sure what that meant; she found Harding's manner of looking at every female with predatory eyes, as if wondering what she would be like in bed, offensive; but there could be no doubt that he was one of the most vigorous members of the local parliament, the States of Guernsey.

The phone buzzed several times before it was answered.

'Yes?'

'Mr Harding? Jack?'

'I am Jack Harding.'

'I hope I didn't wake you up.'

'No, you did not wake me up. Who is this?'

'Sophie Gallagher.'

'Who?'

'Sophie. James Candish's flatmate.'

'Ah . . . oh, yes. How is James? I heard a rumour he'd had an accident.'

'That's one of the things we need to talk about,' Sophie said.

'Oh, yes? Well, I've a rather busy schedule tomorrow. Where is James?'

'He's in hospital, Mr Harding.'

'I see. Well, look, perhaps we could meet for lunch . . .'

'Tonight,' Sophie said. 'We need to meet tonight. Now. It is most urgent.'

'My dear girl, do you know the time?'

'I said, it's urgent. It's a matter of national security.'

There was a moment's silence. 'Something to do with James is a matter of national security?' Harding asked at last.

'Yes,' Sophie said. 'Can I come round?'

'Now?'

'As soon as I can get a taxi.' She had no desire to go back to the Guernsey Island without an escort.

'Well . . .'

Sophie knew he lived in St Saviour's. 'I think I can be there in half an hour,' she said.

She hung up, called the taxi firm, got dressed, waited, drumming her fingers on the table while she looked out of the window, willing herself not to look at the hands on the clock on the mantelpiece slowly moving round – and frowned, as she saw movement on the rainswept street below. The figure had merely been shifting position, and had now disappeared again; but it had been there. Her flat was being watched. *Her* flat! It could be no other. Just as the watcher had to be one of the Arabs. They would have had no difficulty in getting hold of her address, from either the phone book or someone in the hotel. Bertie would have been happy to co-operate, if only to keep her job. But the man was on foot; he would not be able to follow the taxi.

And there it was, sweeping slowly round the corner, following its headlights through the rain. She switched off the flat lights, picked up her coat, and moved back to the window to be sure it had stopped. It had, and as she watched, the man watching the flat detached himself from the shadows and crossed the road.

Of all the cheek, she thought; what was he going to do – ask where his fare was going? She stared down into the gloom, her heart seeming to constrict as she saw the man suddenly reaching into the car, the driver's window having been rolled down for the conversation. There were a couple of quick movements – she couldn't be sure exactly what – then the man opened the driver's door and now reached inside with his entire shoulders. He dragged out the taxi-driver, who was either unconscious or dead, opened the back door, and laid the man on the floor. Then he got behind the wheel and sat down.

He was waiting for her to come down, and then . . . Sophie's throat was dry. She went back to the phone, scrabbled for the number in the darkness as she bent over the table.

'Police station.'

'Sergeant Doofield, please.'

'I'm sorry, Sergeant Doofield has just stepped out.'

'Oh, sh . . . oot. Listen: I'm being stalked.'

'Are you, miss? Where?'

'At my flat. There's a man downstairs waiting to assault me.'

The constable on the phone digested this. 'May I have your name and address, please?'

'My name is Sophie Gallagher, and my address is . . .'

'Sophie Gallagher,' the constable said.

'That's right.'

'You were in here about an hour ago.'

'Yes, that's right.'

'On a charge of illegal entry.'

'For God's sake,' Sophie shouted. 'What's that got to do with it? There's a man outside, waiting to . . . to . . .'

'Yes, Miss Gallagher?'

'I think he's already killed a man. A taxi-driver.'

Some more digestion. 'I'll send someone round,' the constable said at last. 'But if this is some wild goose chase . . .'

'Send two,' Sophie said. 'This man is dangerous.'

'I'll see who I can find,' the constable agreed.

The phone went dead. As it did so, the doorbell rang.

Oh, hell, Sophie thought. Had she forgotten to close the street door? It could have been one of the other occupants . . . but they were mainly middle-aged people, who she didn't think would be too much use in a punch-up with a lethal Arab.

The bell rang again. 'Your taxi, ma'am,' said the voice, in almost flawless English.

The bastard. She had supposed only al-Rakim spoke English.

She listened to a scrabbling sound at the lock. He was using some kind of tool to force an entry, and there was no security chain; in Guernsey it had never seemed necessary. She licked her lips, backed across the room. What to do? Get the big knife from the kitchen and try to take him when he came through? She didn't think that would work against a man obviously trained in unarmed combat.

Call the police? She'd already done that.

Open the window and shout for help? She wasn't likely to get too much of a response on a night like this. But . . . she opened the window anyway. It really was only about twelve feet to the front garden. Twelve feet! So she might break a leg. At least she'd be alive.

She listened to a crunching sound behind her as the lock was forced. She sat on the window sill, then turned and lowered her body, hands tight on the sill. Instantly she was buffeted by the wind and the rain. She looked back into the room, and saw the door opening. Then she dropped, straight down into the flower bed, which unfortunately contained a rose bush. The thorns tore at her clothes and her flesh, but she didn't think she had actually hurt anything serious.

She looked up, saw a face at the window, looking down. She scrambled out of the flower bed and ran down the path to the gate. The taxi waited, engine running. The police were coming, so they said, but she had no idea how long they might be. And she couldn't wait.

She got behind the wheel, gunned the motor. It was a handshift, and unfamiliar, but she managed to get it moving, and drove round the corner.

From behind her there came a groan. She'd almost forgotten the driver; but he could be badly hurt. She twisted the wheel to and fro, skidded round several corners, and reached the hospital. She braked in front of Casualty, ran inside.

'Please,' she told the male nurse on duty. 'There's a man in the car outside. He's hurt.'

Bells rang, and other white-jacketed men appeared to hurry out to the car and bring the driver in.

'What happened to him?'

'Someone hit him.'

'Who? You?'

'Do I look as if I go around hitting taxi-drivers? He was . . . mugged.' To tell the truth might involve her in hours of questioning.

'Good Lord.' The medic was raising the driver's eyelids, peering at his eyes. 'He's been hit very hard.'

'Is he going to be all right?'

'I should think so. But we'd better get him to bed, just in case. You'll have to fill out this form.'

Sophie wrote rapidly. While she did so, she asked, 'May I use your phone?'

'There's a payphone over there, miss.'

'I don't have any coins, and this is urgent. I need to call the police.'

'About the mugging! Yes, I suppose you do.' He pushed the phone across the desk.

A stretcher trolley had appeared, and the taxi-driver was being wheeled away.

'Come on, come on,' Sophie said into the phone. 'Hello. This is Sophie Gallagher.'

'Oh, yes.' It was the same constable as before, and he was sounding rather tired. 'A car is on its way, Miss Gallagher.'

'Well, listen,' Sophie said: 'I'm no longer there. I'm calling from the hospital.'

'Would you repeat that, please?'

'The stalker broke into my flat,' Sophie explained. 'After laying out my taxi-driver. I escaped, and drove the taxi here. I shouldn't think the intruder is still in the flat, but you'd better go there first, just in case.'

'Miss Gallagher . . .'

'Hurry,' Sophie said.

The male nurse had been listening with interest. Now he asked, 'Do you realise you're bleeding, Miss Gallagher.'

'Where?'

'Well, your hand, for one thing. And there's blood on your coat, by that tear. You'd better let me have a look at you.'

'Forget it.' Sophie looked at her watch. It was nearly eleven. 'Listen: I have to go. When the police get here, explain.'

'Explain what?'

'Just explain.' Sophie ran out into the rain and got into the taxi. The radio was spluttering, someone calling Dick over and over again. Sophie switched it off, drove out of the hospital grounds, and then remembered she'd forgotten to ask after James; but that would have involved even more explanations, and time was now very short. She had to assume he was both still unconscious and all right.

Thanks to her years of driving the minibus she knew every road in Guernsey, and found Harding's without any difficulty; but it was still a good distance on wet surfaces and with an unfamiliar car, and it was past eleven before she reached his house, one of several bungalows. She parked the car, ran up the path. The front door opened as she got there.

'You look like a drowned rat,' Harding remarked.

He was a heavy-set man with a bristling moustache and a florid complexion. He was wearing a smoking jacket over . . . she didn't care to think what: his legs were bare except for slippers.

'I feel like a drowned rat. Mr Harding . . .'

He closed the door on them. 'I think you should take those wet things off,' he said. 'I'll lend you a dressing gown.'

Sophie was inhaling not very stale perfume. He had been entertaining. She wondered what he'd done with the bird – sent her off or hidden her in a cupboard?

'I haven't time,' she told him. 'Mr Harding . . .'

'Well, at least let me pour you a drink.' He led the way

into a somewhat overfurnished lounge, which had a very well-stocked bar in one corner. 'Brandy do you?'

'I do not want a brandy,' Sophie said. 'I want help.'

He poured anyway, two goblets, and turned to look at her. 'Did anyone ever tell you what a damned good-looking woman you are, Sophie? Even when soaking wet?'

'For God's sake,' Sophie shouted. 'Listen to me! Guernsey is about to be taken over by a bunch of terrorists.'

He frowned, vaguely, sipping some brandy. 'What on earth are you talking about?'

'Listen! There's a yacht in the harbour—'

'That Arab job? I saw her, this afternoon. Some gin palace. Isn't that the ship on which James had his accident?'

'He did *not* have an accident. He was investigating, trying to find out the truth about her, and they caught him and drugged him.'

Harding put down the second brandy glass. 'Maybe you shouldn't have this, after all. Where have you come from?'

'It would take too long to explain, and we're running out of time. Mr Harding, that yacht is filled with armed men. There are more members of the gang on shore. At midnight, they are going to link up and take over the island.'

'Oh really, Sophie . . .'

'It's true.' She went closer to him. 'Please believe me.'

'How can a handful of men—'

'I've seen the list of what they intend to do. All the key places. By tomorrow morning they'll have Guernsey in the palms of their hands.'

'While Guernsey does nothing about it.'

'What are they going to do, Mr Harding? Tomorrow's Sunday. People will get up late, and maybe go to church, and wash their cars, and have a family lunch, and maybe go for a drive. They won't know anything is wrong. They won't know the island has been taken over.'

'They will eventually,' Harding pointed out. 'And while

this is happening, what do you suppose the mainland is going to do about it?'

'The mainland isn't going to know about it either, Mr Harding, until it is too late.'

Harding considered her for several seconds. Then he said, 'Maybe you should have that brandy after all; you've obviously had a few already.' He poured, while Sophie watched him in total disbelief. 'Now,' he said, holding out the goblet, 'let's get those wet clothes off you, and then we'll put you in a hot shower and warm you up, and then . . . why, we'll sit down together, you and me, and have a little chat.'

He was advancing behind the brandy goblet. Sophie swung her hand and knocked it from his fingers, sending it to the floor where it smashed in a flurry of liquid.

'For God's sake,' he snapped.

'Goodbye,' Sophie said. 'And I hope you're one of those they shoot.'

As she ran for the door, he seized her shoulder and swung her round. 'You little bitch,' he said. 'You come here, in the middle of the night, with your tits hanging out, and—'

'Bastard!' Sophie snapped. 'Let me go.'

'Let you go? We're going to have that hot shower, together.'

'You . . .' She swung her hand and hit him on the side of the head. He gasped, and let her go, but then grasped her again, this time round the waist, as she turned for the door. She kicked behind her, and he grunted. They fell together, Sophie on top, which made him grunt even more. She struck down with her elbows, and he gave another gasp, but was now tearing at her clothes. Sophie rolled over and thrust her fingers at his face. His head reared back and she got to her knees, then her feet, and stamped on him as he tried to rise. He gave a strangled shriek, and fell back, clutching his groin.

'I'll have you in court,' he snarled. 'I'll—'

'Don't hold your breath,' Sophie recommended.

She ran out into the rain, climbed into the taxi, and gunned the engine.

After sending Sophie home, Derek Doofield had a cup of coffee. Then he went for his customary walk about the town. He always did this on Saturday nights, when he was on duty. If there was ever any trouble, now was the time, just as the pubs closed; but tonight all anyone wanted to do was get home and out of the wet.

He agreed with them, and returned to the station, where WPC MacPherson was waiting with another cup of coffee.

'Anything?'

'Donald wants a word.'

'Donald?'

'That woman you brought in a couple of hours ago, Sarge – Sophie Gallagher.'

'Don't tell me she's in trouble again?'

'She's certainly being a nuisance. She telephoned while you were out, saying a man was breaking into her flat.'

'Eh?' Doofield sat up.

'She was talking wildly, about her taxi-driver being killed. Well, I sent a car round right away, but they found nothing – no taxi, no intruder, and no Sophie Gallagher.'

'Oh, my God!' Doofield said.

'But then she telephoned again – from the hospital, where she'd taken the taxi-driver. Seems he wasn't dead after all. Just had a bump on the head.'

'From this intruder?'

'Or from Sophie. It's all very mystifying.'

'But she's at the hospital.'

'No, she's not. She said she had some place to go, and hung up. When I called back, the hospital receptionist said she'd driven off in Dave Williams's taxi. Isn't that stealing?'

'Not if Dave gave her permission.'

'Dave was unconscious, Sarge. I think we should pick her up.'

'Did she say where she was going?'

'No. Just drove away into the night.'

'Well, we'll leave it for tonight. I'll have a word with her in the morning. She'll have gone home by then, or she'll have gone back to the hospital to be with James.'

Donald went off, shaking his head, while Doofield leaned back in his chair, thinking.

Sophie was such an attractive girl – sensible, level-headed as well as good-looking. James Candish was a lucky chap. Then what had activated her tonight into accusing people of being terrorists? Breaking into hotel bedrooms? Claiming that James had been drugged? It just didn't make sense. But she had seemed to believe it.

It could do no harm to make at least a preliminary check. He picked up his phone and called the hospital.

'Who's that? Desmond? Right. This is Derek Doofield. You have James Candish with you tonight, right?'

'Who?'

'James Candish. Assistant Harbourmaster. I've been hearing a rumour that he's had an accident.'

'I'll just check. Yes, here we are: admitted five-fifteen this afternoon. Drug overdose. He is in intensive care.'

'Did you say drug overdose? James Candish? Self-inflicted?'

'Ah . . .' Desmond was obviously checking his computer. 'No. Drugs adminstered by Arab doctor from yacht *Gloriosa*, to subdue patient following a fit.'

'A fit,' Doofield said thoughtfully. 'Can you access Candish's medical history?'

'Well, I can,' Desmond said doubtfully. 'But to release any of it I would need a court order.'

'Listen, Desmond,' Doofield said: 'this is strictly between you and me, and I am not interested in whether James has ever had syphilis or is HIV positive. I just want to know if there is any history of fits or epilepsy. Or even *a* fit.'

81

'Hold on.' Desmond was back in five minutes. 'No, Sergeant – no fits. In fact, until tonight, his only entry is an appendectomy two years ago.'

'Thank you, Desmond. I owe you one.'

Doofield hung up, beckoning Donald. 'Has there been any complaint from this big yacht alongside the Cambridge Dock?'

'Complaint, Sergeant?'

'About the behaviour of any of our people. Specifically, James Candish.'

The constable shook his head. 'I did hear something about an accident . . .'

'This was not an accident. This was behaviour that required a massive dose of sedative to calm him down. Yet the people on the yacht have not reported it. Don't you find that odd?'

'Well . . . they're foreigners,' Donald suggested.

Doofield made no reply, but leaned back in his chair again. Sophie had said Dr Murrain had been the doctor on duty when James had been taken in. He toyed with the idea of calling the doctor, but decided against. It was after eleven, and he did not have sufficient reason for getting the doctor out of bed just to answer a few questions. He brooded for a few minutes longer, then came to a decision, got up, put on his cap and topcoat.

'I'm going out for half an hour,' he said.

'Right you are, Sergeant.'

Doofield got into his car and drove down to the St Peter Port front. The pubs were closed by now, but usually on a Saturday night there would be a throng of young people gathered behind the States Offices. Tonight the weather was keeping them away: the esplanade was deserted and wet, with the wind whipping up little wavelets in the puddles and bigger wavelets in the harbour. But the tide was dead low, and inside the marina all was still save for the clacking of halyards.

Alongside the Cambridge dock he could make out the bulk of the yacht, but she was in darkness. The weather was too much, even for the Arabs; which made having a look at her that much more simple. Doofield drove on to the car park and got out. His was the only vehicle there. He climbed the steps, and checked just before he reached the raised walkway that had once been the harbour wall. Five cars were driving slowly down the road from the esplanade. They had to pass behind him, and thence round the outer end of the harbour before they could approach the yacht. Five cars! Just as Sophie had said.

He waited, as the headlamps slowly rounded the top of the pier and came back down to the Cambridge Dock. This was exactly opposite where he was now crouching. As the cars stopped he could make out the distinctive 'H' attached to each to indicate that it was indeed a hire car.

Just as Sophie had said.

He watched as the men got out, and hurried to the yacht gangplank. Now he saw interior lights as a bulkhead door was opened. He looked at his watch. Eleven thirty. Exactly as Sophie had said.

Still he hesitated. All manner of possibilities ran through his mind. The people on the yacht, and the people in the cars, had still not broken any laws. It could very well be that the people on the yacht had discovered there was another party of Arabs in Guernsey and had invited them on board for a drink. The fact that the yacht was showing no deck or masthead lights was not illegal while she was alongside and on the ground as opposed to being at anchor.

All he had to go on was Sophie's suspicions and James Candish's condition. To start throwing police weight about could well cause international repercussions. But James was a possible entrée: he'd only be doing his job to follow it up.

Sergeant Doofield straightened, walked up the steps and down the other side, and crossed the road. The five hire cars were lined up bumper to bumper in front of him, and to his surprise he saw that each still had a driver behind the wheel.

'Good evening,' he said.

None of the men responded.

'Ah, well.' Doofield walked on to the dock and reached the

foot of the gangplank. There was nobody on deck. 'Hello!' he called. 'Ship ahoy! Shop!'

There was no response. He walked up the gangplank, paused at the top. 'Permission to come aboard,' he called.

A bulkhead door opened and a man came out. 'Who are you?' he asked.

'Sergeant Derek Doofield, Guernsey Police, sir,' Doofield said. 'About this fracas this afternoon. It was reported by the harbourmaster. I wonder if . . .' he checked as the door opened again, and another man came out. This man was carrying a rifle. 'I say,' Doofield said, 'I hope you have a licence for that thing.'

The man squeezed the trigger.

The Fugitive

'What's that noise?' Brian asked.

Charlie, who had just come on duty and was peering into the radar screen in the watch house, asked, 'What noise?'

It was almost impossible to hear anything over the howl of the wind and the slaps of the waves against the harbour wall beneath them.

'Sounded like a shot,' Brian said.

'What – in the harbour, at eleven thirty on a Saturday night?' But Charlie picked up the binoculars and looked back into the harbour. Fishing boats, the pilot boat, the lifeboat, those yachts that had been unable to get into the marina, were all bobbing about, but all were securely moored, and none were showing any lights. The big hydrofoils were also securely moored for the night, hardly moving to the elements. He could just make out the masts of the Arab yacht, beyond the warehouses on the Cambridge Dock; but she was now dry and not moving at all.

'Must've been a backfire,' he said.

'Pretty damned loud backfire in this wind,' Brian commented. 'Well, I'm for bed. See you in the morning.'

He got up, stretched, and the outside door opened, to reveal two men standing there, holding assault rifles.

Sophie drove very fast for a few hundred yards after leaving Harding's house; her entire body was a seethe. Then she slowed, braked at the side of the road and sat there, both

85

hands wrapped around the wheel, drawing deep breaths. That horrible man! . . . But he really was an irrelevance, compared with what was happening.

She looked at her watch: it was twenty past eleven. Whatever was going to happen was about to happen, and she was the only one who knew it . . . save for the Arabs, of course.

So what was she going to do? Quite apart from her tumbling emotions, she was again soaking wet, she was driving a strange car that could almost be described as stolen – if the hospital had managed to bring the driver round he would certainly be wondering where his car was – and she was battered and bruised.

And she could find no one to believe her.

But she did have a legitimate reason to go to the police and *make* them do something. She had reported a crime. Something must have happened there. She engaged gear, drove into town and into the station yard. She ran across the paving stones and tripped as she ran up the stairs, landing on her hands and knees. Her pants tore at the knee.

Muttering curses, she pushed herself up, opened the heavy door, and staggered to the charge desk. 'Sergeant Doofield,' she said. 'I want to speak with Sergeant Doofield.'

The constable raised his head. 'Oh, it's you,' he remarked. 'Do you realise you look like something the cat dragged in . . . and then threw right back out again?' He chuckled at his wit.

'Be funny,' Sophie snapped. 'I told you, I wish to see Sergeant Doofield.'

'He's gone out.'

'That was more than an hour ago.'

'That's right. He went out, and came in, and then went out again.'

'Where?'

'He didn't say.'

'Well, when is he coming back?'

'He didn't say about that either.'

'For God's sake,' Sophie said. 'Well, can't you get him on his mobile?'

'Maybe.' He seemed determined not to co-operate.

'OK,' she said. 'I called you earlier, about a man breaking into my flat after attacking my taxi-driver.'

'And I said you'd be in trouble if it was a wild goose chase.'

'Did you send a man to my flat?'

'I sent two; and they reported there was no one there, and that the front door was open. That's careless, that is.'

'Couldn't they see the lock had been forced?'

'I shouldn't think they looked. Now, this man you laid out . . .'

'I did not lay out any man,' Sophie shouted. 'The Arab did that!'

By now the rumpus at the desk had attracted attention, and several constables, two of them women, had gathered.

'What seems to be the trouble?' asked one of the senior constables.

The policeman sighed. 'This is Miss Sophie Gallagher. At the present time she is in the middle of a one-woman crime spree. Let's see now: at nine o'clock this evening she was arrested on an accusation of unlawful entry into the room of a hotel guest at the Guernsey Island. Sergeant Doofield decided not to formally charge her until tomorrow; I think he is hoping the guest will not press charges. Then at ten fifteen she telephoned to say someone was breaking into her flat. This was a false alarm.'

'That is absolute nonsense,' Sophie said. 'Someone *was* breaking into my flat. An Arab.'

Constable Dickinson had only just come on duty. 'An Arab?' he asked.

'At this moment, Guernsey is crawling with Arabs,' Sophie said. 'You have to do something about it.'

Dickinson scratched his head.

'At this time,' Donald persisted, 'Miss Gallagher appears to have hit her taxi-driver on the head.'

'I did not hit him,' Sophie shouted. 'The Arab did that.'

'The Arab,' Dickinson said again. 'Is he under arrest?'

'I don't think he exists,' Donald said.

'What about the taxi-driver?'

'Dave Williams.'

'I took him to the hospital.' Sophie said.

'Well, yes,' Donald admitted grudgingly. 'She did the right thing there. But then she drove off in Dave's taxi. That's stealing.'

'Can you explain this, miss?' Dickinson asked.

'I needed a car,' Sophie said, wearily. 'I borrowed the taxi. It's outside. But listen: something terrible is happening. You simply have to do something.'

Dickinson looked at Donald. 'Do you know what she's talking about?'

'No I do not,' Donald said. 'She was on at the sarge about something, but I don't know what. He'll be able to tell us when he comes back.'

'The Arabs!' Sophie shouted. 'They're taking over the island.'

'Have you been drinking, miss?' Dickinson asked.

'Oh, for God's sake . . .'

'Let's begin by having a look at this taxi, you . . . borrowed,' the constable decided. He went to the door, but before he could open it, it was thrown in, and a dozen men came in with it, armed with assault rifles.

'What the . . . ?' Dickinson began.

'Jesus!' Donald said, reaching for the phone; but before he could pick it up one of the men fired, to shatter it into a hundred pieces. Donald stared at his bleeding fingers.

WPC MacPherson stifled a scream. The other policemen backed across the room.

'Hands high,' said one of the intruders. 'Obey, and no one will be killed.'

The policemen raised their arms.

For the moment, no one was paying any attention to Sophie, and none of these was from the hotel. She stood against the charge desk, her hands as high as anyone's.

'How many people in the building?' demanded the spokes-man.

Dickinson was recovering from the shock. 'Enough,' he said.

The spokesman levelled his rifle and fired. At such close range Dickinson seemed to disintegrate, his chest falling apart beneath the impact of the bullet, his blue tunic instantly smothered in blood.

Now WPC MacPherson did scream, as she ran forward, to be checked by a gun barrel.

'I said to co-operate,' the leader told them.

From upstairs there came shouts of alarm.

'Get them,' the leader told four of his men.

They ran for the stairs.

'You,' the leader said, 'back up.'

'That man is dying,' MacPherson protested.

'That man is dead,' the leader said. 'Now, you . . .' He pointed at MacPherson. '. . . and you . . .' He pointed at Donald. '. . . will show us how everything works. The rest of you, in there.'

He pointed to the small interview room opening to the right. The policemen hesitated; but they were utterly helpless, and they had seen what might happen if they attempted to resist or even argue. They moved towards the interview room. Again, Sophie was ignored, it being apparently assumed by the Arabs that she was a plainclothes policewoman who would follow her comrades. But to be shut in there while these people carried out their plan . . . and she did not yet know what their ultimate plan was.

To her left there was another door, leading she had no idea where. She had to risk it. As the last of the policemen entered the interview room, those on the upper floor started coming down the stairs, hands held high, looking utterly bemused, followed by the terrorists. For the moment everyone was looking up; the terrorists had no eyes for a single, bedraggled woman.

Sophie took a deep breath and ran for the door; it was only a matter of four steps. There was a shout, and a shot, and a bullet smashed into the wall beside her head; but the door was unlocked and a moment later she was through, slamming it behind herself, shooting the bolt on the inside, wincing as another bullet smashed this time right through the door and hit the inner wall.

She was in a small kitchenette, and there was another door at the back. She reached this in two strides, while more bullets crashed into and through the wood behind her, and there came the thump of a shoulder charge. The door creaked, and would open in a moment.

Sophie tore open the second door and stepped into the rain and wind. She was in a small yard. To her left there was access to the car park, but she didn't doubt they'd have that covered. To her right there was a wall. It was some six feet high, but she threw herself at it, got a leg over, and sat astride.

The door behind her opened, and she dropped down into another yard beyond. To her surprise there were no further shots; but then she realised that it was no part of the terrorists' plan to alert the ordinary Guernseymen and women to what was happening until it was necessary. Already a light had come on in the upstairs of the nearest building.

It was tempting to bang on their door, but what good would that do? They wouldn't believe her, and if they did, and went to investigate, they'd only get themselves killed. She needed positive help, and she needed to alert the world as to what was happening. She had to *make* someone understand.

She tiptoed across the yard, while a dog barked in the house. There was a gate, which she opened, and found herself in one of the narrow streets that composed the

Truchot, surrounded by office buildings, presently closed
and dark.

She heard movement behind her, and the dog was still
barking. She flattened herself against the wall, looked back,
and saw two figures coming through the yard she had just
left. The upstairs light had gone out.

Sophie scooped water from her face and eyes, and tried
to think. There were two of the terrorists following her . . .
but they were not going to use their guns. That was a small
advantage. She needed people, lots and lots of people. She
was only a hundred yards from the front. But there would
hardly be anyone there at midnight on a stormy night. Except
perhaps a policeman.

She ran down the sloping road. There were no shouts from
behind her now, but they were coming too; she could hear
the footsteps.

She reached the pavement, and the street lights. Now she
was utterly exposed, and there was not a policeman in sight.
The front was deserted.

Sophie looked left and right, then opted for the marina.
She ran across the road and on to what was called the
Crown Pier. On her right gangways led down to the various
pontoons, and these were crowded with yachts. This was the
visitors' marina, and the odds were that most of the craft in
here sheltering from the storm were French. None of them
was showing any lights, and in any event she didn't feel her
French was up to explaining the situation. But there were so
many boats and warps and dinghies . . .

Looking over her shoulder, she saw the two men leave the
far side of the esplanade and come towards her. They were
not hurrying; they could see her, and they estimated she was
running out of options.

Sophie ran down the first gangway, on to the pontoon, then
along the pontoon for three-quarters of its length. Then she
looked back. The two men were coming down the gangway. A
light had come on in one of the yachts, its occupants disturbed

by the pounding feet; but again Sophie rejected the option of seeking help where it could be of no use and might just get someone else killed.

She sat down, and slipped her feet over the edge. Even in June, because of the rain and the wind, the water felt freezing. She pushed herself off and slipped into the water. She was a good swimmer, but in any event, at low tide the marina depth was maintained at only six feet; she could go right down, and then push herself back up with her feet.

This she now did, moving between the hulls of the two closest yachts, listening to more feet on the pontoon. She drew a deep breath, and sank below the surface until she touched bottom, then kicked forward; it was only a few feet to the next pontoon, the next row of boats. She held her breath long enough to get right under the pontoon, then came up, her head resting against the wooden slats above her, drawing deep gulps of air.

From her position she could look back at the first pontoon, and see the two men, standing together; but in the darkness they would not have been able to see any movement in the water.

She waited, keeping absolutely still, watching them. They remained on the pontoon for several minutes, obviously deciding what to do next. Then they walked back to the gangway and went up to the pier. Sophie stayed where she was. She had no doubt that at least one of them would remain, watching and waiting for her to surface, literally. The other would no doubt return to the police station, or go on to the *Gloriosa* for further instructions.

What were they afraid of, regarding her? That she might alert the population to what was going on? Chance would be a fine thing, where no one wanted to listen; and by now the deed was done. She couldn't remember the whole schedule, but she did remember that the entire coup was to have been completed in two hours. It hadn't been two hours yet, but all the other units would be in place and

carrying out their tasks, if necessary with deadly inten-
sity.

While she . . . she was shivering now, her teeth chattering.
She had to move. But she had already determined on a way
out. She went down again, under the surface, and reached the
outer pontoon. Here she paused for breath; and from here she
could see the pier. She couldn't make out anyone, but she was
sure he was there. On the other hand, he was clearly under
orders not to shoot.

Once again she dived, this time swimming for the lip.
Above this there was a gate, unnecessary at this state of
the tide, but needed when the water first started to flow
over the lip; yachtsmen had been known in the past to try
to get out before there was enough depth, and go crunching
into the sill. But she was quite sure she could get through.

She surfaced just before the lip, grasped the bars on the
gate and pulled herself up. She waited for a shout from behind
her, turned round with difficulty, and looked up at the pier; but
whoever was there had not made her out in the darkness.

Carefully she wriggled between the bars, tearing her shirt;
as her pants were already torn she did not suppose she could
look any more decrepit, but wished her breasts were slightly
smaller. Then she was on the outside, with a six-foot drop
to the sand of the dry harbour. The tide was actually on the
flood again, but only just; the water was at least a hundred
feet away.

She lowered herself to the full extent of her arms, then let
go, and dropped easily enough, splashing into a puddle. Just
across the way, leaning against the Cambridge Dock, was
the bulk of the big yacht. She was in utter darkness, but
her generator was grumbling away, and a steady stream of
water was exiting from the waste pipe.

But for the moment, *she* was free. To do what? Get to
a phone. She had left her mobile in her flat, but she was
not prepared to go back there at the moment. She had to
go somewhere she would be welcomed, and believed. Her

boss? She doubted she would get much of response from him. Derek Doofield! He would have to believe her now. If only she knew where he was. Perhaps he had gone home; but she had only the vaguest idea where he lived.

Bill Harrison of course! Surely she'd be able to make *him* believe her. And he'd said to call him the moment James woke up. Well, she was sure James would be awake by now. Someone else to call.

She splashed across the sand up the steps against the White Rock Pier. Even if the man on the Crown Pier could see her now, there was no way he could get at her save by coming round the esplanade. She could beat him to that.

Sophie hurried up the hill from the waterfront. She used the main thoroughfare, St Julian's Avenue and then the Grange; the rain continued to lash down and the wind to boom and gust, and there was no one else around. Guernsey was sleeping peacefully, while al-Rakim's people did their work.

Halfway up the hill she left the main road and took the lane leading up beside the brewery on the corner. Ten minutes later she emerged on to flatter ground. She was panting and paining; quite apart from being soaked through she was exhausted by the evening's events. It seemed an eternity since she had received that telephone call to say that James had been hurt. She should be there at the hospital now, to be with him when he woke up; but there was nothing he could do, save become agitated.

She staggered along the empty streets and finally reached the Harrisons' house. Like every other house it was in darkness. She opened the gate, made her way along the path and up the two steps to the front door, and rang the bell. Again and again and again.

At the fourth ring a light came on upstairs, and at the fifth a window was thrown up. 'Who's down there?' Bill called.

'Sophie. Please let me in.'

The window closed, and a moment later the hall light came on. Then the door opened. Bill wore a dressing gown and slippers. 'Sophie? My God, you're soaked through. Come in, come in. Is there something the matter?'

Gratefully Sophie stepped out of the rain. 'Everything is the matter.'

Doris Harrison appeared on the stairs, also in dressing gown and slippers. 'It's James. Something's happened to James.'

'No,' Sophie said wearily. 'James is all right – I think. I need to use a phone.'

'Of course. But first you must get out of those wet things.'

'There's no time,' Sophie said. 'Listen: those Arabs on the yacht and at the hotel – they're terrorists, and they've taken over the island.'

Harrison glanced at his wife, uneasily.

'Do get changed, my dear,' Doris said. 'You'll catch your death. Bill, put the kettle on and make some tea.'

Harrison hurried for the kitchen.

'Now,' Doris said, 'you just come upstairs, and we'll run you a hot bath, and get you something warm to wear.'

Sophie's shoulders sagged, but she was shivering, and she probably *would* come down with something if she didn't change. Anyway, who was she going to telephone?

She allowed herself to be taken upstairs, and a few minutes later was sitting in a steaming tub. 'Can I talk to you?' she asked Doris.

'Of course, my dear.'

'I mean, will you listen?'

'Of course I will. Bill,' she called through the half-open door. 'Put the tea down out there. We'll be out in a moment.' She brought the cup of tea into the bathroom for Sophie to drink and sat on the chair. 'Now, tell me. Something has happened. I know it has. You've been assaulted. Have you been to the police?'

'The police!' Sophie had in any event still been trembling; now she shuddered, and spilt some of the tea. 'Please believe

me, Mrs Harrison.' She outlined what had happened that
evening, omitting only Harding's assault; she merely said
she had been to him and he had laughed at her.

Doris listened to her with growing and obvious incredulity,
clearly trying to decide whether Sophie had gone mad or was
merely drunk.

'That's a nasty cut on your hand,' she remarked, absently.
'I'll put some antiseptic spray on it, shall I?'

'I scratched it on a rose bush when jumping out of my
window,' Sophie said, standing up and drying herself.

'What a night you've had,' Doris agreed.

'You mean you don't believe me.'

'Now, Sophie . . . well . . . it's a little hard to grasp.'

'I'd like Captain Harrison to hear it.'

'Yes, of course. Here.' She held out her spare dressing
gown, and Sophie wrapped herself in it then went into the
bedroom, where Harrison was pacing to and fro. 'Sophie has
something to tell you,' Doris said.

Bill listened, occasionally glancing at his wife.

'You are saying you saw Constable Dickinson shot?' he
asked when she finished. 'And that you were then chased
into the harbour by two terrorists?'

'That is what happened, yes.'

'Do you mind if I check this out?'

'I want you to check it out.'

Harrison picked up the phone and punched the numbers.
'Hello. Would it be possible to speak with Constable
Dickinson, please?' He listened. 'Ah. Right. Well, then,
is Sergeant Doofield there? Ah. Very well, thank you. No,
I'll call back.'

He lowered the phone. 'Constable Dickinson has gone out,
as has Sergeant Doofield.'

'And you believe that?'

'Well . . . it was certainly a Guernsey voice on the phone.'

'With a terrorist standing beside him holding a gun to
his head.'

'Well . . .' Another uneasy glance at his wife.

'Listen,' Sophie said: 'I think Derek . . . Sergeant Doofield . . . must have gone home. He wasn't at the station either when I called them about the break-in at my flat, or when I went there with the taxi. If we can just get hold of him . . .'

'Right,' Harrison said, and picked up the phone again.

'Bill,' his wife said, 'it's one o'clock in the morning.'

He hesitated, then punched the numbers. 'There could be something— Hello, Mrs Doofield? I'm terribly sorry to bother you at this hour, but I wonder if I could speak with the sergeant, please? We've tried the station, but he wasn't there . . . I see. What time do you expect him in? . . . I see. Yes, I suppose there is. But then he'd be at the station, wouldn't he? . . . Yes. Yes, it's Bill Harrison. He has a mobile, I suppose? . . . Oh, I agree, there's been no reason for him to call you at midnight. But I would like to get in touch with him. Would you give me the number?' He waved his hand, and Doris produced a pad and pencil. Harrison wrote down the number. 'Thanks very much, Mrs Doofield. Just in case I don't manage to get hold of him, I wonder if you'd ask him to call me at home the moment he gets in. Many thanks.'

He replaced the phone. 'Doofield was supposed to go off duty at midnight. His wife isn't worried, as she assumed something came up at the station to delay him. But you say he wasn't at the station, Sophie.'

'No, he wasn't. I think he's got tangled up with the terrorists.'

Harrison stroked his chin.

'You don't believe me,' Sophie said disconsolately.

'Well . . .' He scratched his head. 'I'll try his mobile.' He called, and again. 'No reply.'

'I tell you, they've got him. Or killed him. They killed Constable Dickinson. Just like that.' When she remembered, she began to shiver all over again.

'I suppose I could go down to the police station . . .'

'No!' Doris shouted. 'You can't do that. They'll kill you.'

Harrison looked at her for a few moments; then he picked up the phone again. 'Hello, who's that? . . . Brian? You're not on duty now . . . I see. Yes. I was just ringing to make sure everything is all right. . . . Fine. Goodnight.'

He replaced the phone, frowning. 'That was the watch house. Brian is still there. Says it's such a bad night he thought he'd stay and give Charlie a hand. Odd. It's such a bad night there is no shipping movement at all. So why does Charlie need a hand?' He looked at Sophie. 'Do you think . . . ?'

'Yes. They've taken over the watch house. And the airport.'

'But . . . what are they meaning to do? I mean . . . even if there are a hundred of them, they can't hold an island like Guernsey to ransom. I mean, tomorrow . . .'

'Today,' Sophie said, 'is Sunday. Nobody is going to know anything is wrong, if they handle it right. And so far they're handling it very right.'

'What do you want to do?'

'We have to let somebody know what is happening.'

'The Bailiff – I'll call the Bailiff.'

'If I'm right, they already have the Bailiff.'

'Have him? How could they do that?'

'By walking up to his front door, ringing the bell, and when the door was opened, presenting a gun at his head.'

'Doesn't he have an instant link to the police station?'

'It wouldn't matter if he had, Captain. The police station would already have been in their hands. These people are operating on a scale no one in Guernsey has ever experienced. We have to call the mainland.'

'Who?'

'For God's sake, there must be some place to call. The Home Office. The War Office. The Home Secretary. The Prime Minister!'

98

'They've probably all gone away for the weekend,' Harrison said gloomily.

'And if they haven't, they wouldn't believe you,' Doris remarked.

Sophie looked from one to the other in desperation. 'Do you mean to say there is *nothing* we can do?'

'Well,' Harrison said, and snapped his fingers. 'John Hartwell.'

'Who?' Sophie asked.

'*Sir* John Hartwell,' Doris pointed out.

'Who is Sir John Hartwell?' Sophie asked again.

'Chap I served with in the Falklands. I got out after that show. He stayed in and became an admiral. Still is an admiral. I could call him. Come to think of it, he's just been made Commander-in-Chief, Portsmouth. He's the very man.'

'You intend to telephone the Commander-in-Chief, Portsmouth, at two o'clock in the morning?' Doris asked. Her husband's acquaintance with the admiral had been before their marriage. 'He won't be very happy about that.'

'We have to do something. His home telephone number is in the address book.'

Doris fetched the book, and they found the number.

'Suppose he's away?' she asked.

'Oh . . .' Her husband looked at Sophie. 'You do realise that if this is a mistake, or a hoax, I'll lose my job.'

'It's neither a mistake nor a hoax, Captain,' Sophie said. 'People have been killed – are being killed.'

He punched out the numbers. He was using the house phone, and there did not appear to be a problem. Yet the terrorists must already have seized the exchange, Sophie knew. Was there some way they could listen in to conversations, even on an automatic exchange? She didn't know.

'Hello,' Harrison was saying. 'Hello? John? Bill Harrison, Guernsey. Yes, I know the time. We could have a serious emergency here. The island has been taken over by terrorists . . . No, it's not a joke. They've taken over the police station and the generating plant and the watch house; the harbour is in their hands. We believe the airport is too. We think they have kidnapped the Bailiff. We *know* they've killed at least one man already . . . My dear fellow, there has been nothing we *could* do. These people came here as tourists, and suddenly went into action at midnight tonight. Well, there's this girl . . .' He waggled his eyebrows at Sophie. 'No, I am not drunk and this is not a hoax and she is not my bit on the side. She's a friend of one of my assistant harbourmasters. I haven't the time to explain, but she found out what was happening.' He listened. 'I appreciate that . . . No, they've made no demands as yet. We have no idea what they're after . . . Yes, I appreciate that you will have to check; but we are – or we could be – in a desperate situation over here come tomorrow morning. These people are killers.'

He replaced the phone and looked at the two women. 'He has to check. God knows who he's going to check with.'

'Do you think he believed you?' Doris asked.

'He certainly didn't *want* to believe me; but I think I made him understand that something is happening.' He looked at his watch. 'Coming up to two. Well, I don't see there's anything more we can do tonight . . .'

'I need to go to James,' Sophie said. 'He'll be awake by now.'

Pray to God that he is, she thought.

'But, my dear, it's still pouring with rain,' Doris protested, 'and your clothes are sodden . . .'

'Then they'll get sodden again,' Sophie pointed out.

'They're also torn. And you'll catch your death of cold . . .'

'I must go,' Sophie insisted.

Doris looked at her husband, who shrugged. 'We can lend you a raincoat; but . . . suppose you meet some of these thugs on the street?'

'They won't be on the street. They're all in their appointed positions, waiting . . . I don't know what they're waiting for.'

* * *

'It's done.' Honeylee stood on the bridge of the big yacht and looked out at the lights of St Peter Port. Below him he could hear the water slapping against the hull, although it would be at least another two hours before *Gloriosa* would lift. Not that it mattered.

'Everything?' Jeannette asked. The terrier played at her feet; she had not left the bridge since midnight.

'All units have reported in.'

'Fatalities?'

'Just the two policemen. Do you wish more?'

'Only if it becomes necessary. The explosives are planted?'

'That is being done now.'

'And no one suspects a thing. Apart from the policemen, and those we have already taken prisoner. This has been an excellent operation, Captain.'

'Thank you, ma'am. There was that girl . . .'

'What girl?'

'She was on board, earlier today. She's the mistress of that assistant harbourmaster.'

'What is important about her?'

'She is the one who broke into al-Rakim's room at the hotel. Then she was at the police station when we took it, but managed to escape. She was chased to the harbour, but has not been seen since.'

Jeannette frowned. 'You think she is a British agent?'

'No, no,' Honeylee said. 'Just a curious young woman, activated by what happened to her boyfriend.'

'Nonetheless, it would be a good idea to pick her up.'

'That may be difficult. She could be anywhere in the island.'

Jeannette gave a cold smile. 'You are not married, are you, Captain?'

'No, ma'am. Never had the time.'

'So you do not understand women. This woman . . . what is her name?'

'Sophie something-or-other.'

'Well, this Sophie will have gone to the hospital bedside of her lover. You can pick her up there.'

'I'll get on to it.'

'It must be done discreetly. We do not want to alarm the hospital until we are ready to declare our position. That will be at four o'clock.' She smiled. 'While they are still asleep over there. Four o'clock is the most difficult hour of the day at which to have to make decisions.'

Salim appeared at the head of the ladder. 'Al-Rakim is here.'

'Report,' Jeannette said.

Al-Rakim was as flawlessly dressed and debonair as ever, as he stripped off his raincoat and handed it and his hat to the waiting seaman. 'All is as required, ma'am.'

'And there was no trouble? I am told a policeman had to be shot. In addition to the one killed on board.'

'That is correct. The rest surrendered peacefully.'

'The Bailiff?'

'He was taken entirely by surprise. He protested most vehemently, but I don't think he has yet fully accepted the situation.'

'Where is he now?'

'We took him and his wife to the police station, as instructed. We have also arrested the Governor and his wife and aide-de-camp, and taken them to the station. He is very upset, but I think he will be a better spokesman than the Bailiff.'

'Then have him brought on board. And you are firmly in control of the police?'

'With the changeover of duty rosters we should have just about the entire force under restraint in a couple of hours. The senior officers all come in early in the morning, so we will have them too.'

'Excellent,' Jeannette said.

'Do you wish any further action to be taken?'

'What were you thinking of?'

'Well . . .' Al-Rakim looked uncertain. 'Are there any other prominent people you wish rounded up?'

'No, no,' Jeannette said. 'The scenario is as I intended it. Remember, I spent some time here last year.' She smiled. 'I was a genuine tourist then, but I observed a lot. Nothing ever happens here. That is an established fact in the eyes of all Guernsey people. They will not know anything has happened until they are told. There will be no policemen on the streets, but there are never very many policemen on the streets anyway. The Bailiff and the Governor will not be available, but who is going to wish to see them on a Sunday?'

'The wives and families of the police force?'

'Are being told their husbands will be late home because there has been a minor emergency. They will not start to worry for a few hours yet, and that is all we need.' She looked at her watch. 'We will make our demand at four o'clock this morning. It may take about an hour for there to be a response, as it will be a matter of getting people out of bed. Very few people listen to the radio or watch television between four and five in the morning. Besides, it will be a matter of the British government getting their act together and alerting the various television companies. Nothing can be broadcast to the island before seven, I would say. However, we shall close down the generating plant at three o'clock.'

'Won't that get people excited?' Honeylee asked.

'I do not believe so. Very few people will be awake, and that girl told us it happens from time to time. All people have to be told is that there has been a power failure and the service will be resumed as quickly as possible.'

'So,' Honeylee said, 'the British will not be able to broadcast to the island telling them what has happened; but they will broadcast to their own people, and there will certainly be people here calling England during the morning.'

'We will shut down the telephone exchange at the same time.'

'Most people nowadays use mobile phones,' Honeylee pointed out.

'That will be a small number on a Sunday morning. And those who do telephone friends or relatives – what are they going to be told? That they just saw on the television that there is some kind of terrorist takeover in Guernsey? The caller will go to the window and look out, and see life continuing absolutely as normal, and say, what nonsense.'

'They will realise what is happening, eventually.'

'Eventually will be too late.'

'And when the British send in the Navy and the RAF and the SAS? I think we should uncover the gun.'

Jeannette smiled. 'They are not going to do that, Captain. There are sixty thousand lives at risk, here. The British would not wish to have one of those killed. As for the gun, we will keep it covered until we need it. The whole plan is that we should obtain possession of the sheikh and get out of the island before anyone here realises what is happening. Now to your posts. As for your little friend, al-Rakim, she is about to be picked up.'

'And?'

'She is being brought back here. I would like to find out more about her.'

The Alarm

'Do you believe it?' asked Lucy Hartwell. 'I mean, *can* you believe it?'

Lady Hartwell was a plump woman in her early forties who had never quite got to grips with her husband's rapid rise through the service – or the fact that, now he was an admiral, he was home most of the time instead of being absent with his ship for long periods. Having a husband who now virtually had a nine-to-five job and had to be catered for on that basis – and not only as regards food – was taking some getting used to. And if, in addition, he was going to start receiving crank telephone calls in the middle of the night . . .

'I think I must believe it,' Hartwell said.

In the strongest contrast to his wife, he was a big, powerful, energetic man; his energy and determination, as well as his willingness to take decisions, had been what had propelled him upwards.

'Just how well do you know this harbourmaster?' Lucy asked.

'Well, I don't really *know* him. We served together in the Falklands. He got out soon after. I haven't actually seen him since. But we exchange cards at Christmas.'

'He could have gone round the bend.'

'Bill Harrison isn't the type of man who goes round the bend.'

'Seventeen years? People change.'

'Not Bill Harrison.' Hartwell got up and began to dress.

'So what are you going to do? Lead the Navy to sea?'

He glanced at her, suspecting she was joking. As indeed she was.

'Just an idea,' she remarked. 'What *are* you going to do.'

Hartwell sat on the bed, picked up his phone, punched some numbers. He had to wait for some time while the phone buzzed; but at last a sleepy voice answered: 'Yes?'

'Harry?'

'Who *is* this?'

'Johnny Hartwell.'

'Johnny . . .' Air Commodore Harry Crabtree bit off what he might have said, as he remembered that his old friend was now a KCB. 'I say, old man, do you know the time?'

'It is a quarter past two,' Hartwell said, 'and I am most terribly sorry to disturb you at such an hour. But I have a problem.'

There was a rustling sound as Crabtree sat up in bed. There was also a muttering noise in the background. As Hartwell knew Crabtree was not married, he raised his eyebrows.

'Tell me about it,' Crabtree invited.

Hartwell repeated Harrison's telephone call as best he could remember.

'Dashed odd,' Crabtree commented when he had finished. 'Is this fellow Harrison all right?'

'Yes, he is all right,' Hartwell said, somewhat wearily. 'But I do understand that we need to be sure of our ground before doing anything drastic.'

'I should think so,' Crabtree agreed. 'Have you tried telephoning?'

'Who would one telephone in Guernsey?'

'Well . . . the Bailiff? The Chief of Police?'

'According to Harrison, these have already been taken out by the terrorists. Look, Harry, it'll be daylight in a couple of hours. I was wondering if it might be possible to overfly the island, have a look at things, try to talk with the local air traffic control.'

'Guernsey airport closes at night. The first plane, with the mail and newspapers, goes in about six.'

'But there must be someone on duty in case of an emergency.'

'I'm sure there is. But . . . is this an emergency?'

'If what Harrison told me is true, then it is a very serious emergency.'

'And you would like me to scramble a squadron, at this hour . . .'

'One aircraft will do. But you could try calling the tower first.'

'Hm. You realise this will cost money. If it is a hoax . . .'

'I will have to take responsibility.'

'What have you got in the vicinity?'

'We have a fishery protection frigate in the Channel. She can be there in a couple of hours. But I'd really like to know what I'm sending her to, and what orders I'm to give her. We don't want any civilian casualties.'

'Which is what these people, if they are terrorists, are counting on, I imagine. Look, John, do you mind if I take this up with Peart?'

'Who?'

'Charlie Peart. He's GOC South, and the Channel Islands comes into his province, as it were. Between you and me, he's a bit of an old dodderer, but his is the ultimate responsibility.'

'I would have said the ultimate responsibility was the Home Secretary.'

'You're absolutely right; but I reckon I'd rather telephone Charlie Peart at half past two in the morning than the Home Secretary. Let Peart get *him* out of bed.'

'Gracey? Is that you, Gracey?' General Peart always shouted into the telephone; he was slightly deaf.

'I am here, sir,' Paul Gracey said.

The trouble with having young seconds, Peart reflected,

was that they always sounded alert, even at three o'clock in the morning.

'This Guernsey business,' the general said.

But not that alert. 'Ah . . . what Guernsey business, sir?'

'This yacht you were telling me about. She seems to have been full of terrorists.'

'Would you repeat that, sir?'

'I have just had a telephone call from Air Commodore Crabtree,' Peart said, 'who has been in communication with Rear Admiral Hartwell. It seems that all hell has broken loose in Guernsey while we have been sleeping.'

Gracey digested this. 'I'm afraid I will have to ask you to explain, sir.'

'And I am telling you to get dressed and get down to the Home Office within the hour. We have to decide what to do.'

'The Home Office, sir?'

'I am calling the Home Secretary, now.'

The phone was put down, heavily.

'What on earth was that all about?' Joanna Gracey asked, having been awakened.

'I think the old man has finally flipped his lid,' Gracey said. 'But I suppose I'll have to humour him.'

As predicted, the Home Secretary was not in a good mood at being awakened with the birds. 'May I ask what this is all about?' he enquired of the three service chiefs seated across the table.

He listened, firstly to Hartwell, then to Crabtree, then to Peart.

'So,' he said, when they had finished. 'We are gathered here in crisis on the basis of a telephone call from a somewhat hysterical harbourmaster.'

'With respect, sir,' Hartwell protested.

'I know – old chums and all that. But you'll agree that it is a rather wild and woolly tale, unsubstantiated.'

'It has been substantiated circumstantially, sir,' Gracey said.

The Home Secretary regarded the young colonel with suspicion.

'My aide,' Peart hastily explained.

'Speak?'

'Instantly on being informed of the possible situation by General Peart, sir, I made several telephone calls. The first was to Guernsey Central Police Station.'

'And?'

'I was informed that there was nothing happening; the officer I spoke to could not imagine where I might have got my information that there was terrorist activity in the island.'

'As one might have expected. And?'

'I next telephoned the airport.'

'And?'

'The night staff informed me that everything was in order, and that they anticipated opening the airport, as usual, for the arrival of the planes bringing the mail and newspapers at six o'clock this morning. They also could not imagine where I might have got my information that there was terrorist activity in the island.'

'Well?'

'I then telephoned the Chief of Police, and was told that the Chief was out of the island. This answer was given to me by a male servant.'

'Well?' Each 'well' was becoming more of a barb.

'I then telephoned the Bailiff at home, and was informed that the Bailiff was out of the island. This answer also was given to me by a male servant.'

'Well?'

'I then telephoned the residence of the Lieutenant Governor, and was again answered by a male servant, who informed me that the Lieutenant Governor was out of the island.'

'Colonel, you are digging yourself a hole in the ground.

Is this the circumstantial evidence on which you would like me to base some irresponsible action?'

'May I ask you to review what I have just said, sir?' Gracey was unflappable. 'Both the police station and the airport report that there is nothing untoward occurring. That is itself a strange way of replying to an enquiry as to whether there has been any terrorist activity on the island over the past twenty-four hours. And each reply was couched in almost exactly similar words.'

The Home Secretary stroked his chin.

'Secondly, sir, at the houses of both the Bailiff and the Chief of Police, a male servant answered the phone, and told me his employer was out of the island – again, in virtually identical words. As did the servant at Government House. More to the point, sir, while I have no doubt the Bailiff may well employ a servant, in Guernsey it is more likely that she would be a woman rather than a man. The same would go for the Chief of Police. And more important even than that: except in the houses of the extremely well-to-do, your average Guernsey maid, male or female, does not sleep in. Government House may well be an exception to that observation, but the other two are at the least unusual.'

'Those are good points, Colonel,' the Home Secretary conceded, 'but they are still entirely circumstantial.'

'There is one remaining point, sir: I then telephoned the editor of the local newspaper, the Guernsey Press. He wasn't too happy at being got out of bed in the small hours, but he was co-operative. I asked him if he was aware that the Lieutenant Governor, the Bailiff and the Chief of Police were all out of the island together, and he said that he wasn't and he was sure they weren't. It is apparently a requirement that both the Lieutenant Governor's and the Bailiff's offices should inform the media when they are leaving the island, even on a private visit, and the Press had not been so informed. At my request he promised to look into the matter, but said that he could not possibly do so until later on this morning. Not wishing to cause any alarm, I accepted this.'

'Well,' the Home Secretary said, 'I am bound to say that you have been most efficient, Colonel Gracey. However, I am also bound to say that the evidence that something is happening in Guernsey remains very thin. However . . . these people appear to have come in by yacht. I assume you have units in the area, Admiral Hartwell?'

'There is a fishery protection frigate standing by, sir.'

'How powerful is she?'

'Well, sir, she is not designed to fight a sea battle, if that's what you mean. She's a small ship, fifteen hundred tons fully loaded.'

'Crew?'

'A hundred and forty officers and men.'

'Weaponry?'

'Three forty-millimetre guns, four twenty-one-inch torpedo tubes, two small and somewhat antiquated missile launchers, Limbos Mark Ten.'

'Speed?'

'Well, sir, she *can* make twenty-seven knots. But she's been at sea a while. Let's say twenty-five.'

'Fast enough to overtake this yacht?'

'I would say so.'

'Very good. But you have a superior back-up?'

'Several.'

'Put one out in the Channel, just in case.'

'Very good, sir. But may I ask: do you intend to wait for this yacht to leave Guernsey?'

'It seems to me that is the most sensible approach, gentlemen, at least until we have a clearer picture of what is going on. To attempt to go in and seize the yacht inside St Peter Port Harbour might provoke bloodshed, and it would certainly provoke an international incident, just supposing she is legitimate.'

'I would have thought she could be seized from the shore, sir,' Gracey said.

'How would you do that, Colonel, if indeed the Guernsey Police are in the hands of the terrorists?'

'If we could land an SAS company . . .'

'And how would you do *that*, without alarming the terrorists and causing the very bloodshed we are trying to avoid?'

'Well . . . we could fly them in, wearing mufti, as passengers on a scheduled flight.'

'If the airport is in the terrorists' hands, I wonder if there are going to be any scheduled flights. We shall have to wait and see.'

'While the terrorists do whatever they like in Guernsey,' Crabtree commented.

'What exactly do you suppose they can do, in Guernsey?' the Home Secretary asked. 'It has no political or strategic importance. So perhaps they intend to rob all the banks and jewellery stores. They still have no means of getting the loot off the island without being arrested by the Navy.'

'I was thinking of the people,' Crabtree said. 'The harbourmaster chappie said at least one policeman has been killed already.'

'And I am sure he died very gallantly. I also am thinking of the people. The men, women and children going about their normal daily lives who must be protected.'

'There is one factor I feel we haven't taken into proper consideration, sir,' Gracey said.

All the heads turned.

'Well, sir,' the colonel said, 'we are all agreed that there is no way the terrorists can leave Guernsey in their yacht without being apprehended; but surely the terrorists know that as well?'

There was a moment's silence.

'Just what are you suggesting, Colonel?' the Home Secretary asked.

'That they must have some plan for dealing with their situation, sir. In which case, just waiting for them to attempt to leave may not be a realistic option.'

'Back to your SAS, eh?'

'I feel we should try to open some sort of dialogue with these people, as soon as possible.'

'Tell me how we do that, Colonel? Except by means of a public broadcast, which will cause panic and do untold damage. No . . .' He looked up with a frown as the door opened. 'Hargreaves? I said I was not to be interrupted.'

The secretary's face was pale. 'I felt it was necessary, sir. We have just received a radio communication from the Lieutenant Governor of Guernsey.'

The office was still as Hargreaves placed the sheet of paper on the Home Secretary's desk. He scanned it, then read it again, more carefully. Then he leaned back in his chair, staring at the officers waiting expectantly in front of him.

'I'm afraid things are worse than I imagined they could be,' he said. He held up the paper. 'Will you read this aloud, Hargreaves.'

The secretary took the paper and cleared his throat. '"Sir,"' he said, '"I am communicating with you in my capacity as Lieutenant Governor of Guernsey, to inform you that the island is in the hands of a group of Arab patriots, acting in the name of Sheikh Raisul Abdullah ibn Hassan."'

He paused, to allow his boss to speak. 'Who is, as I am sure you know,' the Home Secretary said, 'at present in custody here in London, awaiting transference to The Hague for trial on charges of international terrorism. Continue, Hargreaves.'

Another clearing of the throat. '"Sheikh Hassan's people are demanding the release of the sheikh, forthwith. They wish me to inform you that Guernsey is entirely in their power. Their message reads as follows: *At the present time, the general population are unaware of the situation, and if your government acts promptly and in a co-operative manner there is no need for them to know until after we have left the island. However, we must warn you that refusal to co-operate will force us to resort to selective executions. Again, the general public will not know of these. Do not attempt to broadcast your assessment of the situation, as of this moment we are shutting down the electricity-generating plant and there will be no power for radios or television sets. We are also closing down the telephone exchange. We are aware that it will be possible for you to use mobile phones to call various members of the public here, but we would advise against it. In the first instance, they would not readily believe you, and in the second, anyone discovered using, or having used, a mobile phone, will be shot immediately.*

"'We would also strongly advise against any attempt to take over the island by force. We are determined men who are quite prepared to die for our sheikh. If we are forced to this extremity, we shall take as many of your people as possible with us, causing as much damage as is possible on our way. We should inform you that the oil and gas storage tanks in St Sampson's have been wired to explosives. Explosives have also been placed in the electricity-generating plant and the telephone exchange. We are in control of the local radio and television broadcasting stations, and we are in a position to destroy all the shipping in the harbour, and render the harbour itself unusable for some considerable time. We would therefore ask you to consider our demand very seriously and very quickly.

"'You have two hours to reply. Your reply will be made to the yacht Gloriosa, *in the first instance on the normal shipping band. You will then be given another band to use. When you reply in the affirmative, we will give you our instructions how to proceed. Should you not reply in the affirmative, or not reply at all within the two hours, we shall commence our plan of action, beginning with the Lieutenant Governor and his wife, followed by the Bailiff and his wife."*

That is the end of the message. "I wish you to understand,

114

sir," the Lieutenant Governor has added, "that I regard these people as genuine, and determined enough to carry out their threats. I would therefore ask you to act in accordance with their demands, and free my island from this terrible threat. Sir James Earnestly, Lieutenant Governor of Guernsey."'

The room was again silent for several seconds. Then the Home Secretary said, 'Hargreaves, get me the Prime Minister. Also the Minister of Defence.'

The Prime Minister also disliked being awakened at dawn on what he had hoped was going to be a peaceful Sunday; but his mood of irritation very rapidly changed when he had read the radio message from Guernsey. He raised his head to survey the anxious faces around the Cabinet table. The service chiefs were there by virtue of having been in on the ground floor, as it were; there had been no time to summon a full Cabinet meeting.

The Prime Minister tapped the paper. 'I assume you gentlemen are convinced this is genuine.'

'We are, sir,' Hartwell said.

'Has any effort been made to contact Guernsey?'

'Colonel Gracey,' General Peart invited.

Gracey listed the telephone calls he had made, and the replies.

'Very good,' the Prime Minister said. 'Admiral Hartwell?'

Hartwell listed his dispositions. 'I have not yet ordered HMS *Blackwall Tunnel* to go in, sir, as I did not wish to provoke any counter-action on the part of the terrorists; but she is off Alderney, and could be in the Little Russel in an hour.'

'Very good. Well, gentlemen, let us start at the top. We appear to be dealing with absolutely ruthless people who will stop at nothing, and who have already, if the Guernsey harbourmaster is to be believed, committed at least one murder. One thing in our favour is that these people do not appear to know that Captain Harrison has made contact with us, but apart from giving us a head start in our deliberations I am not sure what other advantage that has conferred. If we do not respond favourably, in just over one hour's time they will shoot the Lieutenant Governor, if we take their threat seriously, and it is your belief that we should. Therefore we must respond favourably.'

'You'll release ibn Hassan?' The Home Secretary was aghast.

'It is not the practice of Her Majesty's Government to release known terrorists in exchange for hostages,' the Prime Minister said.

'Sixty thousand hostages,' Crabtree muttered.

'The exact number is immaterial. In any event, it would appear that only Guernsey's most prominent people are at risk. Not,' he added hastily, 'that I am contemplating allowing *anyone* else to be killed. What we shall do is open a dialogue with these people. You will radio this yacht, Mr Secretary, and say that we are willing to negotiate. Once we have their exact terms and requirements we can take it from there. By then, too, we will have been able to assemble a full Cabinet. However,' he went on, looking around their faces, 'I want us prepared for all eventualities. Admiral Hartwell, you will send out whatever naval force you consider necessary. Your ships will remain out of sight of Guernsey, and will not attempt to enter either of the island harbours without orders from you.'

'Yes, sir. You understand that whatever ships I put out will have to be within radar range of the island.'

'That is quite acceptable. The terrorists will expect to see some activity. Now, Group Captain, you will have a squadron of transport planes ready to deliver a regiment of the SAS to the island at the shortest possible notice.'

'Will do,' Crabtree agreed.

'You, General Peart, will organise these troops and have them on standby.'

'And the people of Guernsey, sir?' Gracey ventured.

'What about them?'

'Well, sir, should they not be informed of what is going on?'

'I don't see how you propose to do that, Colonel, if these terrorists are as good as their word.'

'We could check that out, sir,' Hargreaves suggested. 'By having a news item put out on television. Just in case they *haven't* shut down the generating plant.'

'I'm not sure that would be a good idea,' the Prime Minister said. 'In fact, I don't even want this news to be released to the media here, until and unless it becomes necessary. The one thing we do not want is for the people of Guernsey to panic or attempt to take action on their own behalf, which might result in a bloodbath.'

'You mean they are not to be told what is going on, sir?' Gracey asked.

'That is what I mean, Colonel. Let us hear what these people want, and let us put our possible counter-measures into place. The terrorists don't want the Guernsey people to know what is happening, so we have every possibility of keeping it quiet until we get things sorted out.'

'The media will blow their top when they find out, sir,' Hargreaves remarked.

'I'm sure they will. But if we can handle this with no further loss of life, we will have to be congratulated, even by the Opposition.'

'And without letting ibn Hassan go?' the Home Secretary asked.

'I think we will be able to work something out,' the Prime Minister said. 'Make that call, Ned, and let me know as soon as you hear back from these people. Hargreaves, you'll call a Cabinet meeting for seven this morning. Most urgent – nothing more than that. Gentlemen . . .' He surveyed the faces of the service chiefs. '. . . you have your instructions.'

* * *

117

'Complete surrender,' Honeylee said. 'We just have to tell them what we want, and they'll deliver.'

'Just like that?' Jeannette asked. 'So quickly?'

'They know they are on a hiding to nothing.'

'Or they are laying a trap.'

'If they are, we must call their bluff. Do I deliver the list?'

Jeannette stroked her dog. 'Yes, go ahead. As you say, we shall call their bluff.' She looked out of the bridge windows at the lights of St Peter Port, scanty at a quarter to three in the morning. The yacht was just starting to lift, giving little bumps with each surge of the tide; the wind continued to howl and the rain slanted down. It was a celestial mood that suited her own. She had volunteered to take command of this operation, and Kasim had agreed – not merely because she was Hassan's mistress, but because he knew her hatred for the British who, despite her English mother, had shot her father in Aden. Yet she also knew that he had doubted her ability to carry it through. Like most Arab men, he discounted women as a physical force. Well, she was going to prove him wrong. 'Tell al-Rakim it is time to throw the switch.'

It was five to three by the time Sophie reached the Princess Elizabeth Hospital, once again soaked to the skin despite the borrowed raincoat, and buffeted by the wind as well; and she then had to make her way up the long, winding drive to the main entrance. Fortunately there was a new man on the desk, but he still blinked at the bedraggled figure in front of him.

'You all right?' he asked.

'I have no idea,' Sophie said. 'You have a patient in here I'd like to see.'

'At three in the morning? You have got to be joking.'

'This is important. His name is James Candish and he was brought in about twelve hours ago, suffering from an overdose of drugs.'

118

'And what is he to you?'

'We live together.'

'That's hardly a legal relationship, you know.'

'I don't care whether it is or not,' Sophie said. 'I want to know if he's recovered, and then I want to see him. It really is most urgent.'

The receptionist punched his computer. 'James Candish,' he said. 'Dr Murrain's patient.'

'That's right.'

'Recovered consciousness at ten past one. Condition stable, but weak. Right?'

'Great. Now can I see him, please?'

'I'm sorry, that won't be possible. Come back at visiting hours later this morning.'

Sophie kept her cool with a great effort. 'Dr Murrain said I could spend the night in the ward with him, if I chose,' she said. 'I now choose.'

'There's nothing about that here,' the man said, peering into his screen.

'Well, you can ask the doctor.'

'The doctor is not on duty at this time.'

'Can't you call him at home?'

'I don't think that would be a good idea. This isn't an emergency, and doctors need their sleep as much as anyone, you know.'

'Listen,' Sophie said: 'I have had a very long night. I have been soaked to the skin, time and again. I have been assaulted. I have been swimming in the marina. And I have been nearly killed.'

The male nurse goggled at her.

'So,' Sophie said, 'if you won't allow me in to see Mr Candish, I am going to start screaming, so loud it'll wake up the corpses in your mortuary.'

The nurse licked his lips apprehensively, and pressed a button on his desk. 'I could send for the police and have you removed,' he said.

119

'That would probably be a good idea,' Sophie said.

He scratched his head, and a sister appeared. Fortunately, she was someone Sophie knew. 'Oh, thank heavens,' she said. 'I'm Sophie Gallagher. You must remember me.'

'Of course I do,' Sister Morgan said. 'Your man is in intensive care.'

'Still?'

'Well, he only came round a few hours ago, and we thought we'd let him sleep where he is. We'll be moving him to an ordinary ward this morning. Dr Murrain's note says he's to stay in for twenty-four hours for observation. My dear, you're wet through. You really should go home and change, or we'll have you in here with James.'

She was such a sensible, down-to-earth woman . . . who for that reason, Sophie knew, wouldn't believe a word of what was happening.

'May I see James?' she asked.

'Well . . .'

'He's all right, isn't he?'

'He seems so, certainly. But he's asleep.'

'Can't he be woken up? I really need to speak with him.'

Sister Morgan hesitated, glancing at the receptionist.

'Sophie Gallagher,' he said, obviously remembering what he had been told by his predecessor. 'The police were here last night, asking about her. Bob told me. She stole a taxi.'

'Did you do that?' Sister Morgan was astonished.

'It's a long story,' Sophie said. 'Look, could I speak with you alone?'

'Well . . .'

'Don't do it,' the receptionist said. 'I'm going to call the police.' He picked up the phone, and stared at his monitor. 'Shit! The electrics are out.'

The lights were still on in the lobby. But now these went out as well.

'Check that out,' Sister said. 'See if it's us or the mains. If it's the mains, find out how long the outage is going to last. But first, switch to the emergency generator; and you'd better get the duty engineer up anyway. Be quick; there are people on life support machines.'

'Yes, ma'am.' The receptionist threw various switches. 'None of these is working.'

'Then get Hallam!' Sister snapped. 'It'll have to be started manually.'

'Yes, ma'am.' The receptionist picked up his internal phone and called the engineer.

'Listen,' Sophie said, 'this outage is permanent.'

Sister gave her an old-fashioned look.

'It is,' Sophie insisted. 'The island is in the hands of a group of terrorist thugs.'

'Oh really, Sophie. Look, go home to bed. Call me later this morning and I'll tell you how James is. Right now I have to check those machines.'

'Hallam is coming right up,' the receptionist said. He picked up the outside phone to call the electricity company, and frowned. 'Funny. This is dead.'

'Because they've put the exchange out of action as well,' Sophie said.

'What on earth are you talking about?' Sister demanded. 'Who are *they*?'

'The terrorists I am trying to tell you about,' Sophie shouted.

'Call the police!' Sister snapped.

'The phone is dead.'

'You have a mobile, haven't you? Use that.'

'But if their phones are dead as well . . .'

'Do it,' Sister commanded. 'Sophie, you stay here. Unless you want to take off those wet clothes. We can lend you a bed gown or something.'

'You don't believe me, do you?' Sophie asked.

'Of course I don't believe you. Things like that don't happen, in Guernsey. We've had electricity outages before. And phone failures.'

121

'On the same day, and virtually at the same moment?'

'Oh . . . thank God for that!'

The lights glowed.

'It's the generator, not the mains,' the receptionist pointed out.

'As long as there's power. Now, I simply must check those machines.'

A doctor appeared, looking distinctly hot and bothered. 'What the devil is going on, Sister? The electrics . . .'

'There's been a power failure, doctor,' Sister said. 'We've switched to the generator. I'm just going to check the emergency cases now.'

'I'll come with you,' the doctor said.

'I'd like to see James,' Sophie said stubbornly.

'Sophie,' Sister Morgan said, 'go home.' She didn't seem to realise she had contradicted herself.

'Oh . . .'

The front doors swung in, and two men came in. They were both members of the group who had been staying at the Guernsey Island Hotel.

'That's her,' one of them said.

Plans

'Oh, gosh!' Sophie said, and ran for the inner entrance.
'Get her,' one of the Arabs said.

'Just who do you think you are?' Sister demanded, stepping forward.

The first terrorist drew an automatic pistol and shot her in the chest. She fell over backwards and struck the floor with a thud; the front of her uniform was flooding red.

Sophie, already at the entrance to the inner hall, checked in horror. 'Oh, my God!' she gasped.

'You!' The pistol swung to cover both the doctor and the receptionist, who were in the direct line of fire. 'Move and you're dead. Hands up. High!'

Both men obeyed without hesitation; they were staring at Sister Morgan's body lying at their feet.

'Get her!' the first terrorist said again.

Sophie turned and raced along the corridor. At the far end two nurses appeared, hurrying towards the sound of the shot.

'Take cover!' Sophie screamed, and turned the corner, racing towards the intensive care ward into which James had been taken. This was on the ground floor and the Sister had indicated he would still be there until they were ready to move him to a general ward.

She rounded another bend and felt she had lost her pursuer for the moment. She threw open the door and half-fell in. A nurse standing by the bed turned with a startled expression. Sophie looked left and right, saw a broom and pan leaning

123

against the wall a few feet away. The double doors had no lock, so she grabbed the broom and thrust it through the two handles.

'Hey,' the nurse said. 'Who are you? What are you doing?' She was a pretty little thing – very young, with a plump figure and expressive green eyes to go with her red hair.

Barring the doors with a wooden handle could only be a very temporary expedient. Sophie ran to James's bedside. He had been awakened by the racket, but was still clearly very drowsy.

'Listen,' she said: 'we have to get out of here.'

The nurse stood beside her. 'What are you *doing*?'

'We have to get him out of here,' Sophie repeated.

There came a thump on the door, and behind it an upsurge of noise as the hospital was brought to life, violently.

'Those people are killers,' Sophie said, urgently. 'Help me, for God's sake. Help yourself!'

She had grasped James's shoulders to raise him up. The nurse, still uncertain how to handle the situation, was brought to life by another shot, this one blasting through the wooden panelling of the door, without hitting the broom handle. That made up her mind for her, and she ran round the bed to help push and pull James to his feet. He wore only a green hospital robe, as far as Sophie could make out, but she had no time to look for his clothes. Of course the men were after her rather than him, at the moment, but she was determined that they weren't going to get him either.

'Sophie?' he asked, blearily. 'Where are we going? What's happening?'

Between them Sophie and the nurse pushed him to the window. Behind them the door thumped again, and the broom handle cracked.

'What are we going to do?' the nurse asked. 'Who's out there, anyway?'

'I told you – a killer.'

'But . . . surely they'll have sent for the police.'

'Forget it,' Sophie said. 'Hold him.' She threw up the sash and looked out into the rainswept dawn. Beneath the window there was, inevitably, a flower bed. 'How far is the drop?'

'Eight feet, maybe.'

'Let's go.'

'Sophie,' James protested, as they lifted his legs and inserted them into the window space. 'What are you doing?'

A crash came from behind them.

'You first,' Sophie told the nurse.

The nurse – she was certainly not much more than twenty – gulped, but obeyed, thrusting her black-stockinged legs into the opening and then dropping through. She landed on her feet with a squelch in the mud, and Sophie pushed James after her. He gave a startled exclamation, but dropped beside the nurse, and she threw both arms round his waist.

Sophie dropped behind them, just as the doors burst open. She was not properly prepared, and the shock of landing jarred her and had her staggering; but she was able to grasp James's arm. 'Run!' she screamed, heading for the side of the building.

The nurse grabbed James's other arm, and between them they squelched through the mud, James and the nurse already soaked by the steady drizzle. As they reached the corner, Sophie looked back and saw a man peering out of the window. He held his pistol, but couldn't make up his mind to shoot: he had obviously been told to take her alive.

Then they were round the corner. 'Do you have wheels?' Sophie asked.

The girl nodded, panting. 'In the staff park.'

'Then let's get the hell out of here.'

'I'm on duty,' she said.

'Your first duty is to keep your patients alive,' Sophie told her. 'Let's go.'

Jeannette scanned the list Honeylee presented to her. 'That seems right. Send it.' She frowned. 'What is that bleep?'

125

'One of the mobiles.'

Al-Rakim answered. 'What? What? In the name of Allah, are you madmen? One girl?'

'What has happened?' Jeannette asked.

'Harb and Affan went to the hospital, as instructed, to pick up the woman, Sophie Gallagher. She was actually in Reception when they arrived, but there were some other people present. These would have interfered, and Harb shot one of them – a woman nurse. Now the entire hospital is in an uproar.'

Jeannette snorted. 'I said it was to be done discreetly. I hope your people are not losing their nerve, al-Rakim. What of the Gallagher girl?'

'She escaped out of a window. They wish to know what to do.'

'What is the situation, now?'

'Harb commands the lobby. Affan has joined him. But there are a lot of people milling about, nurses as well as patients. They are afraid of being overrun.'

'They have guns, haven't they? As they have shot one nurse, they may as well shoot as many more as is necessary. Tell them to hold their ground, and send them reinforcements. Ten men should do it.'

'But if the news gets out . . .'

'How is it to get out? The hospital must be sealed. The phones are dead.'

'The mobiles . . .'

'In the first instance, anyone using a mobile will telephone the police. Tell Mustafa to have the police say help is on its way. While they are waiting for that we will have taken over the building, and all the mobiles. Hurry now. Captain, you get Mustafa's people moving.'

'And the terms?'

'Will have to wait for a few minutes while we regain control.' She smiled at the anxious faces in front of her. 'A delay. A small delay. It cannot affect the outcome.'

*   *   *

Sophie and the nurse hurried James across the wet staff car park. 'Isn't there anybody here?' Sophie demanded at large.

'The next shift comes on at six,' the nurse panted. 'That's not for another three hours. Should we wait?'

'Like hell we'll wait. Those people are out to kill me. And you, I shouldn't wonder.'

'But . . . when the new shift arrives . . .'

'We'll have to alert them. But we can't stay here. Do you have a phone?'

'At home.'

She had led them to a small Italian car, and this she now unlocked.

'Sophie,' James said, swaying against her. 'What's happening, Sophie?'

'Just get in,' Sophie said. 'I meant a mobile,' she added to the nurse.

'That's at home too,' the girl said. 'We're not supposed to take them to the hospital.'

'So take us home.' Sophie pushed James into the back seat and got in beside him. 'Home being where?'

'My flat. But . . . it's out of town.'

'Just let's get there.'

The nurse started the engine. 'Shane will still be asleep.'

'Husband, or boy friend?'

'Well . . . we're going to get married.'

'So let's wake him up,' Sophie said. 'If we can get out of here.'

The nurse drove down the drive.

'Can't you go any faster?' Sophie asked.

'There's a ten-mile-an-hour speed limit,' the girl protested.

'There are times when the speed limit just has to be ignored,' Sophie pointed out. 'I don't even know your name.'

'Helen.' The nurse reached the main road and swung left. The street was empty at a quarter past three in the morning.

'I'm Sophie.'

'I know,' Helen said. 'He was muttering your name in his sleep.'

'Was he?' Sophie gave James a hug. 'He's an affectionate beast.'

'Sophie,' James said, speaking with more clarity than before. 'What the hell is happening? Where am I? I'm soaked to the skin.'

'Join the club,' Sophie said.

'You know what?' Helen remarked, now driving quite fast through the deserted streets: 'I should be taking you to your home, not mine. Then you could get changed.'

'No way. Those thugs know where I live. You're going to have to put up with me.'

'For how long?'

'Until I can work out what to do next.'

'Sophie,' James said.

'Listen: how much can you remember?'

'I was on the yacht, seeing what I could find. Then there was this dog, and the voices . . . lots of voices. Then that woman with a gun. Then . . . Honeylee hit me, and that doctor injected me.'

'You listening to this?' Sophie asked Helen.

'Did that really happen?'

'It's still happening,' Sophie reminded her.

'Then they came to the hospital . . . I thought I heard a shot.'

'You did. They shot Sister Morgan.'

'Jesus!' The car swerved to and fro on the wet road.

'Concentrate,' Sophie recommended. 'How much further?'

They were well out of town.

'Half a mile. But . . . shouldn't we be going to the police?'

'They've taken over the police as well.'

'But . . . how could they *do* that?'

'It's very simple, really,' Sophie said, 'as long as you have a lot of guns and are prepared to use them.'

'What are we going to do?' James asked, now fully awake.

'Get to a mobile phone,' Sophie said, and yawned; she had had no sleep.

'Who're we going to ring?'

'I'll think of someone,' Sophie said, and nodded off.

'The Gallagher woman has got away,' Harb said over the phone. 'A nurse helped her. They were away before our people arrived.'

'What about the man Candish?' al-Rakim asked.

'We think he went with them.'

'That is a right foul-up,' al-Rakim said.

'Give me the phone,' Jeannette said. 'Listen: what is the situation at the hospital now?'

'It is under control, madame. We have some men in the grounds, and others patrolling the wards. We have told all the staff, and the patients, that anyone who attempts to escape or make trouble will be shot on sight. They know we mean what we say. We will have no trouble.'

'Very good,' Jeannette said. 'Just remember that in due course there will be the morning shift arriving; let them in, and take them into custody, as quietly as possible. Now, you tell me Gallagher was assisted to escape by a nurse. If Candish went with them, this must have been done from whichever ward he was in. This should not be difficult to ascertain, and the name and address of the nurse on duty should also be easy to discover. Make them show you their duty roster. Once you have established that, send four men to her home. She is to be eliminated, and anyone who is with her. If that happens to be Candish and Gallagher, so much the better. If they are not there, before she is disposed of, make the nurse tell where they have gone. But they must be disposed of, and quickly. Otherwise they may cause a great deal of trouble. Understood?'

'Yes, madame.'

'And Harb, I do not wish any mistakes this time,' Jeannette said, and handed the phone back to Rakim.

'You don't think we are going to have trouble anyway?' Honeylee asked. The yacht was still aground, but she was surrounded by water, and the tide was lapping over the sill to the marina. There was considerable activity on board the various yachts, both inside and outside the gates. 'Those chaps will want to move.' There was also some activity on the fishermen's dock, on the far side of the harbour.

'In this weather?' Jeannette asked. 'Have the Harbour Office make an announcement that because of the storm no yachts are permitted to leave the harbour until the wind abates.'

'You think they'll go for that?'

'They will have to,' Jeannette said. 'By the time they decide to do something about it, we will have left.'

'What about the fishing fleet?'

Jeannette shrugged. 'If they wish to put to sea, let them go. They'll be out of our way. Now let us contact London.'

'No, no,' said the Saudi ambassador. He looked as hot and bothered as anyone at being dragged from his bed in the dawn. 'Those two were born Saudis, yes, but they gave up their citizenship several years ago. I believe they carry Sudanese passports.'

'But they still have oil wealth,' the Prime Minister remarked.

'Well, yes; they inherited it from their father, and reinvested a large part of it, before they became involved in international terrorism. Now, their vast holdings are spread all over the world.'

'Being spent on terrorism. And you have never sought to arrest them?' the Foreign Secretary asked.

The Ambassador spread his hands. 'They are no longer our citizens. We would certainly arrest them should they ever return to Saudi.'

'And lock them up for a long time, I hope.'

The Ambassador smiled. 'We would chop off their heads, Mr Foreign Secretary. But this man Hassan – even if he is found guilty at The Hague . . . you will merely lock him up, eh?'

'It is our custom,' the Foreign Secretary agreed.

'Supposing we can get him there,' the Prime Minister remarked. 'Yes, Hargreaves?'

'The Home Secretary is here, Prime Minister. He has received a further communication from Guernsey.'

'Ask him to come in, will you? Mr Ambassador, I'm sure you'll excuse us. It was good of you to come at this unearthly hour.'

'I would like to help you catch these thugs,' the Ambassador said; 'but all I can do is offer you my best wishes for a speedy and successful conclusion to this affair.'

'I'll say amen to that,' the Prime Minister agreed.

Hargreaves showed the Ambassador to the door, and he was replaced by the Home Secretary.

'They certainly seem to have it all thought out, although they may have missed one or two points.'

'Well?'

'They require a fully fuelled 747, with a crew and Sheikh Hassan, who will be unescorted, to land at Guernsey's La Villiaze airport at ten o'clock this morning. They will then board the aircraft and leave.'

'Just like that?' asked the Foreign Secretary. 'What do they take us for?'

'They have endeavoured to cover themselves against every eventuality. They say they have wired explosives to the storage tanks, for both gas and oil, in St Sampson's, and they have also placed explosives in the electricity-generating plant. These will be on a time switch, the detonators concealed in the ground. They will radio us giving us the code and places for accessing these switches once they are clear away. They are also taking with them, as hostages, the Bailiff and his wife, and the Lieutenant Governor and his wife.'

'Bloody hell,' growled the Prime Minister. 'But wherever they go, we can still track them on radar. And when they land . . .'

'They will find asylum, possibly in Libya, probably in the Sudan.'

'Of which country they are nationals, according to the Ambassador,' the Foreign Secretary remarked.

'Damn, damn, damn,' the Prime Minister said. 'Have they got us, Ned?'

'We can delay things by a couple of hours.'

'They won't accept a delay,' the Foreign Secretary said.

'In this case, they will have to,' the Home Secretary said. 'According to Crabtree, the runway in Guernsey will not take a jumbo.'

The Prime Minister frowned. 'Is he sure?'

'He's sure. He has all these facts at his fingertips.'

'What's the largest it will take?'

'Even a 727 would be chancing it a bit. Anything smaller – well, it'll cut their range.'

'By how much?'

'Oh, they'd still be able to make Libya, certainly.'

'So, are we any further ahead?'

'Well, Prime Minister, as I mentioned, we have at least a possibility for a delay.'

'I don't see how. We tell them we can't use a jumbo; they'll simply settle for the largest plane we *can* put down.'

'Not if we act like a bunch of charlies, Prime Minister. They've asked for a jumbo; they'll get a jumbo. Now, our pilot will of course have been in touch with Guernsey Air Traffic Control from the moment he takes off from Heathrow. They are undoubtedly under the control of the terrorists, but they will still tell the pilot, as they will surely tell the terrorists, that he cannot possibly put the aircraft down on such a short runway. He will reply, sorry, old man, but I have my orders. Then he will make his approach, attempt to put down, discover he can't make it without overshooting and crashing, with his precious cargo, Hassan, probably being killed. He will go up again, and tell the ground, we'll have to try something smaller. The terrorists will have to go along with this. They want him at ten o'clock; well, they'll get him at ten o'clock. He then has to fly back here and put down, and be transferred to another aircraft, while we talk to the terrorists, admit that we had no idea a jumbo couldn't get down in Guernsey, tell them that we are doing our best to co-operate, and that a replacement plane will be along as soon as possible. That's taking us up to eleven o'clock at the earliest. It'll probably be twelve.'

'Will Hassan be on board?' the Prime Minister asked.

'I think he should be. His friends may well wish to speak with him.'

'Is that a good idea?'

'Certainly. What can he tell them, save to confirm that we are doing everything possible to carry out their demands? He won't be anxious to risk a crash landing.'

'It's damned risky.'

'This whole business is damned risky, Prime Minister.'

'OK,' the Foreign Secretary said. 'We can buy ourselves an hour, maybe two. What are we going to do with that time?'

The Home Secretary looked at his watch. It was just coming up to four o'clock. 'Well, we have something like six or seven hours. In that time, quite a lot can happen.'

'That sounds rather like wishful thinking,' the Prime Minister grumbled. 'Has there been any word from anyone in Guernsey?'

'Only that telephone call from the harbourmaster that started our reaction. Of course, ninety-nine per cent of the island is still asleep. It's Sunday morning, it's pouring with rain, and it's blowing a gale. However, people will start to stir in the next couple of hours.'

'According to the terrorist spokesman—'

'It's a spokeswoman, actually,' the Home Secretary murmured.

'That's probably worse. Anyway, in their original message they said they hoped to keep what is happening from the Guernsey population.'

'That was when they were intending to be away by ten. A couple of hours' delay may upset that idea.'

'And supposing somebody does understand, or find out, what is going on?'

'That harbourmaster certainly does,' the Foreign Secretary said. 'But he seems to think he's done his duty by contacting Johnnie Hartwell.'

'As he did,' the Prime Minister said. 'What else was he supposed to do? What are you hoping for, Ned? Those people have no weapons, no organisation to deal with a situation like this . . . if anyone attempted to start something, there would be an absolute bloodbath.'

'There may well be anyway,' the Foreign Secretary grumbled.

'Well,' the Home Secretary said, 'there hasn't been one yet. As far as we know, there has been one fatality, and even that is claimed by the harbourmaster; the Lieutenant Governor did not mention it.'

'So maybe they are not as ruthless as they would like us to think,' the Prime Minister said hopefully.

'If it is true they have killed a man, Prime Minister, then we may assume they are ruthless.'

'But you are still hoping the Guernsey people may start something. Then you have your bloodbath. I must say, Ned, it seems to me that you don't really have a coherent plan.'

'Do you?'

The Foreign Secretary scratched his head.

'What I have done,' the Home Secretary said, 'is contact my opposite number in Paris, and he has agreed that a regiment of the SAS should be flown to Cherbourg airport. That means that they can be over Guernsey in ten minutes, once the order has been given.'

'And who is going to give this order?' the Prime Minister asked.

'Ah . . . it would have to be you,' the Home Secretary said.

'If we send in the SAS . . . talk about bloodbaths.'

'It is a situation – profit and loss – which has to be weighed. We are legally entitled to use them now. A man has been killed.'

'You have no confirmation of that,' the Foreign Secretary reminded him.

'I think we have to assume it is true. So, the decision needs to be taken, now. Are we going to let this man Hassan get away, in which case we will be ridiculed before the world, and, incidentally, be the target of every terrorist organisation in the world, as they will all regard us as a soft touch?'

'We cannot possibly allow that to happen,' the Prime Minister said.

'Absolutely. Therefore, some time between now and say eleven o'clock this morning, we have got to make something happen. If we assume that these people are serious, and are both ruthless and suicidal, there is going to be bloodshed. Our decision must be when to move so as to keep that to a minimum, at least amongst the civilian population of Guernsey.'

'Not to mention the total destruction of the island's infrastructure,' the Foreign Secretary said.

'We can replace the infrastructure, Harry,' the Home Secretary said. 'We can't replace the people who get killed.'

'Amongst whom, we are talking of the Bailiff and his wife, and the Lieutenant Governor and his wife,' the Prime Minister said.

'I'm afraid that is very probably the case, Prime Minister,' the Foreign Secretary said. 'However, if we are going to determine this situation by force, it is my belief that we should use the greatest force possible. Hartwell has two destroyers and a couple of frigates ready to put to sea. He

135

should get them out there, within half an hour's range of the island. Crabtree has a squadron of Tornados standing by . . .'

'Are you seriously suggesting we should bomb or shell the hell out of our own people?'

'I am suggesting that the sight of so much force – warships on the horizon and aircraft flying low over the island – will call these people's bluff. Then if we send in ground troops as well . . .'

'And if they aren't bluffing?'

'Well . . .' The Home Secretary shrugged. '. . . there will be casualties. But the SAS know how to handle these situations. They will keep them to a minimum.'

'I take it you have discussed this with their commanders?' the Foreign Secretary asked.

'No, I haven't, as a matter of fact. I wanted clearance first.' The Home Secretary looked at the Prime Minister.

'Because I think there is a small point you have over-looked,' the Foreign Minister said. 'The SAS are probably the best force of this type in the world. They will, as you say, inflict the minimum number of casualties. However, in all of their past operations they have known exactly where they were going, where their enemies were. Here they are blind. We know absolutely nothing about the situation in Guernsey. They claim to control the harbour. That is probably true. But that can be done, in a harbour as small as St Peter Port, with half a dozen men and a machine gun. The terrorists claim to control the airport. Ditto. But we don't know for sure. They claim to control the police station and a majority of the island force. Perhaps. They certainly seem to be holding the Bailiff and his wife, the Lieutenant Governor and his wife, and the Chief of Police and his wife. Where? We don't know that. They claim to hold various key positions in the island; but again, we don't know how true this is or in what strength those positions are held. Nor do we know what other positions are held, which have not yet been specified. At the very least it means that after we put down the SAS, it could be a matter of some time, perhaps even hours, before all of these people can be taken out – hours during which they can be wreaking all manner of death and destruction.'

The Home Secretary gulped.

'Yes,' the Prime Minister said, glad to have something on to which he could latch, and which might postpone taking the dreadful decision for a little while. 'We need a more accurate picture of what is happening over there.'

'And how are we supposed to get that? Both the electrics and the telephones are out.'

'We'll use a mobile.'

'To telephone whom? Someone who is enjoying his Sunday morning breakfast? We call him and say, I say, old man, can you nip out and discover just how many terrorists there are on your island, exactly where they are situated and what they are doing?'

'Simmer down, Ned,' the Prime Minister said, not taking offence; he knew the enormous strain they were all under. 'We do have a contact in Guernsey: the harbourmaster. If we can get in touch with him, and explain the situation – as much of it as he should know – and that we need information as to the terrorists' dispositions before making our own, well, I think he might be of great help.'

'You'd be asking him to stick out his neck a mile.'

'Well, we'd have to explain the risk, but equally, the risks to so many other lives if we don't get that information.'

'Do we have his mobile number?' the Foreign Secretary asked.

'Hartwell will probably have it. The two are old buddies.'

'Well, get hold of Hartwell and ask him to follow that line up. Meanwhile, I approve of all your other dispositions, Ned. Tell the terrorists their plane, and their man, will touch down at ten o'clock as agreed; and you'd better arrange to have Hassan transferred from the Scrubs to Heathrow.' The Prime Minister leaned back in his chair with a sigh. At least he had things moving, even if he had no idea where they were going to wind up.

'As before,' Honeylee said. 'Total surrender. The plane will touch down at ten o'clock as arranged. Hassan will be on board, and we will be airborne within an hour.'

'Sooner than that, I hope,' Jeannette said. 'Although I don't like the way they are giving in to all our demands without a question. That is suspicious. They have something up their sleeves.'

'What, do you suppose?' Honeylee asked. 'We hold all the high cards.'

Jeannette looked at al-Rakim. 'Can we have overlooked anything?'

'I do not think so. I think our planning is perfect.'

'I still do not like it. Their response almost leads me to believe they knew we were here before we informed them, and have been anticipating our demands. Is that possible? Could someone have found out and telephoned before we shut down the system? Or used a mobile?'

Honeylee snapped his fingers. 'That Gallagher woman.'

'Shit, yes!' Jeannette said. 'She certainly knew of it. But we're going to get her. I am going to make her squeal. Call Harb and tell him I have changed my mind and wish her taken alive. I think we will take her with us, when we leave, and throw her out of the aircraft over the desert.'

'But this girl drives a minibus, taking tourists for trips around the island,' al-Rakim said. 'Who is she going to contact in the British government? All right, so she discovered that we were planning something. That fool Sufyan whom I sent to deal with her made a mess of it, and she's been on the run ever since; but she did the obvious thing, and took her story to the police station. She got there just before our people, and managed to escape again. Hashim and Sufyan followed her down to the harbour, and she went into the water. They didn't see her again, and supposed she must have drowned.'

'Instead she went to the hospital, as madame said she would,' Honeylee put in.

'She must have more lives than a cat,' al-Rakim complained. 'The point is, she has been rushing around Guernsey. She has made no effort to get a message off the island, so far as we know.'

'Well, I believe someone did,' Jeannette said. 'Get Yusuf up here.'

Yusuf was their communications expert.

'What time was the telephone exchange put out of action?' Jeannette asked him.

'It took longer than we anticipated. But all lines were dead by three o'clock.'

'And before then? I assume you were monitoring all calls between midnight and three?'

'That is correct, madame. I have made a list.' He held it out. 'You will see there were very few.'

'But this number has made three calls.' Jeannette jabbed the paper with her nail. 'One at a quarter to one, one at a quarter past, one at half past. It is not usual for people to make three telephone calls in rapid succession in the middle of the night. Was someone having a baby?'

Yusuf checked his list of numbers. 'I do not think it was a pregnancy, madame. The three calls were made from the house of the harbourmaster.'

Jeannette frowned. 'To whom?'

The first was to the house of Sergeant Doolittle. The second was to the watch house.'

'Sergeant Doolittle?'

'That was the police officer who came on board last night,' Honeylee said. 'Harb shot him. I examined the body and found his identification.'

'That man is completely trigger-happy,' Jeannette growled. 'But this happened at eleven thirty. Why should the harbour-master telephone his wife two hours later?'

'I presume he was trying to reach him. As a matter of fact,

the sergeant's mobile buzzed while I was checking him out, but I thought it best not to answer, and switched it off.'

Jeannette raised her eyes to heaven, but perhaps it was a good thing. 'So, none other than us know what happened to this sergeant. But the harbourmaster, two hours later, is trying to reach him. Then he telephones the harbour watch. But they were already in our hands.'

'So what did they tell him?' Honeylee asked.

'I assume they obeyed their instructions, and had one of the watch-keepers answer him. If anything had been wrong, they would have contacted us. So he must have been satisfied.'

'You think so? You are a fool,' Jeannette said. 'You are all fools. You have this harbourmaster, apparently peacefully at home, until some time after one o'clock. Then he suddenly starts telephoning all over the place. Don't you realise why? It was because that girl Gallagher had got to him – the harbourmaster. He is the boss of her lover, who we sent to hospital with a drug OD! Who was the third call made to?'

'England, madame.'

'England?' Jeannette shouted. 'My God, that is it. Who was he telephoning in England?'

'I have the number; but I don't who the person was.'

'Well, find out. There must be an English directory at the exchange.'

'The harbourmaster will know,' al-Rakim said.

'Yes,' Jeannette said. 'Bring him here, al-Rakim.'

'Is it important?' Honeylee asked. 'They have agreed to all our demands.'

'Far too quickly,' Jeannette said. 'That telephone call was made just before two this morning. The harbourmaster was calling someone in England at that unholy hour. Therefore it is possible that the British government knew all about us at least an hour before we contacted them. An hour in which to make plans.'

'But they have agreed to our demands,' Honeylee said again.

'As I said, far too quickly. Something is up, and we must know what it is. Al-Rakim, fetch that man here.'

Pursuit

'I'm afraid Admiral Hartwell doesn't have the number for the harbourmaster's mobile phone, Prime Minister,' Hargreaves said. 'Only the house phone. And that is dead.'

'Damn!' the Prime Minister said. 'Surely it'll be listed in the Guernsey telephone directory?'

'Ah . . . I'm sure it is, Prime Minister. But we do not have one.'

'Well, find one. Get hold of someone at the Post Office. I want a Guernsey telephone directory on my desk in fifteen minutes.'

Hargreaves gulped.

'Eh? Eh?' Sophie woke up as the car stopped. 'Where am I?'

'You were having a little nap,' James explained.

The sound of his voice brought back memory, and she blinked at the rather large house looming above them. 'You live here?' she asked Helen.

'It's divided into flats,' Helen said.

It was still raining and blowing; the trees lining the drive were waving to and fro. Sophie got out and began to shiver. 'What time is it?'

'Half past three,' Helen said, hurrying from the car and up the steps to the front door, key in hand.

'Come on.' James was now wide awake, and he held Sophie's arm to escort her to shelter.

'Sssh,' Helen begged, letting them into the house and

leading them up the stairs. 'The first thing we have to do is get you out of those wet clothes.'

'We must find out what's happening,' Sophie repeated. She was still half asleep and was, in addition, feeling unwell, mainly the result of having been continuously wet and cold for several hours.

Reaching the first floor, they tiptoed along a corridor, where Helen unlocked a door and let them into a small lounge.

'It's only a one-bedroom,' she apologised, opening an inner door and switching on the light.

'What? Ah . . .' A bulky, craggy-faced young man, long hair tangled, sat up with a start. 'Oh, Helen.' Then he saw James and Sophie, and grabbed the sheet to cover his naked body. 'What the . . . ?'

'Go in there.' Helen pointed at the bathroom door. 'And strip off. You'll find a dressing gown hanging on the hook. I'll put some coffee on.' She looked at James. 'You'd better do the same. You're soaked.'

'How many dressing gowns do you have?'

'Use a towel.' Helen began to undress herself; she was as wet as either of them.

'What the hell is going on?' Shane enquired from the safety of the bed.

'All hell is going on,' Helen said, wrapping herself in her own dressing gown and bustling into the lounge, off which there was a kitchenette.

'She's a remarkably composed young woman,' James remarked, closing the bathroom door. 'You have got the shakes.'

'And how.'

Sophie had a hot shower.

'You need to take something,' he said, joining her. 'Helen is a nurse. She's bound to have something.'

'If I take anything,' Sophie said, towelling herself, 'I am going to pass out cold. I haven't had any sleep, save for that

143

five minutes in the car, and I've had quite a night.'

'I hope you're going to tell me about it.'

'When I have the time.' She wrapped herself in the dressing gown hanging behind the door, and went into the bedroom. Shane had at least got up and pulled on his pants.

'Please tell me what's going on,' he begged. 'You look familiar.'

'I drive for DriveRite,' Sophie said. 'Maybe you've used our bus, sometime.'

'And you're a friend of Helen . . . Have you had an accident?'

'Several. And I only met Helen tonight.'

The door opened, and Helen brought in a tray with four steaming mugs of coffee. 'What are we going to do?' she asked.

'You believe me, about what's happening?' Sophie asked.

'You haven't told me what's happening,' Helen pointed out, 'but I believe you that something is.'

Sophie outlined the situation. Shane sat on the bed with his mouth open. James stood in the bathroom doorway, wrapped in a towel, with *his* mouth open. Helen drank coffee.

'You mean you're actually being hunted by a bunch of Arab terrorists?' Shane looked at Helen for confirmation.

'I saw it happening,' Helen said.

'But . . . if they come here . . .'

'They won't,' Sophie said. 'No one knows I'm here. The question is, what are we going to do now. It's four o'clock. Soon people will start to wake up; and they don't have a clue what's happening. We have to tell them.'

'Hang about,' Helen said. 'Is that a good idea? Those thugs shot Sister Morgan, just like that. You say they shot a policeman, as well . . .'

'At least one,' Sophie muttered.

'That means they'll be quite happy to shoot anyone else who gets in their way.'

'Sixty thousand people?' Shane asked. 'They couldn't

possibly have that much ammo.'

'Oh, for God's sake,' Helen snapped. 'You expect the people just to march against their machine guns and Kalashnikovs and get mown down till they run out of ammunition?'

'Minimis,' James said absently.

'Eh?'

'They're not using Kalashnikovs. They're using Minimis. Those aren't assault rifles. They're virtually small machine guns in themselves, only much more powerful than a tommy gun.'

'Cheer me up,' Helen said.

'You said you were in touch with the harbourmaster,' Shane said. 'He was going to call England.'

'He did.'

'Well, then, they know over there. They'll be doing something.'

'What, do you suppose?' James asked.

'Captain Harrison might know. Anyway, if he's the only other person in Guernsey who knows what's happening and hasn't been shot or picked up by the terrorists, it seems to me that we should get together with him and decide what we do.'

'Good thinking,' Helen said. 'Do you have his number?'

'No, I don't,' Sophie said. Her brain was beginning to go dead with exhaustion again.

'It'll be in the book,' Helen said, locating it.

'They've closed down the telephone exchange,' James warned.

'His mobile number is here.' She handed the phone to James, who punched the keys.

'Captain Harrison? James Candish.'

'James! My God, it's good to hear your voice. Are you all right?'

'I'm getting there. You've seen Sophie?'

'A couple of hours ago. I hope nothing has happened to her.'

'She's with me,' James said. 'What we want to know is if there has been any reaction from England?'

'Not to my knowledge. I'm not sure there will *be* any reaction. Admiral Hartwell didn't sound too convinced. And frankly, well . . . it's been two hours since Sophie was here, and nothing has happened. The island is completely quiet. Well, if you can call it that with a gale blowing. If this is some mistake . . .'

'It isn't, Captain,' James said. 'It's happening. Can't you call this admiral back, and find out what he's doing?'

'Ah . . . I really don't think I can do that, James. Anyway, all the phones are dead.'

'Captain,' James said patiently, 'you're speaking with me on your mobile.'

'Why, yes, so I am. But still, to call the Admiral again . . .'

'Well, will you give me his number?'

'You, James?'

'I'll call him myself,' James said. 'I'll let Sophie speak with him. What she has seen and experienced should get him going.'

'James,' Harrison said, 'if this *is* a foul-up, you could lose your job.'

'It isn't,' James said. 'Please give me the number.'

'Oh, very well. Wait a moment.' Harrison fetched his address book, read out the number. 'Now, James . . .'

James wrote the number on Helen's desk diary. 'You won't be involved. Thank you, sir.'

'Well . . . hold on; there's someone at the door. I'll be right back.'

'Don't answer it!' James shouted. 'Get Mrs Harrison and leave by the back.'

There was no reply.

'Shit!' James said.

'What's happening?' Shane asked.

James held up his hand, listened to a series of odd noises, gasps and thumps, and then a scream from Doris Harrison.

'Shit,' he muttered again.

'Excuse me, please,' said a voice into the phone. 'What number are you calling from?'

James switched off. 'They've got him.'

'Oh, no,' Sophie said, waking up again.

'So much for forming our own resistance group. It's us chickens, and nobody else.'

They gazed at each other.

'But at least I have Hartwell's home number.'

James punched the numbers. 'Hello? Hello? May I speak with Admiral Hartwell, please? . . . No, he doesn't know who I am; I'm the assistant harbourmaster in Guernsey . . . Yes, Bill Harrison's second . . . Yes . . . Well, could you give me a number where I can reach him? This really is a matter of life and death. . . . Thank you, Lady Hartwell.'

He wrote down the new number. 'She seems to know what's going on.' He tried the next number.

'I'd like to speak with Admiral Hartwell, please. This is the assistant harbourmaster, Guernsey. No, I cannot prove who I am, but it is essential that I speak with the Admiral.' He waited, drumming his fingers on the desk. 'Admiral Hartwell? James Candish here, sir. Assistant harbourmaster, Guernsey . . . Yes, sir. They seem to have taken Captain Harrison . . . I don't know, sir. Ah . . . as far as we know, sir, the terrorists control the harbour and the police station, the electricity-generating plant, the telephone exchange, the local television and radio stations, and the hospital. Several people have been killed . . . Yes, sir, several. And we believe they have taken the Bailiff and his wife, the Lieutenant Governor and his wife, and the Chief of Police and probably his wife as well. I believe they have now also taken Harbourmaster Harrison, and probably his wife as well . . . No, sir, at the moment all seems calm. The thing is, no one apart from those I have mentioned, and us here, knows that anything is going on. We would like to know if there is anything we can do. Well . . .' He looked at the anxious faces watching him. '. . . I'm afraid there seem to be just four of

147

us . . . No, we have no weapons . . . Yes, sir. Rather goes against the grain . . . Yes, sir. I understand.' He switched off the phone.

'Do absolutely nothing. Do not endanger lives. The terrorists have apparently been in touch and have made certain demands. These are being processed; but the situation is under control. Shit!'

'Actually, I do have a weapon,' Shane said. 'A shotgun.'

'I'm not sure I'd back a shotgun against a Minimi,' James said. 'Anyway, that was a direct order. Do nothing. Do not endanger lives.'

'While those thugs take a life whenever they feel like it,' Sophie muttered.

'I'll make breakfast, shall I?' Helen volunteered.

But by the time it was ready, Sophie was fast asleep.

'The watch house reports some activity on radar,' Honeylee told Jeannette. 'There are two large blips just off Alderney. Those are clearly warships.'

'That is reasonable,' Jeannette said. It was just past six, and full daylight, although the low cloud made the morning dull, and rain squalls continued to lash the island, while in the Russel the seas still showed white teeth. The yacht was now well afloat, rising and falling on the swell, grinding against the fenders holding her from the dock. Several fishermen had put out, despite the weather, but the gates to the marina remained closed.

'There is also a good deal of activity over Cherbourg. Several blips have gone in over the past half-hour.'

'They are putting men on the ground,' Jeannette said. 'But these are just motions. There is nothing they can do.'

'There is also considerable agitation at the airport.'

'Because the mail plane was turned away?'

It had tried to come down a few minutes before, and been told by Air Traffic Control, under the guns of the terrorists, that the airport was closed.

'I don't know about that; but it appears that there are several early-morning flights to England, even on a Sunday. Passengers are turning up, to find the airport buildings closed. There is apparently a good deal of unrest.'

'How many people have we got out there?'

'Three in the control tower, another six commanding the buildings and those members of the staff we have taken prisoner.'

'Have one of those make an announcement to the passengers that, because of the weather, all flights have been cancelled.'

'This is apparently unusual, except in cases of fog.'

'They will still have to accept it. These people are sheep. They accept whatever authority tells them to accept. Tell them that it is expected normal flying will be resumed this afternoon.' She looked at her watch. 'Perhaps sooner than that. Ah, al-Rakim. You have the man?'

'And his wife. Below.'

'I will come down.'

Jeannette picked up her terrier and went down the ladders to the saloon. Bill Harrison and Doris were both seated on the settee. The harbourmaster's face was bruised, and he looked dazed; both wore only nightclothes, which were soaking wet.

With them were the two other women in the 'tourist' party. Both were anxious. 'What is happening?' one asked.

'Everything that is happening is as was planned,' Jeannette told them; they were only window-dressing anyway. 'We shall be leaving on schedule.'

'Are you in charge?' Doris Harrison demanded.

'I am in charge,' Jeannette acknowledged.

'I wish to protest most strongly,' Doris said. 'Your thugs beat up my husband.'

'He endeavoured to resist us,' al-Rakim explained.

'He may well be beaten up more than that,' Jeannette said. 'Give him a glass of brandy.'

149

The steward poured and gave Harrison the glass. He sipped; his hand was shaking.

'Now I wish you to answer a few questions,' Jeannette said, sitting down herself, and putting the terrier on the carpet. 'You telephoned England this morning at about two o'clock. Whom did you call?'

Harrison drank some more brandy; he was getting his nerves under control.

'Listen to me,' Jeannette said, leaning forward: 'we are not playing games. If you made that telephone call as a result of a visit from the woman Gallagher, you will know that we are very serious indeed. If you do not answer my questions . . .' She snapped her fingers, and al-Rakim, standing at her shoulder, drew an automatic pistol. '. . . we shall shoot your wife.'

Doris gave a little gasp.

'So?' Jeannette asked.

Harrison drew a deep breath. 'I telephoned a friend of mine.'

'At two o'clock in the morning? Who was this friend? Please do not lie to me. If I do not like your answer, your wife will die.'

Harrison looked at his wife, who looked back. Then he drew another deep breath. 'I telephoned Rear Admiral Sir John Hartwell, Commander-in-Chief, Portsmouth.'

'For a friendly chat. At two o'clock in the morning?'

'I felt he should know what was going on here.'

'And how do you know what is going on here? You were acting on what the Gallagher woman told you. Is that correct?'

Harrison sighed. 'Yes. Sophie told me.'

'Thank you. Now, what was the reaction of this admiral?'

'I don't think he believed me.'

'I see. And have you spoken with him again, since?'

'No.'

'But you were speaking to someone on your mobile phone when my people called.'

Harrison's head jerked at the choice of words.

'Who was it?'

Another sigh. 'I was speaking with my assistant, James Candish.'

'The young man who came aboard yesterday afternoon and caused so much trouble? Well, well. I know he has left the hospital. Where is he now?'

'I have no idea.'

Jeannette snapped her fingers, and al-Rakim levelled his pistol.

Doris gave a little shudder, and held her hands to her mouth.

'It is the truth,' Harrison shouted. 'He telephoned me, using my mobile number. He didn't say where he was calling from.'

Jeannette gazed at him for several seconds; then she nodded. 'We will find him. Come to think of it, Captain, contact Harb and find out why he has not yet caught up with Gallagher and Candish.'

Honeylee, who had followed them down to the saloon, nodded and went out.

'What do you wish to do with these?' al-Rakim asked.

'Lock them up for the time being,' Jeannette said. 'I will tell you later.'

Al-Rakim summoned the steward, and the two of them shepherded Harrison and Doris to the inner door.

'You won't get away with this,' Doris said. 'You're going to spend the rest of your life in prison.' It was a stupid, fatuous remark, but she felt compelled to say something.

'You must come and visit me,' Jeannette said, voice thick with sarcasm.

The door closed behind them, and the terrier barked.

'I know, darling,' Jeannette said, and picked the little dog up. 'But you know what? I think we can go walkies . . . ashore.'

She went to the door, and the saloon phone buzzed. Jeannette turned back to answer it.

'We have an address for that nurse, at last,' Honeylee said. 'Seems the staff at the hospital weren't exactly co-operative.'

'Well,' Jeannette said, 'tell Harb to get her.'

'And her companions?'

'They had better be disposed of; but I wish to ask Gallagher some questions.'

'Will do.'

The phone went dead, and Jeannette looked at her watch. It was just coming up to seven o'clock. Everything was going according to plan. Even that damned woman was just a blip. But she would soon be history.

'I have been unable to get in touch with Harbourmaster Harrison, Prime Minister,' Hartwell said, standing in the centre of the hastily convened operations room. 'In fact, I believe he may have been taken by the terrorists. I have, however, spoken with his assistant, James Candish, and he has been able to give me an update on the situation, in so far as he knows it.'

'And?'

'It seems that the terrorists' claims are all accurate. They do control every vital installation in the island. Candish did not mention the placing of bombs at the fuel depot, but as he confirmed every other claim, it seems likely that is also true. What he did say, however, was that there have been several deaths.'

The Admiral paused, glancing at General Peart and Colonel Gracey, who were also present.

The Prime Minister gave a grim smile. 'Back to the SAS, eh, Colonel?'

'With every justification, sir.'

'Absolutely. Providing only terrorists get killed in the shoot-out. Supposing you did go in, give me, roughly, your dispositions.'

'The big factor is time, sir. The terrorists have the airport, and thus the radar installation. They will be monitoring Cherbourg as well as the Channel.'

'Then they will have seen the SAS battalion go in.'

'No, sir. They will have seen increased activity over Cherbourg airport. They will not know precisely what that activity consists of. However, if several aircraft were to take off and fly to Guernsey, they would certainly have something like fifteen minutes warning that an invasion force was on its way. That would give them ample time to carry out their various threats, if they are sufficiently determined to do so. Then, of course, the aircraft can only be put down at the airport. Even if they can carry their own transport, it would take at least another fifteen minutes for them to reach the various positions, most especially the fuel depot in St Sampson's.'

'Helicopters,' General Peart said. 'If we used helicopters, we could put our people down exactly on their targets.'

'The same objection applies to helicopters, sir,' Gracey said. 'Even more so. The terrorists would see them coming on radar in ample time to carry our their executions and demolitions.'

'Paras,' Crabtree suggested. 'They'd do the job.'

'Guernsey is a very built-up island, sir,' Gracey pointed out. 'Putting down paras amongst all those houses and then assembling them would again be a very lengthy business, and the same objection remains: that the aircraft would be spotted long before they reached their targets. We must act on the assumption that these people mean what they say – that they are prepared to go down fighting, destroying everything possible as they do so.'

'Are you telling us that there is no way we can counter-attack?' the Prime Minister asked.

'Only by complete and total surprise, sir.'

'You have just explained that that is not possible, Colonel Gracey.'

'By any conventional means, sir. However, the terrorists have themselves requested the use of a very large aircraft. A jumbo could carry four hundred men, and sufficient light equipment to do the job.'

'But we can't put a jumbo down in Guernsey,' Crabtree said.

'We could, sir. It wouldn't ever take off again, but we'd have four hundred men on the ground. If they acted sufficiently promptly, they could take over the airport before the terrorists knew what had hit them.'

'Won't work,' Crabtree said. 'You are accepting the fact that the jumbo will have to overshoot the runway and crash-land.'

'Yes, sir,' Gracey said. 'If we load her with just sufficient fuel to get to Guernsey, there should be little risk of fire. There will be some injuries to the personnel, presumably, but these will have to be accepted.'

'We're back to time, Colonel. I have flown into Guernsey several times. An overshoot will leave the aircraft something like half a mile from the terminal buildings and air traffic control. Even the best-trained soldier is not going to cover that distance, fully equipped, in under three minutes.'

'Yes, sir, but surely the crash will have the airport in some disarray.'

'Not sufficiently. All it would require is one telephone call from the men in the control tower to their central command, and the show would go up. Oh, your people would no doubt take all the terrorists out, but the cost to the island and the islanders would be unacceptable.'

There was a brief silence while the men round the table looked at each other.

'That's quite a doomsday scenario,' the Prime Minister said at last. 'Are we licked?'

Once again glances were exchanged.

'If we're down to a damage-limitation exercise,' Hartwell

said, 'there is one possible way to wind it up with the least loss of life, at least amongst our people.'

'Yes?'

'Well, sir, we have agreed to their demands. We can do just that: provide them with an aircraft to take them and their sheikh out of Guernsey . . . and then shoot it down.'

There was another brief silence.

'What about the hostages?' the Home Secretary asked.

'At least four,' Hartwell said.

'The Bailiff and his wife, the Lieutenant Governor and his wife. There are also the explosive charges.'

'I would say our people could find those in time, once the terrorists had left.'

'I wonder.'

'In any event, such a drastic course would have to be a last resort,' the Prime Minister said. 'It wouldn't do our international reputation any good.'

'It would show that we mean business when it comes to combating terrorism,' Hartwell argued.

'Hm,' the Prime Minister said, and looked at his watch. 'Half past eight. Is the plane all ready?'

'Yes, sir,' Crabtree said.

'And the sheikh?'

'He is at Heathrow, under guard.'

'Yes. Well, gentlemen, I think we will proceed as originally planned, for the time being. The 747 ploy has bought us at least an hour of time. I will make a decision as to how we handle the situation by ten o'clock. Air Vice Marshal, would you remain behind, please. And you, Colonel. Thank you, gentlemen.'

The other officers and the various secretaries filed from the room, casting curious and envious glances at the two chosen to remain.

'Close the door, Colonel Gracey,' the Prime Minister said. Gracey obeyed.

'Now, gentlemen,' the Prime Minister said; 'it is not my

155

intention to permit that terrorist thug to escape, or to allow Her Majesty's Government to be blackmailed. However, nor is it my intention to murder the Bailiff of Guernsey or the Lieutenant Governor, not to mention their wives. If they are to die, it will have to be by terrorist action, not ours. Now, Colonel, I was intrigued by your idea of crash-landing a plane filled with members of the SAS; but as you, Air Commodore Crabtree, have pointed out, the distance between where the plane will come to a halt and the control tower is such that it will still give the terrorists the time to react positively. However, I have a plan that might just overcome that difficulty.'

He outlined his idea.

'Gosh,' Sophie said, staring at a strange ceiling. 'Where am I?'

'In my bed,' Helen said.

'In bed?' Sophie cried, sitting up.

'You just passed out cold. You were totally exhausted. I'd say mentally as well as physically. I think you should stay put.'

'But . . . what time is it?'

'Half past eight. You've only been down four hours.'

'God Almighty!' Sophie leapt out of bed but checked when she realised she was naked. 'My clothes!' She looked at the bedroom door, but it was shut.

'They're in the drier, with my uniform,' Helen said; she was still wearing a dressing gown. 'I imagine they're wearable by now; but they're pretty torn up. Listen: calm down.'

'Where are the boys?'

'In there. Your James is still pretty done up.'

'But . . . what's happening?'

'Nothing's happening. There are no electrics and no telephones. I've checked with the other flats and they're the same.'

'Did you tell them why?'

'I didn't think I should. I don't want to cause a panic.'

'But you have a battery radio, haven't you?'

'I do. But there's not a lot on it. Guernsey Radio is dead. Well, that figures. But the BBC is exactly as usual. Not a mention of anything happening in the Channel Islands.'

'It'll surely be filtering through by now,' Sophie said. 'We have to do something.'

'Sophie, there is absolutely nothing we *can* do,' Helen said. 'That admiral James spoke to said that everything was under control. We have to believe that.'

'That's military-speak for "we don't have a clue what to do next,"' Sophie said. 'There must be something . . . what's that?'

Helen went to the window. 'Just a car in the drive.'

'A car?' Sophie joined her, and they watched the four men get out. 'Oh, my God! They're coming for us.'

'For us? But how? It can't be true. How did they find out where I live? How can they possibly know I brought you here?'

'You were looking after James. They checked duty rosters and then got your address,' Sophie said. 'My clothes! The drier!'

'In the kitchen. But—'

'Get dressed,' Sophie told her, and wrenched open the bedroom door.

'Sophie!' Helen shouted. 'The boys . . .'

Who were both staring at the naked body running past them for the kitchen. 'We have to get out,' Sophie shouted.

She opened the drier, pulled out her clothes and began dressing.

Helen appeared in the inner doorway, pulling on her own clothes, looking thoroughly bemused.

'What . . . ?' James stood up.

'Is there another way out?'

'Only that window, again.' Helen gave an almost hysterical giggle. 'It's only about twelve feet.'

'I seem to have been jumping through windows all of my life,' Sophie said, and threw up the sash.

'Would someone mind telling me what's going on?' Shane enquired, somewhat plaintively.

'We are about to be killed if we don't get out of here,' Sophie told him.

He stared at her with his mouth open, then twisted his head as there came a knock on the door. It wasn't a loud knock, but it was still filled with menace. Instinctively Shane moved towards it.

'Don't open it,' Sophie snapped, pulling on her shoes and looking out. It was a miracle she had already jumped out of so many windows with only a scratch from a rose bush to show for it; but here again there were flower beds.

'Open the door,' said a voice. 'We know you are in there, Miss Gallagher.'

'Out you go,' Sophie told Helen.

Who hesitated. 'You guys *are* coming?'

'Just as quickly as we can,' Sophie assured her.

'I have no clothes,' James pointed out.

'Here.' Shane threw him a pair of pants and a shirt. 'They'll hang a bit; pull the belt tight.'

Helen hitched up her skirt, got one leg out, then the other, and gave a little shriek as she plummeted downwards; but as she was back on her feet in a moment, Sophie reckoned she was all right.

Sophie also got one leg out, and listened to the explosion behind her. Splinters flew away from the door panelling.

'Holy Jesus Christ!' Shane remarked.

'Don't hang about,' Sophie said, and got her other leg out. She went down with a thump and fell to her knees in the soft earth, turned to mud by the rain.

Helen dragged her up, and they heard another explosion. The noise was alarming the rest of the building. People

158

were shouting questions and some windows were being
opened.

Shane was next down, with a splash and a thump, and
James was immediately behind him, while from above there
came a third explosion.

'That did it,' James gasped.

'Round the front,' Sophie shouted. 'Run.'

They ran across the lawn that led round the building.
Behind them there were more shouts, some from the terrorist
looking out of the kitchen window, the others from people
higher up, also looking out of windows.

They rounded the building into the front drive, where
Helen's car was parked, as well as several others and the
terrorists' hire car – and the fourth terrorist, who had remained
with the car.

He was equally surprised to see them, reached inside his
jacket for his pistol, and was struck with a rugby tackle by
Shane, who was still travelling at full speed. He went over
backwards, hit his head on the side of the car, sat up, shaking
his head in a daze, and was hit again, this time by a chopped
fist where his neck joined his shoulder. Now he went down
for good.

'Hell!' James commented admiringly.

'My car!' Helen shouted.

'No, this one,' Sophie said, and they scrambled into the
hire car; the keys were still in the ignition, and as Helen had
hers, they would have a certain start.

James got behind the wheel, and they raced out of the
drive.

'Those other people . . .' Helen said.

'Let's hope they keep their doors locked,' Sophie said.
'They're after us, not anybody else.'

'Where'd you learn to put a man away like that?' James
asked.

'Army training,' Shane explained.

'You were in the army?'

'Territorials. But we trained with the SAS. Would someone like to tell me where we are going?'

James had been driving west, and now they topped a rise and looked down on the sea, whipped into whitecaps by the wind. 'You'll be telling me next you're a crack shot,' he said.

'Actually, I'm not. I was trained in explosives. Shit! I left my shotgun behind. We going down to the coast?'

'For starters,' Sophie said.

'Explosives?' James asked.

Shane grinned. 'Take me to your semtex, and I'll show you how to blow yourself up.'

'Stop the car,' Sophie said. 'Down there.' She pointed to a side lane leading off the road.

James obeyed.

'What's wrong?' Helen asked.

'I have an idea.'

'What?'

'You say you know how to handle explosives, Shane?'

'Time was, I was an expert.'

'Well, I reckon the time has come again. Listen: the terrorists have blanked out all communications, right, save for mobiles. But they are communicating with England, because Admiral Hartwell said so. Now, how do you suppose they are doing that?'

'They're using the ship's radio,' James said. 'She has some outsize equipment, and her own electricity.'

'Exactly. That yacht is the hub of their whole operation. Not only is she their communicating centre with England, but I would say all the orders to the various groups on the island are coming from her. So, put her out of action and they're up the creek.'

'And just how do we do that?'

'We fix some explosives to her bottom and blow her up.'

There was a brief silence.

'There would be one or two problems,' James said at last.

'List them.'

'Well . . . we don't have any explosive charges. Or any explosives, for that matter.'

'We can get them.'

'How?'

'From the pre-set bomb sites,' Helen said excitedly.

'No way,' Sophie said. 'For one thing, they probably have people on guard there, and for another, if they're wired up, we'd probably blow ourselves up. No, listen: just up north there is a quarry being worked. They're blasting regularly. They must have explosives in store there.'

'You mean, we just go along there and ask for some?'

'I mean, we just go along there and take some. It's Sunday. They don't work on Sundays.'

James scratched his head.

'You could fix it so that ship blows up, couldn't you, Shane?' Sophie asked.

'Ah . . . if I can get to the ship, sure.'

'We'll work that one out after we get the explosives.'

'You won't be able to sink her, you know,' James said. He looked at his watch. 'She'll just about be taking the ground again, now. For the next six hours. And even if she were floating, she'd still only go down about six feet.'

'We're not interested in sinking her,' Sophie said, 'just in destroying her communications system; and maybe spreading a little alarm and despondency. Up till now they've had it all their own way. A couple of shocks could throw them right off track.'

James looked at Shane, who grinned and shrugged. 'Sounds like fun. Helen?'

'If you're game.'

'You realise we could all be killed?' James asked.

'They'll give us posthumous medals,' Sophie told him. 'Let's go.'

161

Awakening

'Let me get this very straight,' Jeannette said. 'You let her get away *again*, with her friends? And in your car? Where are you now?'

'We are still at the nurse's house, madame. In her flat.'

'How did you get in?'

'It was necessary to break in, madame.'

'So the whole building knows what is happening?'

'Well, madame, there was some shooting . . .'

'God give me patience,' Jeannette said. 'Where did you get these characters from, al-Rakim?'

'Harb is one of our best and most experienced men,' al-Rakim protested.

'Show me your worst and I'll scream. Very well, Harb,' she said into the phone. 'I suppose you have no idea where they have gone?'

'None, madame. They turned to the right – that is, to the west – when they left the drive.'

'OK,' Jeannette said. 'I assume the other residents have cars?'

'Yes, madame.'

'And they are all under guard?'

'Yes, madame. Shall we shoot them?'

'Control yourself, Harb. Find a safe room into which they can be put, tie them up, and lock them in.'

'With respect, madame, they will get free, eventually.'

'Eventually. If you make a good job of it they won't get free for at least two hours, and that is all we need. When you have

162

done that, commandeer two of their cars. Send two of your men back to the hospital. You and one other, see if you can spot their car – your car, remember? It is early on a Sunday morning, and the weather is very bad. There will not be very many cars on the road. And, Harb – there really cannot be any more failures.'

Harb could be heard to gulp at the end of the line. 'There will not be, madame.'

'Thank you, Harb.' Jeannette switched off, and looked at her watch again. 'A quarter to nine, and the aircraft is due here at ten. How long will it take them to fly from Heathrow to Guernsey?'

'In a jet? Half an hour,' Honeylee said.

'She won't be able to climb to her proper height or develop her proper speed,' al-Rakim said. 'She will barely take off before she will be coming down again.'

'So, say forty-five minutes,' Jeannette said. 'They will be preparing to leave now. How long will it take all of our people to assemble?'

'Well . . . not more than half an hour,' al-Rakim said, 'providing they are all in contact.'

'Well, alert them all for the signal,' Jeannette said. 'Call that idiot Harb and tell him he has half an hour to find that woman.'

'And then?'

Jeannette made a face. 'We shall have to forgo the pleasure of teaching her a lesson, I suppose. At least on this occasion.'

Pete Smith rang the doorbell on the Bailiff's house. This was situated down a quiet lane a couple of miles outside St Peter Port proper, and on a rainswept Sunday morning the lane was empty.

The Bailiff was apparently sleeping in. Smith turned up the collar on his waterproof coat, watched water dripping from the brim of his hat, and gave a little shiver. The *Guernsey Press* did not publish on Sundays, although news still had to be gathered for the Monday edition, work on which would commence that evening; but still he felt that to be sent out in the pouring rain just to call on the Bailiff and make sure he was there was a bit much. He rang the bell again, and again, and then realised the door was not going to be answered.

He wiped rain from his glasses, and went round the house to look at the garage. It was closed.

He walked along the lane to the next house, and rang this bell in turn. The door opened in seconds. 'Hello, Mr Waterman,' Pete said. The reporter was well known on the island.

Waterman was wearing a suit; he was clearly planning to go to church. 'It's a rum do,' he remarked.

'What is? May I come in?'

'Oh, yes. Wet out there.' Waterman stood back and allowed the young reporter into the dark hallway. 'This electricity failure. Island-wide, is it?'

'I'm afraid so. And the phones are out too.'

'Is that a fact? I haven't tried mine this morning. What's your problem?'

'I'm trying to get in touch with the Bailiff.'

'Oh, yes?'

'My boss received a phone call in the middle of the night, apparently, suggesting that Sir William had left the island. He just wanted to check that out. But as I say, the phones are out, and he isn't answering his mobile. Or his front door.'

'He isn't there,' Waterman said.

'Ah, he has left the island, then? Without notifying any-one?'

'Oh, I don't think he's left the island,' Waterman said.

'You mean he's at his office? We've tried there, but he hasn't gone in.'

'He left last night,' Waterman said.

Pete frowned as his ears pricked up. 'Last night? What time last night?'

'Must've been about midnight, I suppose. I was up late

watching the telly. And I heard this car draw up outside his house. Well . . .' He flushed. 'It was an odd hour, so I looked out. There was a car waiting, and after a few minutes, Sir William and Lady Martel came out. They got into the car and drove away.'

'In the middle of the night,' Pete said thoughtfully. 'You're sure about this?'

'Of course I'm sure,' Waterman said indignantly. 'You think I'd been drinking?'

'Had you?'

'Well . . . I'd had a couple. But that was before dinner. Hours earlier.'

'What's the trouble, Bob?' a woman called from upstairs, and a moment later Mrs Waterman appeared, also wearing her Sunday best. 'Oh, it's you, Mr Smith.'

'Morning, Mrs Waterman. OK, Mr Waterman, can you tell me what the Bailiff was wearing?'

'Well, coat and hat. It was raining.'

'But he wasn't carrying any bag, or anything to indicate he was leaving the island.'

'Of course not, young fellow. How was he going to leave the island in the middle of the night?'

'You know what I think,' Mrs Waterman said. 'I think there's a serious illness in the family. That nice son-in-law of theirs. I think he's been taken poorly. Or maybe his wife. They'll be at the hospital, you mark my words.'

Pete nodded, then had a thought. 'This car that took them away – was it from the hospital? Or one of the States Offices?'

'No, no, it was a hire car.'

'A hire car came for the Bailiff in the middle of the night?'

'I saw the "H" stuck on the back.'

'You didn't find that odd?'

'Well, it was none of my business, right?'

'I suppose it wasn't,' Pete said thoughtfully.

'You'll find them at the hospital,' Mrs Waterman said

confidently. 'Don't you see – with the electricity out, and the phones, they had to send a car for them.'

'The electricity didn't go out until just before dawn,' Pete said. 'I'll try the hospital. Thanks for your help.'

He hurried through the rain to where his car was parked.

'Hey!' called the watchman. 'Just what do you think you're doing?'

The four young people were just getting out of their car. Now they looked at each other in dismay.

'I hadn't thought of a watchman,' Sophie said. 'Shit!'

The middle-aged man splashed through mud and water towards them, an umbrella held above his head, swaying uncertainly in the wind. 'You're on private property.'

'Ah,' Sophie said. 'I think you're going to have to do your stuff, Shane.'

'And we'll all go to gaol,' James groaned.

'Won't matter, if, as you say, we're going to be killed first.'

The watchman peered from one to the other, unable to grasp what they were saying. 'You're drunk,' he suggested.

'I'm sure he's a reasonable man,' Helen explained. 'What have we got to lose? Listen,' she said: 'we need some explosives. Urgently. It's to save Guernsey from being taken over by terrorists.'

The watchman gaped at her.

'What have you got in that shed?' Shane asked.

'Gelignite.'

'Any plastic?'

'Some.'

'And detonators?'

'Of course we have detonators. How else are we going to explode the gelly?'

Shane nodded. 'We need some. Quite a lot.'

'You're drunk,' the watchman repeated. 'Or crazy. You think you can just walk in here and take some of our gelignite? You'll be breaking the law.'

'There isn't any law, right this minute,' Sophie said.

'Drunk,' the watchman said again, and reached for the mobile clipped to the back of his belt.

Shane grabbed him, pinning his arms. 'Listen, mister: I know it's bloody hard to believe, but the island is in a state of real emergency. Real bad. People have been killed by terrorists who have taken over the entire island. We haven't time to tell it all now and we don't want to have to hurt you; but if you don't help us get what we need, we're going to have to tie you up, see?' He was really a very mild young man – until roused. Now he relieved the old man of his mobile.

'Jesus,' James muttered.

The watchman gasped. 'I'm not fighting you, son, but I'm not giving you any explosives. I'd lose my job. All that rubbish about terrorists . . .'

'Get those keys,' Sophie commanded.

Shane took the keys from the watchman's belt before tying him up, gently but firmly. Then he unlocked the shed. 'Holy Mary, Mother of God,' he remarked. 'Will you look at all of this. Even timers.'

'Hurry,' Sophie said.

'We'll use this carryall,' Shane said, tipping out the watchman's flask and sandwich box. 'Easy now. Make sure they're dry. And we need a waterproof bag. More than one. Make sure they're waterproof, now.'

He loaded the plastic explosive – TNT 808 – in preference to the gelignite while the women hunted for the bags.

'Just what are we going to do with all this stuff?' James asked.

'Get it on to that ship and blow it up.'

'How?'

'Under water.'

'You serious? We'll need wetsuits. Where are we going to get wetsuits?'

Shane looked at Helen. 'Think we can risk going back to the flat?'

'No,' Sophie snapped.

'Ah . . . Pete Smith.'

'You mean that Press reporter?' Helen asked.

'Right. He does a lot of scuba. If he doesn't have a wetsuit at home, he'll know where we can get hold of some, and cylinders as well.'

'Listen,' James said. 'Those people command the entire harbour.'

'So we'll have to go in from outside the harbour. What state is the tide?'

James looked at his watch. 'Quarter past nine. It'll be getting on to half-tide down. She'll be on the bottom.'

'But there'll be water, right?'

'A few feet, and dropping.'

'Enough, we can get through those piles underneath the dock.'

'We?'

'Well, I hope you're coming with me, chum,' Shane said. 'This is your show.'

The Prime Minister himself went to Heathrow, together with several service chiefs; this was the most serious emergency of his term of office, so far, and as they were now working to his plan, even if it was known to only two other people, he felt he should take full responsibility for what was going to happen. By now rumours were beginning; there had already been calls from one of the tabloids as well as a television company asking what was happening; the pilot of the mail plane due to land in Guernsey at six o'clock had been turned away, merely being told that the La Villiaze airport was closed. He had flown over the airport twice, and although, with driving rain and low cloud, visibility had not been good, he was fairly certain there had been no emergency on the ground. At least as regarded other aircraft. Now the various airlines that serviced Guernsey were also telephoning about, trying to find out what was going on. None of the several flights due out of Guernsey that morning – the planes were normally on the ground, in Guernsey, overnight – had left, and their base controllers were unable to get in touch with them.

There had even been a reference to 'odd happenings in Guernsey' on one of the television news programmes.

Thus far the government had maintained absolute silence on the matter. But reporters were starting to accumulate. 'We're going to have to tell them something,' the Home Secretary pointed out.

'In due course,' the Prime Minister said, maintaining his reputation for unflappability. 'Is everything prepared, Air Commodore?'

Crabtree nodded. He was very nervous.

'I'd like to meet the pilot.'

Squadron Leader Mallon was introduced.

'Have you ever flown a jumbo?'

'As a matter of fact, no, sir; but I've flown heavy bombers, and they've given me a quick run-down of the instruments.'

'You understand what you have to do?'

'Yes, sir. I don't see any problems. This time.'

'And the next?'

The squadron leader grinned. 'I understand that's a matter of playing it by ear.'

'Which of your crew speaks Arabic?'

'My co-pilot, sir.'

The Prime Minister nodded and shook hands. 'Good luck. Where is the sheikh?'

'We have him over here, sir.'

The Prime Minister was escorted into a small waiting room off the VIP lounge, which had been closed for the morning. Sheikh Hassan was a small man, very well dressed in a business suit, who wore a pointed beard and horn-rimmed spectacles. He was in excellent spirits and greeted the Prime Minister with a smile. 'Well, Prime Minister, I understand it is all going according to plan.'

'Absolutely. You appear to hold all the trumps.'

'The fortunes of war,' Hassan said equably. 'Perhaps we shall meet again. On more even ground.'

'I wouldn't hold my breath, if I were you,' the Prime Minister said.

Outside Gracey was waiting.

'All correct?' the Prime Minister asked.

'Yes, sir.'

'Where are they?'

'Safely out of anybody's sight. Obviously we can't produce the 727 until the jumbo has been turned back.'

'Oh, quite. Well, let's get things rolling.'

On Jeannette's instructions, al-Rakim drove to the airport to supervise the landing of the jumbo.

A cautious man by nature, he was extremely anxious about the next hour. The weather continued to be very bad, with low cloud scudding across the sky in a succession of rain squalls: suppose the big plane couldn't get down?

He also felt that it was necessary for them to be off the island just as soon as possible. Guernsey was certainly filled with discontented people. They were just starting to go to church, and were gathered on street corners, in the rain, grumbling about the electricity and telephone failures, about their blacked-out television screens, about the lack of information as to when this crisis was going to be over.

In the yacht marina, groups of equally discontented yachtsmen were gathered on the pontoons, grumbling to each other. Those who had wanted to brave the storm earlier that morning, and had been refused permission – by the harbour authority, as they supposed – were most discontented. But in any event the tide had now fallen too far for the sill to be crossed; they would have to wait until later that afternoon. Those who were still on the lay-by pontoons were less upset; only one yacht had attempted to put out. Honeylee and his people had made no effort to stop her, but in the event she had no sooner encountered the very big seas in the Russel than she had turned back and moored up again.

Al-Rakim didn't suppose all these people were going to remain quiescent much longer. He used his mobile to call Harb.

'Not a sign of the bitch,' Harb said. 'This island has got so many little lanes, she could be anywhere.'

'All right,' Rakim said. 'Forget her, and report to the airport. We are nearly at zero hour.'

He switched off the phone and watched the road, which was now becoming quite busy as the morning advanced. This island, he thought, might have a lot of little lanes, but it also has one hell of a lot of traffic.

He swung into the airport and pulled to a stop in the forecourt. The only people about were a clutch of taxi-drivers, some still in their cars, others gathered beneath the overhang. They watched al-Rakim get out of his car with interest.

'You can forget it, mate,' they told him. 'The whole place is closed down.'

Al-Rakim ignored them and headed towards the terminal building; he had called ahead and one of his people was waiting for him, to guide him across the parking apron towards the tower.

'Hey!' one of the taxi-drivers shouted after him. 'Who're you then?'

'Tell us what's happening,' shouted another.

Al-Rakim was escorted up the stairs. Two white-faced traffic-controllers were there, with three of the terrorists.

'Would you mind telling us what is going on?' one of the controllers asked, shakily.

'There will be a plane coming, in about fifteen minutes,' al-Rakim said. 'You must have it on radar.'

'I have an aircraft on my screen, approaching us.' The emergency generator was in use. 'But he can't mean to land.'

'Why not?'

'He is too big. His transponder indicates that he's a jumbo –

a 747. You can't put a 747 down on Guernsey: it'd overshoot the runway by a mile.'

Al-Rakim stared at him in consternation.

The radio came to life: 'Guernsey, Guernsey,' the voice said, 'Golf Alpha Charlie George. You are expecting us.'

'No, we are not expecting you,' the controller replied.

'I am carrying with me Sheik Hassan, as instructed,' the pilot said. 'I am required to put him down on Guernsey at ten o'clock. That is precisely five minutes from now. Will you kindly give me clearance and approach instructions.'

'But . . . you can't do it!' the controller shouted.

'Give me that.' Al-Rakim took the microphone. 'This is al-Rakim,' he said. 'I am in charge here. Did you not know you could not land an aircraft that large on Guernsey?'

'Mr al-Rakim, I was merely told to take the aircraft and its passenger up, then put it down, and do what I would be told. No one told me I couldn't land.'

Al-Rakim hesitated, then said, 'You say Sheikh Hassan is on board?'

'As instructed.'

'Let me speak with him.'

'Al-Rakim! It is good to hear your voice.' The sheikh spoke Arabic.

'And yours, Your Excellency. Are you all right?'

'I have never felt better. What is this nonsense about being unable to land in Guernsey? Are you not in complete control?'

'We are in complete control,' al-Rakim said. 'But there seems to have been a foul-up. Frankly, it did not occur to us that Guernsey airport is too small for a jumbo. It does not seem to have occurred to the British government, either.'

'That is strange,' Hassan said. 'Do you think it is some kind of trick?'

'Did you see any evidence of trickery in England?'

'It all seemed very straightforward to me. But al-Rakim . . . what is to be done?'

Al-Rakim would dearly have liked to consult with Jeannette, and hand the responsibility over to her. But there simply wasn't time. 'Give me the pilot,' he said, and switched back to English. 'What do you propose to do?'

The jumbo was now directly overhead, circling at about four thousand feet, only occasionally visible as the clouds scudded past.

'Bit of a foul-up, what?' Mallon remarked. 'But I'd say there is no possibility of my putting down on that little strip. There are going to be a few heads rolling over this, I can tell you.'

'I'm glad to hear it,' al-Rakim said. 'However, you still have not told me what you intend to do. You know our terms, I presume. We want Sheikh Hassan, and we want a long-range aircraft. Now.'

'Well, old man,' Mallon said, 'now isn't on. What I can do is return to Heathrow and change to a smaller plane. What is the largest aircraft I can put down on Guernsey?'

Al-Rakim looked at the controller.

'He might just get a 727 down,' the controller said. 'There's a strong westerly wind.'

'Did you hear that?' al-Rakim asked.

'I did. Right. We'll go get a 727.'

'How long is this going to take?'

'Well . . . I can radio ahead, of course. But it's a matter of an aircraft being made available. Say an hour. Maybe a little longer.'

'Is that all right with you, Your Excellency?' al-Rakim asked.

'I see no alternative. One hour. I can wait,' the sheikh said.

'Then do it,' al-Rakim said. 'One hour.'

'I'll be in touch,' Mallon said, and the jumbo soared back out of sight.

Pete Smith swung into the hospital drive, slowed to the

regulation ten miles an hour, and watched a man emerge from the bushes beside the road. The man was waving, and Pete slowed to a halt, frowning. The fellow was dark-skinned and black-haired, conventionally dressed in a raincoat and a slouch hat; he carried one hand behind his back.

'Can I help you?' Pete asked, rolling down his window. As he did so, he saw another man, standing by the bushes.

'You cannot come in,' the man said.

'Eh? Oh, I know it's not visiting hours,' Peter said. 'But I'm Pete Smith. Savvy? I'm a reporter for the *Press*. I'm following a story.'

'You cannot come in,' the man said again. 'The hospital is closed for the day.'

'Closed for the day?' Pete was incredulous. 'The hospital can't close.'

'It's closed for the day,' the man said. 'Back up, turn and go away.' They both heard the drone of the aircraft, low overhead. The man grinned. 'Come back this afternoon.'

'You must be joking,' Pete said. 'Just get out of my way.' He gunned the engine and took his foot off the brake. The car surged forward and the man jumped back.

'Stop there,' shouted the second man, and brought his hands round in front, holding an automatic pistol.

'Holy shit!' Pete muttered, and pressed the gas pedal as hard as he could.

There was a clunk as a bullet smashed into the bodywork, and then another on the other side; both the bastards were firing at him.

Men, firing guns, in the grounds of the hospital, on a Sunday morning, in Guernsey? His head spun. But the bastards were firing at *him*! There was another crunch as a third bullet slammed into the back of the car, but then he had turned a corner and was racing past the first car park.

The hospital buildings were on his right, and he felt a great temptation to swing into the main entrance and ask them if they knew what was going on. As he reached it, however, the doors opened and a man came out, obviously alerted by the shooting and perhaps by a call on a mobile phone as well; he too was carrying a gun, only this was some kind of automatic rifle.

Already having started to turn, Peter wrenched the wheel the other way, skidded against the pavement, and then, regaining control, drove at speed through the remainder of the hospital roadways to reach the second entrance. But here also there were two men, waving at him to stop. He ignored them, driving as fast as he dared. They too fired and hit the car, one shot shattering the windscreen; but he was only slightly cut by flying glass and then was on the road beyond, twisting the wheel to send the car towards town.

There were people on the streets now, and they were staring, both at the car and in the direction of the shots. Pete felt he should tell them to keep away, but he was too confused and disorientated to stop. He felt he was living a bad dream. His sole idea was to get down to the police station just as quickly as possible, to let them know that the PEH had been taken over by a bunch of trigger-happy madmen – with whom the Bailiff was involved? – and then . . . what a story he was going to have.

Pete Smith lived in a house rather than a flat, a little cottage tucked away down a side lane. But . . . 'He's out,' Sophie said, eyeing the empty driveway.

She was sitting in the back of the hire car, with the box of explosives on her lap. What a way to go!

'Maybe Jennie's home.'

James swung through the open gate and braked before the front door. He got out and rang the bell.

'James?' The door opened to reveal a rather untidy-looking young woman, whose basic good looks were distorted by the uncombed hair, just as her figure was invisible behind her baggy pants and loose shirt. She gaped at the bare-footed figure in front of her. 'I thought you were in hospital. Pete said . . .'

'I was. Do you know where Peter is?'

'Hello, Mr Candish,' a small voice piped up, and the child clung to her mother's leg.

'Hello, Christine. About Pete . . .'

Jennie was looking past him at the other people in the car. 'Shane Richings? You look all hot and bothered. Helen?' She didn't know Sophie.

'It's very urgent,' James was saying.

'I think you should come in out of the wet and have a cup of coffee. Peter had to go out. The editor telephoned – oh, at some ungodly hour – and said he should go and interview the Bailiff. Can you believe it? At eight o'clock on a Sunday morning.'

'The Bailiff?' Sophie shouted. 'Did he?'

'I suppose so. He hasn't come home yet. Do come in.'

Sophie hesitated. 'Can I bring this into the house?'

'Of course.' Jennie stepped back, the door held wide.

'I think you should know that it contains a box of explosives.'

'Ah . . . say again?'

'We're going to blow something up,' Shane explained.

Jennie scratched her head, not relieving the tangle. 'Maybe you should come back when Pete is home.'

'But you don't know when he's coming home,' Helen said, 'and we can't wait.'

They listened to the roar of an aircraft engine, low overhead.

'Someone else trying to get in,' Sophie suggested. 'They must be queuing up for miles.'

'Let's hope that one isn't,' James said. 'That sounds like a bloody big plane.'

'Listen,' Jennie said. 'Oh, Chrissie, run along and play.'

The child scampered into the house.

'Perhaps if I knew what was going on,' Jennie said.

'We'll tell you.' Shane took control, ushered them all into the house, carefully placing Sophie's box on the floor just inside the door; the porch was constantly being swept by the rain.

'That's not going to go off, is it?' Jennie asked.

'Only when I tell it to,' Shane assured her. 'Now come and sit down, and listen.'

Jennie obeyed, her mouth sagging as she heard of the night's events. When Shane was finished, she said, 'But . . . you can't just blow up those people's yacht? It must be worth millions.'

'We happen to feel that Guernsey is worth a few millions more,' Helen said; 'and they're meaning to blow *it* up.'

Jennie swallowed. 'So . . . you want Pete to make a story of it? I'll get him on his mobile.'

'It's too late for that,' Shane said. 'What we're going to do has to be done in the next hour or so. Before they can leave. What we would like is to borrow Pete's wetsuit. Actually, we need more than one.'

'I have one,' Jennie said absently.

'Ah!'

'But I'm not going diving under any yacht with a bag of explosives,' she said. 'I've Chrissie to think of.'

'Absolutely. I don't suppose your suit would fit either me or James?'

Jennie looked at the two large men. 'No,' she said.

'It would fit me,' Sophie said.

'Why yes, I think it would.'

'Are you out of your tiny mind?' James demanded.

'I don't think so. I've done quite a lot of scuba diving.'

'Not with a bag of plastic explosive draped round your neck. I absolutely forbid it.'

'Listen,' she said. 'Who created this whole situation? Anyway, you couldn't possibly do it even if you had a suit. Look in the mirror. You're still groggy as hell from that drug overdose.'

James bit his lip; he knew she was right.

'I'll need the loan of a swimsuit as well,' Sophie said.

'I think we can manage that,' Jennie said.

'Let's get with it,' Shane said. 'Jennie, I'm going to need some props.'

'I still think I should call Pete,' she grumbled, as she led him towards the back of the house.

Still drawing the attention of various people on the streets, Pete swung down the narrow lane that led to the police station, turned into the yard, and braked. For a few moments he just sat there, panting and shaking, attempting to get his nerves under control. Only gradually did it dawn on him that there were a lot more cars parked in the yard than usual; it was as if the morning shift had come on duty, and the night shift hadn't gone home.

He opened his door, got out, and walked to the steps, turning up his coat collar against the still rain-filled wind. The door was closed, but not locked. He pushed it in, gaining the impression of hasty movement on the other side, and looked at the charge desk. There was a constable seated there, but no one else to be seen.

'Donald!' Pete said, going towards the desk. 'Do you have any idea what is going on?'

Donald opened his mouth, and closed it again, and Pete heard movement behind him. He swung round, instinctively ducking, as the man who had been standing behind the door came towards him, pistol levelled.

'Run!' Donald shouted, picking up a heavy paperweight and throwing it as hard as he could. 'Warn people!'

The Arab took the weight on his chest, coughed and fell to his knees. Pete was already at the door, pulling it open and racing for his car. Behind him he heard a shot, and several shouts, in a language he did not understand. He reached his car, turned the ignition, and there were several more shots, a couple of which struck; but then he was swinging out of the yard and gunning his engine.

He swung down the Truchot, braked, and again sat panting for several seconds. Then he picked up his mobile. He was

178

tempted to call and Jennie and tell her to . . . do what? She
was better off at home. Besides, he had a job to do. He punched
the numbers of the editor's house.

'Hello? Mrs Lucas? Is Joe there? Pete Smith. It's very
urgent. Hello, Joe? Listen: all hell is breaking loose. I don't
know where the Bailiff is – he's disappeared. Some men came
for him and Lady Martel at midnight, and they haven't been
seen or heard of since. I tried the hospital, and was shot at by
a bunch of thugs. Yes, that's what I said – shot at. So I went
to the police, and was shot at again. I am not drunk. My car
is full of bullet holes. What the hell are we going to do? Go
home? OK. I'll wait for your call.'

Jack Harding drove slowly into town. His car was a large
Mercedes and was inclined to tremble every time it was
caught by the wind, which was gusting a good thirty to
forty knots; he thought he wouldn't be surprised if some trees
came down. Certainly he assumed it was the weather that had
caused the infuriating electricity and telephone outages; but
he was driving slowly because he was still trying to decide
what to do.

He had been an utter fool. The fact was that it had been
an unsatisfactory evening with Marcia; evenings with Marcia
were nearly always unsatisfactory. Then that strange phone
call, and that very odd but so very attractive young woman,
appearing when he had had too much to drink and was
very randy.

He must have been mad; but the fact was, he supposed he
had assaulted her. He could still feel the bruises she had given
him. Silly bitch! He wasn't at all sure what she had been
nattering about. Something about terrorists; but there were
no terrorists in Guernsey, and there never had been.

The problem was that he *had* assaulted her. That wouldn't
look very nice if it appeared in the *Guernsey Press*, or if she
went to the police. What to do? James Candish! She was
James's girlfriend. If he could have a word with James, and

179

explain the situation . . . James was a very level-headed, laid-back young man. How on earth had he accumulated such a hysterical weirdo as a mistress? But if anyone could calm her down, James was the man.

But James was in hospital. Damn! Harding looked at his car clock as he turned on to the front, deliberately, as he wanted to look at the weather; he was actually on his way to the local marina to make sure his Sunseeker was all right. He'd have to go up there afterwards.

The Russel was an impressive mass of large whitecaps. The tide was dead low, so quite a few of the rocks were uncovered, surrounded and smothered by flying spray. No day to be at sea. Or even in the air. He heard the drone of an aircraft engine, and looked out of his sunroof and up, and the huge plane seeming to hover very low overhead. A 747! What the hell was a jumbo doing trying to land in Guernsey? Then it was lost again in the clouds.

This was obviously going to be one of those very odd days.

He turned on to the White Rock, the roadway that divided the commercial harbour from the local marina, glanced to his right across the car park at the big yacht, on the ground, he supposed; her only movement was the occasional tremble.

He wondered what it must be like to own something like that – a boating man's ultimate dream. He slowed to admire her before pulling into his reserved place above the pontoons, and frowned as he heard some very odd sounds coming from the town.

Someone had just fired several shots, in the middle of St Peter Port, at ten o'clock on a Sunday morning. He had to be hallucinating. Just like that girl last night.

Harding frowned, and braked. Just like that girl, he thought.

A man came pounding up the gangway from one of the pontoons, seaboots slipping on the wet surface. 'Jack!' he shouted as he saw the States member. 'Those were shots!'

Harding got out of his car to gaze at the town. Everything

looked normal, but clearly everyone on the front – and there were quite a few people about despite the weather, which meant that none of the small ferries were running to Herm – had also heard the shots.

'I'd better get up there and see what's happening,' Harding said.

'I'll come with you,' said his friend, a businessman named Tom Lowndes. He got into the other side of the car, while Harding made a face at the wet oilskins being dumped on his immaculate upholstery.

He drove round the one-way system. This brought him close to the moored yacht on the other side of the pier. There were people on her deck as well, and on the bridge wing, staring at the town. Shooting was not what a wealthy Arab yachtsman expected to hear when on holiday in a place like Guernsey. One of the officers, he noticed, was speaking into a mobile phone – probably, he thought, calling his base and asking if they could come home now.

He swung on to the esplanade. 'Where do you think, exactly?'

'Sounded like the police station,' Lowndes said.

Harding did a U-turn, causing others cars to stop and hoot, then drove up St Julian's Avenue. As he did so, a car emerged from the lane beside the pub and all but hit him. Harding braked violently, causing a skid. The other car had stopped against the pavement, the driver slumped over the wheel.

'Shit! he's had a heart attack,' Harding said, getting out of his car and running to the other, around which several people had gathered.

The driver raised his head and blinked at them.

'Pete Smith?' Harding was incredulous. 'What the hell is going on?'

'The police station,' Pete gasped. 'It's full of terrorists. They shot at me.'

A ripple of alarm went through the growing crowd.

'Those shots were at you?' Harding demanded. Then he saw the bullet holes in the car. 'Jesus Christ!'

'Aaagh!' A woman screamed.

'Stop that,' Harding barked. His brain was tumbling over itself. That girl had been telling the truth after all. But what to do? For a moment his brain seemed to have gone blank. He snapped his fingers. 'The Bailiff! He'll have to be informed.'

'I think he already knows,' Pete groaned.

'Then what's he doing about it?'

'They have him. And his wife.'

Harding stared at him in disbelief. 'Well, then, the Lieutenant Governor . . .'

'I think they have him too.'

'Good Lord! The Chief of Police . . .'

'As they're holding the police station, I'd say they have him too.'

Harding scratched his head. Another woman started to scream, and was hastily hushed by a friend, while Harding tried to think. So the weather had nothing to do with the power failure or the telephone system breakdown.

'What do you reckon these people want, Mr Harding?' someone asked.

Harding looked at Pete.

'God knows, Mr Harding,' Pete said. 'Joe Lucas may. I believe he's been in contact with the mainland. And by the way, they've taken over the hospital. I got shot at there, too.'

'You mean they know over there what's happening? On the mainland?'

'I believe so.'

'Right. Who was Joe talking to?'

'I don't know. Somebody important, I think.'

'Right,' Harding said again.

'What are we to do, Mr Harding?' someone repeated.

'Spread the word,' Harding said. 'Discreetly, now. We don't want anyone to be killed. Use your mobile phones where you have them. Otherwise word of mouth. Get hold of your neighbours, your friends, and tell them what is happening.'

'But what *is* happening?' someone asked.

'What is happening is that a group of terrorists seems to have snatched the Bailiff and the Lieutenant Governor and is holding the police station. They also seem to have knocked out our communications, except for mobiles.' He snapped his fingers again. 'The airport – we must get all planes out, right away, to tell the world what's happening.'

By now the crowd was several hundred strong, with cars backed up to the front as people spilled across the street.

'The airport's closed,' someone said.

'Eh?' Harding swung round to face the speaker.

'Fact. Norman Plant – he's my next-door neighbour – was due out on the seven o'clock. He came home an hour ago, steam coming out of his ears. The entire airport building is closed. All they were told was that there would be no flying until this afternoon.'

'Who told him this?' Harding demanded.

'One of the staff. But he says there were a couple of foreign-looking characters standing beside him.'

'Shit,' Harding said. 'They seem to have the whole island. Right. Continue as I said. Warn everyone. Tell them to stay indoors and away from the police station or any public buildings. They are to do nothing until further notice.'

'Who'll give this notice, Mr Harding?'

Harding drew a deep breath. 'I will.'

'When?'

He got back into his car, restarted his engine. 'Just as soon as I find out what's going on.'

The Time Factor

'There!' Jeannette stood with Honeylee on the bridge wing, Lulu in her arms, and pointed up through the clouds at the jumbo jet, appearing briefly as it began its approach to Guernsey airport. 'She'll be down in a few minutes. Are all your people ready?'

'Standing by.'

'And that is enough transport?' She looked down at the three buses waiting in a row on the road beside the Cambridge berth.

'That is more than sufficient. Cars are being sent to the hospital and the generating station. The charges have been placed.'

'And the police station?'

'They have been instructed to withdraw and make their way to . . .' He returned inside the wheelhouse and leaned over the plan of St Peter Port spread on the chart table. '. . . here. This is called St Julian's Avenue. They will also be picked up by bus.'

'You do not suppose there could be a reaction to this?'

'From whom? The police have been disarmed, and Mustafa says they are thoroughly cowed. No one else even knows what is going on. Now, madame, what is to be done with our prisoners here?'

'They will be coming with us as hostages.'

'That is the Governor and the Bailiff. What about the harbourmaster and his wife?'

184

'Oh, let them stay on board. They will be picked up soon enough. What is that plane doing?'

The jumbo had disappeared behind the clouds, still at several thousand feet.

'I think he is circling,' Honeylee said. 'They must be giving him instructions.'

Jeannette placed the dog on the deck and looked at her watch. 'It is past ten. It must be down by now.'

She went outside again to stare at the clouds. 'What is that noise?'

Honeylee joined her. 'Shots, by God – coming from the town.'

They looked at each other, then Honeylee dashed inside to pick up his mobile and call the station.

'Some madman tried to break in,' he told Jeannette. 'Apparently he was known to the police. One of them tried to help him and has been shot.'

'And you said they were cowed,' Jeannette said angrily. 'What about this intruder? Has he been shot too?'

'He got away.'

'God give me patience,' Jeannette snapped.

'Look there!' Honeylee pointed.

From the bridge of the yacht they could see the World War II memorial at the landward end of the White Rock Pier, and the beginning of St Julian's Avenue leading away from it and up the hill. This corner had suddenly become crowded with cars and people, being checked and agitated by something that had happened some way up the hill and out of sight of the harbour.

'They know what's going on,' Honeylee said. 'What are we to do, madame?'

'Nothing,' Jeannette said. 'They have no weapons. They cannot harm us. And we will be away in a few minutes.' She took the mobile and called al-Rakim's number. 'Al-Rakim! Is the aircraft down?'

'No, madame. The aircraft has gone away again.'

185

'Would you repeat that?'

'It could not land, madame. It is too big.'

Jeannette stared at the telephone. 'Too big? How can it be too big?'

'This is a small airport, madame. A jumbo would overshoot the runway and crash. I have spoken with Sheikh Hassan, who was on board. He agreed with me that they should return to England and change to a smaller aircraft, probably a 727.'

'Hassan decided this? He does not realise it has to be some kind of a trick?'

'Sheikh Hassan does not think so, madame. He believes it is a genuine mistake.'

'You are telling me that a professional pilot did not know he couldn't put a jumbo down in Guernsey?'

'Well, madame . . .'

'And when is this 727 going to be available?'

'The pilot was radioing ahead to arrange it, madame. He thought they might be able to return in perhaps two hours.'

'Two *hours*!' Jeannette shouted. 'Listen. Get back here. We may have some trouble.'

'I am on my way, madame.'

Jeannette looked at Honeylee. 'Did you get that?'

'If it is a genuine mistake . . .'

'Oh, don't be as foolish as the rest of them. Of course it is not a genuine mistake.'

'Then . . . ?'

'They are playing for time. Two hours.' She went to the radar screen, where Salim was on duty, with him watched the sweep going round and round. Alderney and the other islands were clearly depicted, as was the coast of France behind them. To the west of Alderney was a cluster of blips. Some of these were from the islands and reefs of the Casquets group, she knew. Others, more clearly delineated, were ships – at least four, and she had to assume they were warships. But they were fifteen miles away, and they could not get to St Peter Port for half an hour. The only aircraft to be seen was the blip of the jumbo, rapidly receding.

What could the British be planning? What could she have overlooked? It was simply not possible that any British government would risk a military assault on this heavily populated island, with the consequent enormous loss of life; but equally it could not be possible that any British government, with its host of experts and advisers, would not know that it was impossible to land a jumbo on Guernsey without crashing.

'Keep watching,' she told Salim, and rejoined Honeylee, who was studying the crowd on shore through his binoculars.

'They seem to be breaking up,' he said, as the cars began to move. 'Do you think there could have been an accident?'

'Possibly. With no police and no ambulance available they will be confused.'

'So what are we going to do? You know, we'll be floating this afternoon. We have our hostages. They won't dare touch us if we just steam out of here.'

'And Hassan?'

'Ah. Yes . . .'

'We will wait for this new plane, and the sheikh; but in any event, call up London and let me speak to their man in charge – the Home Secretary. We need to convince them that we mean business. You asked me what we should do with the harbourmaster? Have him brought up here.'

'There,' Shane said with some pride. 'This can be attached to any surface, and detonated by means of a time switch.'

The other four had been watching him with a mixture of admiration and apprehension. Even little Christine had come into the kitchen to watch, despite the efforts of her mother to keep her out.

'Will it blow a hole in the hull?' James asked.

'It certainly will. A wooden hull? It'll fall apart.'

'That won't stop them using their communications,' Helen pointed out.

'Yes it will, once water gets into the engine room and floods the generator. Equally, it'll make sure they don't move again.'

'That is supposing they mean to use the yacht again anyway,' James pointed out. 'And what happens after you've planted the bomb?'

'We set the timer to give us time to get away, and we get out of there.'

'You and Sophie. You don't think you'll be spotted?'

'Now, don't start that again,' Sophie begged.

'Those thugs are armed with Minimi rifles. One shot from of those could blow you into several hundred pieces.'

'So we make sure we don't get shot,' Shane said.

His confidence was almost frightening. Sophie felt that he was recapturing the glory days of his service years.

'What about that plane?' Helen asked. 'It's gone away again.'

'Well, if the terrorists control the airport, it'll simply have been turned away,' James said.

'What I mean is: don't you think it was sent for their getaway? You said it sounded very big.'

'Could be.'

'So why was it turned away? If it was their plane. They should have been on their way by now.'

The two men looked at each other.

'Good point,' James said.

'That doesn't alter what we have to do,' Shane said. He had the bit between his teeth.

'Listen: if that *was* the getaway plane, and for some reason it couldn't get down, they'll have to try again – quickly. It seems to me that it's rather pointless to risk your life, and Sophie's, if these people are going to be up and away in an hour or so in any event.'

'If only we had some idea of what is going on,' Sophie said.

'You could try your friend the admiral again,' Helen suggested.

'Ah . . .' James looked at Shane, uncertainly.

'All right,' Shane said. 'Do that. But do not, under any circumstances, tell him what we are planning to do. That way he can't tell us not to do it; and we are going to continue with our plan. You with me, Sophie?'

Sophie, having been shown a possible out, gulped. But she nodded. 'All the way.'

'Right. Next thing we need is a boat. Something small and rubber, which isn't going to be picked up on radar or even noticed, unless they know where to look.'

'We have a rubber dinghy,' Jennie said. 'It's in the garage.'

'If you keep this up I am going to fall in love with you,' Shane said. 'Right. James . . .' he looked round. 'Where's he gone?'

'He's in the other room, telephoning,' Helen said.

'Right. We'll check with him in a moment. Jennie, take me to your rubber.'

Now he was on a high, Sophie estimated; and she was placing her life in his hands.

Jennie opened the back door and led them to the garage. Here there was a good deal of scuba gear, including spare tanks. The rubber dinghy stood on its end against the inner wall; on a bracket beside it was a small outboard motor.

'Isn't it a bit small?' Sophie asked.

'It's eight feet long: ample for two people.'

'But there are big seas in the Russel.'

'We'll be wearing wetsuits. Let's get it on top of the car. You got any rope?'

'Over here.'

Getting the dinghy in place took several minutes, as the wind was still gusting gale force and it needed all three women to hold the light rubber boat while Shane lashed it down. Then he returned to the garage and brought the outboard, which he fitted into the boot. By the time they had finished, pouring sweat, James had emerged, cheeks pink.

'Well?' Shane enquired. 'You seem to have had quite a conversation.'

'We did,' James said, 'the gist of which is that we have been told to sod off.'

'Eh?'

'I didn't get to speak with the Admiral,' James confessed. 'It was his ADC. He was bloody rude. Everything is under control, he said, and they don't want any interference from effing amateurs. As for whether that plane had anything to do with an escape for the terrorists, we should mind our own bloody business.'

'I hope you told him to fuck off,' Helen said, aggress-ively.

'He hung up.'

'Right,' Shane said. 'We're on our own, and we can give him two fingers after it's all over. Now James . . .' He turned to watch the car turning into the drive.

'Pete!' Jennie shouted. 'Am I glad to see you!' She peered at her husband as he got out of the car. 'You all right, honey?' She gazed at the shattered windscreen, the bullet holes in the bodywork. 'My God! What happened?'

'I've been shot at,' Pete said, 'again and again and again. And I've seen a policeman shot. Jesus!' He was trembling. 'And then Harding . . .'

'Harding?' Sophie snapped.

'I think he needs a drink,' Shane decided. 'You have any brandy?'

'At ten fifteen in the morning?' Jennie demanded.

'I don't think the time is relevant.'

They helped Pete inside, sat him down, and Jennie gave him a tiny measure of brandy in a large tumbler.

'Did you say Harding?' Sophie asked. 'Has he been shot?'

'No, no,' Pete said. 'But he seems to have an idea what's going on.'

'The bastard,' Sophie said.

'Why don't you tell us exactly what happened?' Shane asked. 'Quickly now; we're short on time.'

'My editor, Joe Lucas, sent me to interview the Bailiff first thing this morning,' Pete said, glad of the opportunity to get things straight, at least in his own mind. He sipped some brandy. 'But he wasn't there, and his neighbours said he and Lady Martel had left around midnight, with some men. Mrs Waterman thought they must have gone to the hospital, so I went along there, and people began shooting at me. God, it was terrifying. I drove straight through the grounds, and down town to the police station to report what had happened; but the people in the police station started shooting at me too. It was like a bloody nightmare.' He spilt some of the brandy as he raised the glass to his lips. 'I got out of there and telephoned Joe. He told me to come home. But on the way, on St Julian's, I ran into Jack Harding – well, literally. We collided. I told him what had happened, and he said he'd take it from there.'

'How the hell did Harding get in on the act?' James asked.

'I told him,' Sophie said. 'I went out to see him, to ask for his help. He wasn't the least bit . . . co-operative.' There seemed no point in raising questions of assault right this minute.

'Well, he seems to have changed his mind,' James said. 'Good old Jack.'

Sophie made a hissing sound.

'The point is, if he's taking over –' James said '– well . . . shouldn't we try to co-operate with him? At least tell him what England has been saying?'

'No way,' Sophie said.

'I agree,' Shane said. 'That would foul everything up. First thing, he'd try to pull rank on us and tell us not to do anything. Second thing, what is *he* going to do? Assault the police station with an unarmed mob? No, we go in on our own. Now, James, what's the state of the tide?'

James looked at his watch. 'Just about right out.'

'So how's it running?'

'South.'

'OK, so we go in north of the harbour.'

'That's going to be tricky. All those rocks are uncovered.'

'We'll use the local marina. That has a channel leading out to the Russel.'

'There won't be much water in that either, right now.'

'There'll be enough for a rubber dinghy,' Shane said. 'Now, Pete, there's just one thing; we are going to have to jettison the outboard as we approach St Peter Port, right?'

'Jettison?'

'Let it go. We can't afford to reveal ourselves by either wake or sound. We're going to motor out of the marina channel, drop the outboard, drift down, using our paddles to keep as close inshore as we can without hitting any rocks, and when we're within about a hundred yards of the pierheads, we'll abandon the dinghy as well, and swim and drift down to the entrance. How much water will be there?'

'About ten feet. But you realise the tide will be running pretty hard by then. If you miss the pierheads . . .'

'We'll come ashore in Havelet Bay. Quit worrying.'

'Listen,' James said. 'Can't we raise another wetsuit from somewhere? I should be doing this.'

'Come off it,' Sophie said. 'I'm much better at scuba than you, and you know it.'

Pete had only slowly been grasping what they were talking about.

'Let me get this straight,' he said; 'you aim to swim into the harbour, get under the yacht, and blow a hole in her?'

'I couldn't have put it better myself,' Shane agreed.

'You'll be killed. These people are trigger-happy.'

'They have to spot us first.'

192

'Well, hold on a minute while I get my camera. Just in case you don't come back.'

He staggered off.

'Sophie,' James begged, 'please don't do it.'

'I'd like positive support, not negative.'

He sighed, while Peter arranged them like a wedding party, all together for one shot, and then Shane and Sophie alone for another.

'Let's go,' Shane said.

It was half past ten.

'Here she comes now, Prime Minister.' Gracey indicated the radar screen.

A special incident section of several rooms had been set up at Heathrow, in which a good deal of gadgetry had been installed, including both the radar and a radio, as well as a complete communications centre. Now the various ministers crowded round to peer at the screen and the large blip approaching; commercial traffic had been put on hold for the moment.

'I take it Mallon is playing the game to the last?' the Prime Minister asked.

'He is, sir. He has already called the tower here raising all kinds of hell because no one told him he couldn't put a jumbo down in Guernsey, and has demanded that a 727 be made ready for a return flight. This is of course being done.'

'And . . . ?'

'My people are standing by. I intend to lead them myself.'

'Is that necessary? Does General Peart know?'

Gracey grinned. 'General Peart does not know, sir, or he would probably forbid it.' Nor did his wife, he thought; Joanna would have a fit if she knew what was going on, what he was planning to do. 'And yes, I think it is necessary.'

'Hm. Well . . . you have an Arabic-speaking officer?'

'Both the co-pilot and my second-in-command, Captain Lewis, speak Arabic fluently.'

'Very good. Well . . . yes, Hargreaves?'

The secretary stood in the doorway. 'The press conference is assembling, sir.'

'Yes. Well, I can't speak with them until our next phase is under way. If the terrorists got wind of it we'd be up the creek. Tell them I'll be with them in half an hour.'

'I wish someone would tell me what is going on,' the Home Secretary said.

'Very simply, Ned, we are going to take those people out, hopefully before they can do any damage.'

The Home Secretary gulped. 'You're going to assault Guernsey?'

'Yes.'

'But . . . the casualties . . .'

'Are going to be kept to a minimum, and hopefully will only involve the terrorists.'

'How can you be sure? What are you planning to do?'

'Our business is to put down sufficient men to launch a counter-attack on the terrorists before they can react. You will remember Colonel Gracey's plan that we should load the jumbo with SAS men, have it attempt to land and, after it crashed over the end of the runway, carry out an assault on the terminal buildings?'

'But . . .'

'That was proved impractical because of the time factor. But supposing, using a smaller aircraft – a 727, which can certainly get down, and which will be equally loaded with SAS men – we land, only instead of carrying out a proper procedure, once the aircraft is down, the pilot swings hard to his left when abeam of the terminal buildings. It will certainly take the terrorists a few seconds to react to that, and a few seconds will be all we need. The aircraft will crash into the buildings, the troops will disembark, and hopefully the airport will be recaptured before any message can be got to the yacht or wherever is now their command centre. We believe it is still the yacht. Once the airport

194

is captured, not only will we be able to land additional troops at will – the regiment waiting in Cherbourg, for example – but our people already on the ground will be able to proceed into St Peter Port, using civilian transport, and hopefully reach the harbour and take the yacht by assault, again before the terrorists have worked out what's going on.'

The Home Secretary gave another gulp. 'My God! If something were to go wrong . . .'

'It is a high-risk operation, I agree; but . . .' The Prime Minister paused as one of the radio operators came in.

'I have Guernsey, sir.'

They hurried to the next room.

'To whom am I speaking?' Jeannette enquired.

Gracey looked at the Prime Minister, and received a quick nod.

He picked up the mike. 'Lieutenant Colonel Ian Gracey,' he said.

'Are you in command?'

'Ah, yes.'

'So tell me, what are you trying to do? Do you doubt we will carry out our threats?'

'No, no,' Gracey said. 'We don't doubt that for a moment. We are doing everything to co-operate.'

'Such as sending an aircraft you knew could not land in Guernsey?'

'That was a genuine error.'

'I do not believe you. Let me speak with Sheikh Hassan.'

Gracey looked at the Prime Minister, who again nodded.

'He will be here in a moment,' Gracey said.

The Home Secretary made a phone call downstairs, and a moment later the sheikh came up, guarded by two MPs.

'Your lady friend would like a word.' Gracey indicated the radio, and Hassan picked up the mike.

'Jeannette?'

195

'Hassan? Are you all right?' She spoke Arabic.

'I am all right.'

'What is happening at your end?'

'They are arranging for a smaller aircraft to bring me in,' Hassan said.

'Do you trust them?'

Hassan looked at the assembled men. 'They have no choice but to obey us. Is that not right?'

'They are still hoping to wriggle out of it somehow. Well, we will not allow that. Let me speak with Colonel Gracey.'

Gracey took the mike.

'You are playing a game, Colonel,' Jeannette said in English. 'We are not the sort of people with whom you can play games. Do you know the Guernsey harbourmaster? Captain Harrison?'

'I do not know him personally. I have heard of him.'

'He is here with me. Say something to the colonel, Captain Harrison.'

'Ah . . . good morning, Colonel. For God's sake get us out of this mess,' Harrison said.

Jeannette snatched the mike back again. 'Thank you, Captain. Do you believe that was Captain Harrison, Colonel Gracey?'

'Well, yes. Wasn't it?'

'It was. Listen very carefully.' There was the sound of a shot. 'As you said, Colonel, it was.'

Gracey stared at the Prime Minister in consternation.

'The time is now twenty past ten,' Jeannette said. 'I will allow you an extension of one hour and forty minutes to find and deliver a replacement aircraft. If that aircraft is not on the ground, fully fuelled and ready to take me to a destination of my choice at twelve o'clock precisely, I will shoot the Bailiff. At half past twelve I will shoot the Lieutenant Governor. At one o'clock I will shoot the Bailiff's wife, and at one thirty I will shoot the Governor's wife. As by then you will have made it clear that you do not intend to co-operate, I will put Operation Destruction into effect: the charges will be fired, we will open fire on any of your populace who show themselves, we will utterly wreck St Peter Port harbour and bombard the town, and we will await your assault with equanimity. Do I make myself clear.'

Gracey swallowed. 'Yes. You do.'

'Well, understand that I will permit not one second's delay in the above timings. *Gloriosa* out.'

Gracey continued to stare at the set for several seconds. Then Sheikh Hassan coughed.

The Prime Minister turned toward him. 'I ought to send you outside and hang you, here and now,' he said.

Hassan held up a finger. 'But, Prime Minister, you no longer have capital punishment in this country; and in any event, that is not how the British do things, is it? I am sorry about your harbourmaster. Jeannette is a very strong-minded woman.'

'Oh, take him away,' the Prime Minister said, and turned to the Home Secretary. 'Do you still have any doubts as to how this has to be played, Ned?'

Jane Lucas opened the door to Harding's knock. 'Why, Mr Harding, how nice to see you.'

She sounded doubtful. She had only a nodding acquaintance with Jack Harding, but on both the occasions they had met at cocktail parties she had discovered he was the world's number one groper. A good-looking woman in early middle age, Jane was acutely aware that she was wearing only a dressing gown over her nightdress.

'Joe in?' Harding enquired, brusquely.

'Why, yes; he's in the bath. Did you wish to see him?'

'That's why I'm here,' Harding pointed out.

'Oh, yes, of course. Do come in.'

The Lucas's house was situated at L'Ancresse, overlooking

the common that was also the principal island golf course; the lowest part of Guernsey, it could also be the bleakest when a gale was blowing driving rain.

Harding stepped inside, took off his hat, and shook himself. Water scattered from the raincoat.

'I'll just call Joe,' Jane said, and hurried up the stairs.

She returned a moment later. 'He'll be down in a minute. Would you like a cup of coffee?'

'I'd rather have a drink,' Harding said. 'Have you any Scotch?'

Jane looked at the clock on the mantelpiece.

'So it's early,' Harding agreed. 'Don't you have any idea what's going on?'

'Do forgive me for not being dressed,' Jane said, as she went to the sideboard and poured some Scotch, 'but we had a disturbed night.'

'What disturbed you?'

'Well . . .' She held out the glass, looking gratefully at her husband coming down the stairs. Joe Lucas was a large man, totally bald, with a big nose.

'Jack?'

'Don't you know what's happening?' Harding asked again.

'You mean that phone call?' Joe glanced at his wife.

'Jane was about to tell me,' Harding invited.

'Well, some chap in England, a Colonel somebody-or-other, telephoned me in the small hours to ask me if I knew what had happened to the Bailiff. Can you believe it? He had the idea that Sir William had left the island without telling anyone. Well, I didn't like to be rude to the chap, so I told him I'd look into it this morning.' He frowned. 'Is that Scotch you're drinking?'

'You'll be drinking it too in a moment,' Harding told him. 'So you sent out Pete Smith to find the Bailiff; and he ended up with a car shot full of bullet holes.'

Joe stared at him, and Jane dropped the whisky decanter, which shattered on the floor.

'Oh, my God!' she said. 'I'll get a dustpan.' She tiptoed through the mess and ran for the kitchen.

'You mean what he said was true?' Joe asked. 'I thought he was drunk.'

'So you sent him home. It's true: people have been killed, Joe. At least one policeman, and possibly some more. The way they seem prepared to open fire at the drop of a hat would indicate that.'

Joe sat down, staring morosely at the whisky splashed across the floor. Jane hurried in with a dustpan and brush.

'But what's happening?' Joe asked.

Harding eyed Jane's bottom speculatively, but kept his mind on the job. 'The island has been taken over by a terrorist group. Don't ask me why, but it's happened.'

'Then that colonel fellow . . . ?'

'Oh, I imagine they know what's happening. I suppose these people have made some kind of a demand. Didn't you hear that plane just now?'

'First one today,' Joe said. 'The weather, I suppose.'

'The weather hell. They've got the airport as well. I suspect that plane was an attempt to land troops on the island, and it didn't work.'

'Well,' Joe said, 'first thing we must do is contact the Bailiff.'

'Joe,' Harding said patiently, 'please get it through your head: the Bailiff and Lady Martel are in the hands of these people. I expect that goes for the Governor too, and as the police station is in their hands, it would go for Billy Arkwright as well. That's all the top brass taken out. Meanwhile, Guernsey is in the hands of a bunch of thugs.'

'But . . . if the British government knows about it . . . ?'

'Oh, I'm sure they're working on plans,' Harding said contemptuously. 'But what is the usual way of handling terrorist ransom demands? They indulge in dialogue, hoping to talk the thugs into surrendering. These people aren't going to surrender. If they've been killing people, they

can't surrender. So . . . it's up to us.' He watched Jane
retreat to the kitchen with a pan full of glass shards. The
lounge had taken on the rich smell of good Scotch.

'Up to us to do what?' Joe asked. 'I'll get out a special
edition. That'll shake people up.'

'By when?'

'Well . . .' He looked at his watch. 'We could have at least
a broadsheet out by this evening.'

'Fat lot of good that will do. Anyway, I've an idea you may
find your offices have been taken over. I've spoken with quite
a lot of people, told them to pass the word to everyone, to stay
indoors and keep out of trouble until further notice.'

'You mean we do nothing? But you just said it was
up to us.'

'It is – you, me, the leaders of the community.'

Joe scratched his head. He wouldn't have described either
Harding or himself as a leader of the community. 'The Dean!'
he said. 'We could try the Dean.'

'Oh, for God's sake,' Harding said. 'He'd recommend
appeasement.'

'So what do we do?' Jane asked from the doorway, where
she was standing with a mop and a vague expression. 'We
have no weapons, no organisation . . .'

'A force of picked men,' Harding said.

'And women?'

'Well . . . if they want to come along,' he agreed conde-
scendingly.

'To do what?' Joe asked. 'March on the police station with
our arms linked singing "We shall overcome"?'

'They'd mow us down,' Harding said. 'Anyway, the police
station isn't the answer to this. They've occupied it in force
because there is our only apparent source of resistance.'

'Well, it is,' Jane pointed out; 'or it was.'

'But it's not their command centre,' Harding said. 'As
they've knocked out our electrics and main-line telephones,
and we must presume they're still negotiating with the

mainland, they have to have an independent source of power, and that can only be the yacht, with its generator. The yacht is also almost certainly their escape vehicle.'

'A yacht?' Joe asked incredulously. 'Making maybe twenty knots?'

'They'll have hostages to ensure they aren't attacked,' Harding said. 'On both of those counts, if we knock out the yacht, we knock them out. They'll be cut flowers in a vase, with no communications, and no transport.'

'Knock out the yacht,' Jane said, and snapped her fingers. 'Just like that.'

'Listen,' Harding said: 'the yacht is lying at the Cambridge berth, on the south side of the White Rock. On the north side of the White Rock is the home marina, filled with yachts, almost all the owners of which we know and can contact. We start now, using our mobiles and telephoning every one of those who can respond. All they have to do is go down to their boats. Well, I imagine most of them are meaning to do that anyway, just to make sure all the moorings are in good shape after the storm. From the marina it is only a couple of hundred yards to the Cambridge berth.'

'Across an open car park,' Jane said. 'They'll see you coming.'

'Could be done at night, I suppose,' Joe mused.

'We can't wait until tonight. The yacht will float again about five or just after, and they may be planning to leave. It has to be done while she's stuck on the bottom.'

'We can't charge her across that car park in broad daylight without weapons,' Joe pointed out. 'It'd be a massacre.'

'But we *have* weapons,' Harding insisted. 'I have a Very pistol, with several cartridges. Most of the other skippers have them too. A Very pistol can be a very effective weapon when aimed at a ship or at people. And I'm not talking about a direct assault across the car park – at least, not by everybody. When we've finished working on our boats, what do we do? We get into our cars and drive round the one-way system. That

brings us back to the Cambridge berth; on the east side we'll
be out of sight of the yacht behind those big warehouses, but
within fifty yards of it. If we get three or four blokes to a car,
we could have a sizeable force going before the thugs know
what has hit them.'

Joe stroked his chin.

'God give me patience,' Jane shouted. 'Do you really
suppose your average Guernsey boat-owner is going to be
prepared to start acting like a commando? Just like that?
Without any preparation? Jack Harding, don't you realise
people are going to get *killed* if you go ahead with this
crazy scheme? And for what? You yourself say these people
probably mean to take off on the next tide.'

Harding stood up. 'I had hoped for better. Just in case
you've forgotten, Jane, people have already been killed.'

'You don't *know* that.'

'It's pretty certain. And when those people go, they are
going to take hostages with them. We can't let this happen.
Let's get started.'

Onslaught

It was twenty to eleven by the time al-Rakim regained the yacht. There were people about, but fewer than he had expected. No doubt the weather had something to do with that; it was still blowing very hard and the streets were wet. As he was driving a hire car, no one paid him any attention.

The three commandeered buses waited patiently, and Jeannette, wearing oilskins, was walking Lulu up and down the dock beside the ship. The other two women were in the saloon, drinking coffee. It was the most peaceful of scenes.

But Jeannette was not in the most peaceful of moods. 'Well?' she demanded, as al-Rakim got out.

'The jumbo should have landed at Heathrow by now.' He grinned. 'If they can get it down in this visibility.' He ran up the gangplank and into shelter.

Jeannette gathered Lulu into her arms and followed. 'I do not understand how people can survive in a climate like this.'

'At least they have no water problems,' al-Rakim pointed out, and went up to the bridge, where Salim continued to peer into the radar screen and Honeylee walked up and down morosely. Captain Harrison's body had been removed, and the deck scrubbed clean of bloodstains.

'Well?' Honeylee demanded.

'It is happening,' al-Rakim said. 'The jumbo will have regained Heathrow by now. Then it will be a matter of obtaining the 727 and transferring the sheikh. This should not take long. They will be back before twelve.'

203

'I do not like it,' Honeylee said. 'You know it was a trick?'

'Perhaps it was. I do not see what they hoped to gain from it.'

'They must have had something in mind. Anyway, hopefully they have learned their lesson.'

'Eh?'

'Madame executed the harbourmaster while they listened; and she will start executing the other hostages if that plane is not back by twelve.'

Al-Rakim licked his lips. 'All of this killing . . .' He had not actually been present at any of the deaths. 'You know, Jerome, even if we get away from here, they will hunt us down. They always do. You will never be able to return to America.'

'I'll be happy in the Sudan,' Honeylee said. 'All I want to do is get back there.'

'I hope we do.' Al-Rakim went on to the bridge wing to survey the town. There were still very few people to be seen, and almost no cars. Most of the people were gathered in shop doorways, perhaps sheltering from the rain; but all were looking at the yacht.

Honeylee joined him. 'You heard the shooting just now?'

Al-Rakim frowned. 'What shooting?'

'Some madman tried to rush the police station, all on his own and apparently unarmed.'

'And they shot him too?'

'No, they shot at him; but he got away in his car – caused quite a row. There was a big crowd on that street over there.' He pointed at the bottom end of St Julian's Avenue.

'Shit,' al-Rakim muttered. 'So the whole island knows what is happening.'

'Well, quite a few of the people must do.'

'That is something we wished to avoid.'

Honeylee shrugged. 'Nothing has developed from it. And what can they do? If we're away from here by twelve . . .'

'That is still over an hour away. I think you should break out the gun.'

'I have thought this too,' Honeylee said; 'but madame will not permit it. She says it would provoke people.'

'And she doesn't think shooting at them in the streets will provoke them?' Al-Rakim pointed. 'Who is that?'

They watched a Mercedes come down the Glategny Esplanade from the north, and turn on to the White Rock.

'Is he coming here?'

'No,' Honeylee said. 'I think I saw him about half an hour ago. He's a yacht-owner – must keep his boat in that marina across there.'

'That's for local boats,' al-Rakim said.

Honeylee nodded. 'There he goes.'

They watched Harding swing into parking, get out of his car and walk down the steeply sloping ramp.

'As I said,' Honeylee pointed out.

Al-Rakim stroked his chin, then pointed again. 'And him?'

Another car was turning on to the White Rock.

'Him too, I'd say,' the captain said. 'There.'

The car pulled into the park; this time two men got out and walked down the ramp.

Jeannette arrived on the bridge, having taken off her oilskins.

'Call London,' she commanded.

The radio operater obeyed.

Jeannette took the mike. 'Let me speak to Lieutenant Colonel Gracey.'

He came on the air a few minutes later. 'Yes?'

'I hope you absorbed our example, Colonel?'

'You, madam, are guilty of cold-blooded murder.'

'So issue a warrant for our arrest, Colonel. The time is now three minutes to eleven. Where is our aircraft?'

'It is being fuelled now, madam. It will take off at eleven fifteen, and be over Guernsey at eleven forty-five.'

'Be sure that it is,' Jeannette said. 'Out.'

She handed the mike back to the operator, frowning at Honeylee and al-Rakim, both still on the bridge wing, and both using binoculars. She went to the door. 'What are you staring at?'

'Just several cars coming on to the White Rock,' al-Rakim said. 'It seems they all belong to boat-owners who have come down to check their boats after the storm.'

'Give me those glasses,' Jeannette said.

She studied the various cars, the little group of men gathered on one of the pontoons, heads bowed together against the wind and the rain.

'What do you suppose they're talking about?'

Honeylee shrugged. 'I suppose word is spreading, about the shooting, maybe about the takeover.'

'That is exactly right,' Jeannette said. 'Word is spreading. And yet these yachtsmen still come down to the harbour to look at their boats?'

Al-Rakim levelled his glasses again. 'You think they are going to try something?'

'I don't know. But we must be prepared. Captain, break out the gun; but keep it covered until we need it.'

'Aye aye,' Honeylee said thankfully, and hurried aft to give the necessary orders.

'I don't see what a bunch of unarmed yachtsmen can do,' al-Rakim said. 'But . . . by Allah!'

'What is it?' Jeannette demanded, raising her own glasses again.

'That last car,' al-Rakim said.

Jeannette focused on the small hire car that had just pulled in to parking beside the other yacht-owners' vehicles. It had a rubber dinghy strapped to its roof.

'What is important about this one?'

'Look at the man getting out,' al-Rakim said.

There were actually two men getting out, and two women. One of the men was wearing a wetsuit and carrying a pair of flippers. The other . . .

'That looks like that assistant harbourmaster who caused all that trouble last night,' Jeannette said.

'It *is* the assistant harbourmaster who caused all that trouble last night,' al-Rakim said. 'And the woman in the wetsuit is his girlfriend, Sophie.'

'The one we have spent the night looking for?' Jeannette asked. 'Well, well. They do say everything comes to he, or she, who waits. Who are the other two?'

Al-Rakim shook his head. 'I can't say.' He watched them unstrap the rubber dinghy, while the women took the air bottles out of the back of the car. 'What do you think they are doing?'

Jeannette watched James carrying the dinghy down the ramp, blown from side to side by the wind. Shane was lifting the outboard out of the boot. Helen and Sophie were also descending the ramp, each carrying a cylinder. 'It is something to do with us, you can be certain of that.'

'Shall I go down and get them?' al-Rakim asked.

Jeannette lowered her glasses.

'I'd take some men with me,' he said.

'You would provoke an incident. How many men would you take? You get yourself on those pontoons with even a dozen men and anything could happen.'

'I thought you wanted her.'

'I do,' Jeannette said; 'but I can wait a little longer. I think she is coming to us.'

Jack Harding was well pleased with the response to his various telephone calls. A good dozen men had volunteered to meet him at the marina, and if the terrorists were manning the police station, the airport and the hospital, as well as various other vital places in the island, he doubted they would have as many as a dozen men left on board. As he watched his supporters coming down the ramps, his heart swelled with pride. Not a Guernseyman himself, he had invested heavily in the island, partly as a means of avoiding English income tax, and had gradually come to consider himself, and be considered, an important member of the community. He was well aware that many people who knew him well did not like him – he had a weakness for female flesh that was apt to surface whenever he had had a few drinks – but the people of Guernsey as a whole saw him as a bluff bon viveur who had ideas, and the time and the money to put those ideas into practice. They had now re-elected him to the States twice.

Now he felt he was being given the opportunity to prove himself on a far larger stage, gain international renown, and certainly enter the realms of Guernsey folk hero. And, incidentally, put himself out of reach of any crazy allegations by that Sophie character, which could so easily ruin both his political career and his social standing.

As for any danger involved – well, he did not himself intend to be directly in the firing line, and in any event, he was only dealing with a bunch of wogs who probably couldn't shoot straight, as they had proved in their inability to hit Pete Smith.

He shook hands with each man in turn as he came down the ramp.

'Good to see you all,' he said. 'Now, we mustn't hang about in a group too long; they can see us from the bridge of the yacht.' He looked at his watch. 'We'll all go to our boats, and get our gear together. Very pistols, eh? Each with a couple of spare cartridges. It's ten to eleven. At eleven fifteen we start leaving our boats, and get into our cars. I'll lead. We drive slowly round the White Rock, following the one-way system. Now, they'll undoubtedly be watching us. That we all leave within a few seconds of each other need not necessarily upset them. They will lose sight of us when we go round the top and, in fact, we will be out of sight until we reappear at the western end of the Cambridge Dock – that is, right alongside the yacht. But we're not going to do that. I will stop on the eastern arm, where we will still be out of sight because of the high buildings. Then we have to act very

quickly. You will all pull in behind me, and we will round
the buildings and assault the yacht, firing our Very pistols as
we do so. Now, we must be very clear about this. We aim at
the bridge and the superstructure of the yacht. In effect, they
will be assaulted by some twenty small rockets. As you fire,
reload. Our initial volley will have them in a right mix-up,
and we should get on deck without any real trouble. Then I
will head for the bridge, with . . . you three.' He picked out
his men. 'The rest of you get below and free the hostages;
but remember: don't hesitate to shoot.'

'We could start a fire,' someone said.

'So we start a fire.'

'But, if the yacht were to be burned out . . .'

Harding grinned. 'No one is going to send us a bill, Jerry.
These people are terrorists. Whatever they get was coming
to them. Right?'

They nodded, uneasily.

'Right. Quarter past eleven. You . . .' He gazed at the
gangway in consternation. 'What the fuck . . . ?'

James swayed towards him, the dinghy constantly caught
in the wind. 'Hello, Jack. What are you up to?'

'What . . . ?' Harding looked past him at the second man,
whom he didn't know, and then at . . . Shit, he thought. If
that little bitch has come here to cause trouble . . . 'Where
the hell are you going?' he demanded.

'Scuba-diving,' James said.

Harding gazed at him, and then looked out of the marina
mouth. This faced north, and at this stage of the tide revealed
mainly rocks, which were acting as breaks; what sea there
was inside them was quite calm. But in the distance, outside
the St Sampson's breakwater, was all tumbling white.

'You need your heads examined,' Harding said.

'Good morning, Mr Harding,' Sophie said composedly.
'Going sailing?'

They regarded each other for several seconds.

'Perhaps,' Harding said at last.

209

'Well, have fun.'

James lowered the dinghy into the water, and Shane bolted the outboard into place on the wooden frame situated on the after transom. Then he sat on the pontoon to pull on his flippers while Helen strapped his air bottle on to his back.

James was doing the same for Sophie.

Harding scratched his head.

'OK,' Shane said. 'You OK, Sophie?'

Sophie nodded. Her stomach was rolling and she was sure she was going to be sick; but she also knew she was going through with it. This was her baby – had been from the beginning.

James placed the waterproof bag in the bottom of the boat; his head was close to hers. 'You can still change your mind,' he whispered. 'I wish you'd change your mind.'

'We're going to do it, James.'

'Well, promise me one thing: if they spot you and call on you to surrender, no heroics.'

'And then? These people shoot people in cold blood. I've seen them do it.'

He bit his lip.

'Let's go,' Shane said, and started the outboard. The dinghy moved away from the pontoon towards the entrance. There was just enough water for them to scrape across, with the outboard raised. The man in the watch house shouted at them, but they ignored him, and disappeared round the harbour wall.

'I don't know whether to cheer or scream,' Helen confessed. 'What do we do now?'

James realised they hadn't thought of that. 'We get as close to the yacht as we can, and wait. Hopefully for a bang.'

Harding approached. 'Just what are those two up to?'

'We told you: scuba-diving,' Helen said.

'Mad as march hares,' Harding growled. 'Look, James, we're going to assault that yacht. You game?'

'Eh?' James stared at him in consternation.

Harding looked at his watch. 'Ten minutes. Using Very pistols, I reckon we can overrun her before those wogs know what's happening. How about it? I've a spare pistol.'

A chance to do something – if he could get aboard that ship . . . 'You bet.'

'You'll be killed,' Helen protested.

'We'll be helping Shane and Sophie.'

She hesitated. 'Then I'll come too.'

'No, you won't,' Harding said. 'This is man's business. You can stay here, on board my yacht, until it's over.'

Helen looked as if she would have argued, then changed her mind and allowed herself to be escorted aboard Harding's yacht, a forty-foot ketch, very comfortably appointed below decks. He opened a locker and took out the two pistols. Each had an enormous bore of at least an inch, into which, when the gun was broken, the equally enormous Very cartridge was inserted. He gave James one, took the other himself, gave them each two spare cartridges.

'Now will you tell me what Sophie and that chap are doing?'

'They're going to blow the bottom out of the yacht,' James said.

Harding stared at him, his mouth making an enormous O. 'That little girl?'

'Shane is an ex-territorial,' James explained. 'Knows all about explosives. He's made up a sort of limpet mine that they can attach to the hull. The yacht is dry right now, so they don't even have to make it waterproof.'

'Great balls of fire,' Harding said. 'They have guts. If they're spotted . . . How long will it take them to get into position?'

'About half an hour,' James said.

'We can't wait that long. We'll beat them to it.' He looked at his watch. 'Ten minutes.'

From inside the wheelhouse, Jeannette and al-Rakim could

continue to study the marina through their glasses. They
watched the rubber dinghy ease its way through the entrance,
but then it was lost to view.

'What do you think?' al-Rakim asked.

'I think they are mad. Call Abdullah in the watch house
and tell him to keep his eye open for a rubber dinghy with
two people on board, which may try to enter the harbour. As
for the others . . .'

'They've all disappeared,' al-Rakim said, 'on board their
yachts. That harbourmaster and the other woman have gone
with them.'

'Let's hope they have the sense to stay there.'

'Heathrow is calling, madame,' said the radio operator.

Jeannette went to the set.

'Gracey here. We shall be taking off in ten minutes.'

'Very good,' Jeannette said. 'Let me speak with Sheikh
Hassan.'

'Jeannette?' the sheikh said. 'Is all well?'

'All is well,' Jeannette said reassuringly. 'And with you?
You are boarding now?'

'Ah . . . yes, I think so.'

Jeannette frowned. 'You do not know? The colonel said
you were about to take off.'

'I believe that is correct,' Hassan said.

'Well, I will call you again at half past. Out.' She handed
the mike to the operator and turned to al-Rakim. 'They are
about to leave, but there is something going on that I do
not like. So at half past eleven, when they will be airborne
and halfway here, you will call the aircraft and speak with
the sheikh – make sure that all is well – and report back to
me here.'

Al-Rakim frowned. 'If they are about to leave, why do we
not just call in all our people, and abandon the ship, before
any of these people do something stupid.'

'Because if we do that, and they are planning something
stupid, as you put it, they will know, or quickly discover, that

we have left, and follow us out to the airport. We want to get
safely away, not be hampered by a mob of angry islanders.
Now go. I will call our sub-commanders and tell them to
stand by for departure.'

'And the people in the dinghy?'

'Two people?' Jeannette's lip curled. 'If they attempt to
enter the harbour we will blow them out of the water. Now
hurry. And listen: once the aircraft is on the ground, set up
a defensive perimeter until we are all assembled and ready
to take off.'

Al-Rakim slid down the ladder, shaking his head. It had
all been supposed to go much more smoothly than this.
He got into his car and drove away; the time was ten
past eleven.

'Jesus,' Sophie muttered, as she knelt in the bow, holding the
painter, while Shane motored into the approach channel to the
marina. Here they were still completely sheltered by the rocks
– quite a few of these were higher than themselves – but in
front of them the whitecaps raced by, the waves tumbling
over themselves as the south-going tide hurled itself against
the southerly wind.

'We're not going into that,' Shane shouted, 'but we have
to get an offing so we don't get thrown into the rocks. Now
listen: once you're in the water, go down and stay down.
Make for the harbour wall. I'll be right with you all the time.
Got it?'

She nodded.

'Once inside, still stay down, and make for the hydrofoil
berth. I'll join you there.'

This berth was on the outside of the second jetty, one away
from the Cambridge Dock.

The dinghy surged past the outer buoy, and was immediately seized by the tide. Even here there were whitecaps,
although the waves themselves were small. Shane cut the
outboard, and let them drift, while he opened his bag and

made some adjustments. 'I'm setting the timer for ten past twelve,' he said.

'But . . . that's an hour.'

'We need to give ourselves ample time to get well away before it explodes. Go,' he commanded.

Sophie bit on her regulator and went backwards into the water. Even in June and wearing a wetsuit it was colder than she had expected as she sank below the surface. She looked around and saw Shane descending beside her, his waterproof bag strapped to his shoulder. He gave her the thumbs-up sign, and pointed ahead of them. The time was thirteen minutes past eleven.

'OK, Sheikh, it's time to go,' Gracey said.

Hassan peered at him, realising for the first time that the colonel had a revolver strapped to his belt and a tin helmet hanging from his shoulder.

'You are coming with me? You did not come the last time?'

'We believe in personal delivery,' Gracey said. 'Even of soiled goods.'

Hassan frowned, mystified. 'You look as if you are about to fight a battle.'

'That is my intention,' Gracey said. 'Shall we go?'

Hassan now discovered that two armed MPs were waiting for him. This was totally unlike the VIP treatment he had been accorded on the first flight. He went down the stairs and got into the waiting car. The MPs sat on either side of him, Gracey in the front beside the driver, and they were taken across various parking areas to a remote corner of the airport, where a 727 was waiting, engines already a low rumble.

'I want you to know,' Gracey said, as they got out, 'that from this moment on, should you say, or do, or even think anything I don't like, Sheikh Hassan, I am under orders to shoot you. Please remember this.'

Hassan swallowed, went up the steps, then swallowed

again as he entered the cabin and gazed at the rows of seats, each occupied by a battledress-clad soldier, helmeted and equipped with an automatic weapon. It was exactly eleven fifteen.

'Let's go.'

Harding stuck his pistol into the back of his pants, beneath his windcheater, and climbed the ladder into the cockpit of his yacht.

James made to follow, and had his hand clasped by Helen. 'For God's sake be careful,' she said. 'And come back.'

'I mean to.' He followed Harding into the cockpit and stepped on to the pontoon. The wind still howled, but it had stopped raining, and there was even some blue sky to be seen.

He wondered if he was afraid? Unlike Shane, he had had no military training, and his few years in the Navy had been spent mainly on fishery protection vessels, with no likelihood of ever actually coming under fire. Certainly his heart was pounding, but that was because the adrenalin was flowing.

Harding went up the ramp, James immediately behind him. At the top he unlocked his car and glanced back at the marina. Several other men had left their boats and were strolling towards the ramp.

Harding got into his car, started the engine and pulled out of parking. He drove towards the head of the dock, very slowly, glancing at James. 'OK?'

James licked his lips. 'I think so. Where do you suppose Sophie is now?'

'She won't have reached the harbour mouth yet,' Harding said. 'We'll be done long before she gets here.'

He looked in his rear-view mirror. Several of the other cars had pulled out of parking and were following him, slowly.

'We're nearly there,' he said.

'They're all going home,' Honeylee said. 'There's a relief.'

215

Jeannette stood beside him, glasses levelled. Harding's Mercedes had disappeared behind the Customs buildings at the head of the dock, but several of the other cars were still in sight, following each other, slowly.

'They're not going home,' she said. 'Uncover the gun.'

Honeylee gulped, then ran for the after deck, where one of his men stood by, holding the plastic-shrouded gun. This was a Carl Gustav eighty-four-millimetre recoilless M2. Although described as an anti-tank device, and firing a one-pound warhead, it was a multi-purpose weapon, which could not only destroy tanks or even concrete bunkers, but was equally effective against personnel. Honeylee plucked the plastic cover away, and the sailor immediately fed in the first warhead. A tray of spare cartridges lay on the deck.

Jeannette ran on to the bridge wing, with a loudhailer. 'Move those buses!' she shouted.

It took some seconds for the three drivers to respond. Then they started their engines. But now several men, led by Harding, debouched round the buildings. There was a succession of flaring lights, and the big yacht was shrouded in flying mini-rockets.

'Open fire!' Jeannette shrieked.

Honeylee hesitated a moment – the buses had not yet cleared the dock – then he levelled the gun and squeezed the trigger. By now a second wave of Very cartridges had seared into the yacht. One smashed into the wheelhouse and struck the radar set. Salim jumped away from it with an exclamation of alarm as sparks flew and the set went dead. Jeannette ducked below the rail level and heard another cartridge smash into the bridge. Now she smelt burning.

But Honeylee's first shot had struck the corner of the row of buildings, the warhead exploding with a great whumpff. The women looking out of the saloon screamed and dived for shelter, while the yachtsmen were totally taken aback: they had expected only rifle fire. Several were knocked from their feet by the blast.

Up till now Harding had been leading; now he suddenly also went down, shouting curses. James hesitated, looking down at him; he couldn't see any blood.

'I tripped, goddamit!' Harding bellowed, rolling away from the line of fire.

Tom Lowndes pushed James to one side and took up the lead, James immediately behind him; but Honeylee had reloaded and fired again. Now he aimed down at the gang-plank. As Lowndes reached it, he seemed to dissolve into blood and bone, and tumbled backwards, cannoning into James, who fell with him, right off the shattered and now collapsing gangplank and down between the ship and the dock. The tide was right down, but the yacht was surrounded by shallow water and his fall was broken; yet he hit the bottom with sufficient force to send a jolt of pain up his leg.

Lowndes had inadvertently saved his life, he realised, as he watched another body plummeting down beside him, and this man was also dead. He had dropped his pistol and had no idea where it was. Desperately he rolled away from the hull and beneath the thick piles supporting the dock – knelt there, up to his thighs in the water, holding on to one of the piles and gasping for breath.

'Cease firing,' Jeannette shouted.

Honeylee took his fingers from the trigger and wiped his brow. He had spent three years in the Marines, but that had been a long time ago, and he had never had to shoot at virtually unarmed men.

Virtually.

'Fire extinguishers!' Jeannette shouted.

Salim was back on his feet, and now he played the foam over the interior of the burning wheelhouse. The radio operator used the other extinguisher; his set had also been damaged.

Jeannette had withdrawn to the wing.

'Is it bad?' Honeylee panted.

'It's a good thing we're not going to sea,' Jeannette

said. 'The bastards have knocked out both the radar and the radio.'

'Shit,' the captain said. 'I'll get Yusuf up to repair the radio; it doesn't look too bad. Who'd ever have supposed they had the guts.'

'They haven't any more,' Jeannette said, looking down on the dock. There were two bodies sprawled there, and she supposed more had gone into the water. There had been more than that in the assaulting group, she was certain, even if she didn't know how many; but the others had all gone to ground. In any event they would have expended their Very cartridges, and the fire in the wheelhouse was now under control. The only real problem was the communication loss, and as Honeylee had said, the radio at least could easily be repaired. Until then . . . She picked up her mobile.

'Keep your eye on that dock,' she told Honeylee, 'and if any of those idiots shows his head, blow it off.'

'Yes, ma'am,' Honeylee said. 'What about that lot?'

The sounds of the firing had reached the town. People were gathered on the esplanade to stare at the yacht. Visiting yachtsmen had left their boats and their pontoons to gather on the Crown Pier, chattering amongst each other.

'Ignore them,' Jeannette said; 'but I think we will take the gun with us when we go.' She switched on her mobile. 'Al-Rakim,' she said, 'where are you?'

'Just coming up to the airport, madame.'

'Any problems?'

'None. There is hardly anyone to be seen. Even the taxi-drivers seem to have gone home.'

'Well, we have had a problem here. We have lost the use of both our radar and our radio.'

'Madame?' His voice was anxious.

'I will explain it to you when we are airborne; but for the time being, we will have to use the airport facilities.' She looked at her watch: it was twenty-five past eleven. 'That aircraft is on its way. Get in there. The plane should be on their radar. Call the sheikh at half past eleven to make sure everything is all right, and then call me back here. Once we are sure the plane is coming in on time, with no more tricks, we will call in our people and assemble for departure. Understood?'

'Understood,' al-Rakim said.

'Abdullah is calling from the watch house, madame,' Salim said.

Jeannette took the other phone. 'You have seen the dinghy?'

'Yes, madame. It has just drifted past on the tide. But . . . it was empty.'

'I see,' Jeannette said. 'They were wearing wetsuits and had air bottles. They are probably in the harbour by now. Keep your eyes open.' She handed the phone back to Salim. 'How many men have we got on board?' she asked Honeylee.

'Seven. And us three.'

'And Hafsah and Raqayyah,' Jeannette reminded him. 'They will have to earn their keep. How deep is that water?'

'Only a couple of feet at the moment; but it is rising.'

'Very well. Salim, you and Yazid get down on the bottom. Arm yourselves. I believe people may attempt to approach us underwater; but they cannot reach us underwater at the moment. You will see them long before they can get to us.'

'Do you wish them killed, madame?'

'You may shoot the man. I want the woman alive.'

Salim beckoned the radio operator, and went down the ladders. Honeylee stared morosely at the burned-out radar set. 'God, to be blind at such a time.'

'Al-Rakim will take care of it,' Jeannette assured him. 'Now, man that gun, and if any of those men sheltering behind those buildings shows himself, blow him away.'

She went down the ladders herself, then aft, to the saloon, where the two women were crouching, sheltering from the shooting even though it had stopped.

219

'Such courage,' she commented. 'Get up and arm your-selves.'

'The prisoners,' Raqqayah said. 'They are banging on their doors and shouting.'

'Ignore them,' Jeannette told them, and summoned Dr Hamath. 'We will be leaving in a few minutes,' she said. 'Get your gear and the rest of your people together.'

'The other plane is here?' Hamath asked, anxiously.

'It is on its way.'

'Shit,' Jack Harding muttered. 'Shit, shit, shit.'

He had crawled to shelter inside one of the warehouses. From his position he could just see the remains of the yacht gangway hanging down the side.

'You OK?' asked Harry Lewis. With the other yachtsmen he was crouching a little distance away. 'We saw you go down.'

'I tripped, goddamit,' Harding said. With James Candish dead, no one could prove otherwise.

'Maybe you were lucky,' someone said. 'Did you see those chaps? They never stood a chance.'

'It was a right royal cock-up,' someone said.

'I didn't know they had a fucking bazooka,' Harding complained. 'How the hell was I supposed to know that?'

'We should've known they'd have *something*,' someone complained.

'The point is, what do we do now?' asked Lewis. 'Four good fellows dead, and all we've accomplished is a small fire. Which is now out. And we're pinned down here, by that gun.'

'Come on, Jack,' someone said. 'You got us into this. Tell us how we get back out.'

'We'll have to wait a while,' Harding said.

He didn't want to admit it, even to himself, but they were entirely dependent on that little girl and her high-powered friend.

*   *   *

'Seems your friends are late,' Gracey told the sheikh. It was twenty-five to twelve, and the 727 was beginning its descent.

Hassan said nothing. He knew he was about to witness the destruction of his entire organisation. And perhaps of Jeannette as well. Unless . . .

'Guernsey's on the air, Colonel,' said the radio operator. 'They want to speak with the sheikh.'

'Now remember,' Gracey told Hassan as they went forward. 'Captain Lewis speaks Arabic. Say anything he doesn't like, and it's curtains. They can't stop us going in now, anyway.'

Hassan put on the earphones, as did Lewis with the other set.

'Hassan here,' the sheikh said.

'Your Excellency,' al-Rakim said. 'Is all well?'

Hassan glanced at Gracey. 'Yes,' he said. 'All is well. Where is Jeannette?'

'Still on the yacht. They are having a slight communications problem; but they will be joining us as soon as I have spoken with you. We are anxiously awaiting you.'

'As I am anxious to be with you,' Hassan said. 'Tell Jeannette for me that I send her two hundred red roses of blood.'

Lewis started.

Al-Rakim hesitated for a moment before replying. 'Two hundred red roses of blood,' he repeated. 'I will tell her. Al-Rakim out.'

'Just what the hell is going on?' Gracey demanded.

'The bastard sent some kind of coded message,' Lewis said.

Hassan shrugged. 'It is the customary greeting of my people.'

Gracey glared at him, and Hassan knew his life was hanging by a thread. But he also knew that Gracey's superiors

221

would far rather have him standing trial in The Hague than shot dead on one of their aircraft, with certain condemnation from around the world that he had been murdered.

Gracey grinned. 'Well, like I said, we're going in anyway. You could try holding your breath, Your Excellency.'

'Refuse them permission to land,' al-Rakim told the controller.

'I can't do that,' he protested, 'not now. They're making their approach.'

Al-Rakim bit his lip. Again he was being forced to take a decision, and a very serious one; but Sheikh Hassan's message had been clear: there were two hundred enemy soldiers on board the aircraft. The fools were going to try retaking Guernsey by storm! And the sheikh was in their midst!

'How long?' he asked.

'Three minutes,' the controller said.

Al-Rakim peered at the sky. But the cloud cover was still too thick for him to see anything.

'Right,' he said. 'You, get out of the building – all of you.'

The controllers gaped at him. 'We can't leave as a plane is landing. He has to be given instructions. Look . . . there he is.' He pointed at the radar screen and the steadily approaching blip.

'Guernsey,' said the radio, 'Guernsey. Wind speed and direction, please.'

'I said out,' al-Rakim told them, as they turned back to their mikes. He drew his pistol, and before anyone realised what he was doing, fired into the radar screen. The men gasped and jumped back as the screen dissolved into a thousand splinters. 'Out,' al-Rakim repeated.

The controllers ran for the door and stumbled down the steps.

'Prepare to evacuate,' al-Rakim told his three men. 'Set the charges for five minutes from now.'

He picked up one of the Minimi rifles, and went outside.

222

Settling Up

'They've gone dead,' Squadron Leader Mallon said. 'Sounded like a shot. Do you want to abort?'

Gracey was standing immediately behind the pilot. 'Can you get her down?'

'Providing this cloud cover doesn't go right down to the runway. It'll be dicey.'

Gracey grinned. 'What isn't, about this business?'

He went back into the cabin. 'Stand by,' he said 'We're going in, virtually blind. There may be a bit of a bump.' He sat next to the sheikh and strapped himself in.

'This is madness,' the sheikh declared. 'We will all be killed. Take me back to London. I will go to The Hague and stand trial.'

'It's just a bit late for that now,' Gracey told him.

Al-Rakim stood on the platform beside the control room, the rifle in one hand, his mobile in the other. He stared at the clouds. 'Madame?' he asked.

'Is it down?' Jeannette asked.

'It is coming down. But it is full of soldiers. I am taking it out.'

There was a moment's silence. 'You are doing what?'

'It hasn't worked, madame,' al-Rakim said, and watched the 727 break through the clouds, a mile from the airport, at a height of about two thousand feet.

'But the sheikh is on board!' Jeannette shouted.

223

'It hasn't worked, madame,' al-Rakim said again. 'Implement Operation Destruction.'

He switched off the phone. The aircraft was coming closer, dropping down to make a visual landing. Behind him his men ran down the stairs to get out of the building. Al-Rakim levelled the Minimi rifle. He had telescopic sights, and he was a superb shot. He aimed at the flight deck; through the sights he could see the face of the pilot quite clearly. But he still hoped to save the life of the sheikh.

The 727 touched the runway, bounced, settled again, raced along the runway to the halfway mark. It was still travelling at well over a hundred miles an hour, but al-Rakim thought it might just be able to stop before overshooting. Only it wasn't going to do that. As it reached the halfway taxiing runway used by the small aircraft based on Guernsey, it swung hard right – so hard its wing actually struck the tarmac and sent sparks flying in every direction. But on its new course it was headed straight at the terminal buildings and the control tower.

Al-Rakim grinned. Now he understood their plan. The rifle was still levelled, tucked into his shoulder. He squeezed the trigger, and kept it squeezed, emptying all thirty cartridges in the box magazine at the flight deck.

'My God, my God, my God!' Jeannette screamed, hurling her mobile at the deck.

Yusuf, who had been working on the radio, picked the pieces up, somewhat curiously; he had never before actually seen a telephone smashed into several pieces.

Honeylee ran into the smouldering wheelhouse. 'Trouble?'

'Trouble,' Jeannette snarled. But she was already recovering from her initial panic, her brain working; there were still alternative plans to be made, and carried out. 'When will she float?'

'The tide has only just turned. Not before five this afternoon.'

224

Jeannette made a low guttural sound at the back of her throat; she reminded the captain of an angry tigress. 'Right,' she said. 'Hashim, get on to all our people and tell them to set their charges.'

'For how long, madame?'

'I will control them from here,' Jeannette said. 'Then tell everyone to withdraw from their positions.'

'To the airport, madame?'

'No, not the airport. Here. I want them all on board this ship. Yusuf, call the police station and tell Mustafa to evacuate and return here, with his hostages. That is most important. Send him one of the buses. Captain, blast those bastards away from those warehouses.' Her head jerked. 'What was that?'

'Shots,' Honeylee said. 'From below the dock.'

'Well, find out who has been shot. After you have destroyed those men.'

Honeylee ran back to his bazooka.

Jeannette picked up Lulu and went down, through the saloon, and along the corridor between the cabins. She heard Doris Harrison banging on the door and shouting, but she ignored her. Telling her what had happened to her husband was a pleasure that could wait.

She went to the master stateroom, in the very stern of the ship. This was more than just a stateroom. It was a large cabin tailored to the requirements of pleasure, with dark-panelled bulkheads and locker doors, thick carpet on the floor, mirrors in the ceiling, and in the centre, a free-standing double bed, bolted to the floor but raised on several legs; the covers and pillows were mauve. Jeannette placed Lulu on the floor, and the terrier immediately scuttled beneath the bed.

'That's the best place for you,' Jeannette told her, 'for the next couple of hours.'

She sat at her dressing table, unlocked a drawer, and took out her remote control box. Despite the damage done to the wheelhouse and the instruments, and her initial reaction to it, she still had every intention of escaping, with Hassan if possible, without him if that was the decree of Fate; and this box, together with her hostages, was her principal guarantee of safety. With it she could detonate any of the explosive charges from up to twenty miles away. She could utterly destroy Guernsey's infrastructure.

But she reckoned the threat would be sufficient. She arranged the settings.

Al-Rakim's bullets shattered the 727 windscreen and tore into the flight deck. Mallon died instantly, struck in the head. The aircraft immediately slewed sideways. The co-pilot grabbed the wheel but was too late to prevent the plane from performing an almost complete circle before coming to a halt. That probably saved his life, as the rest of al-Rakim's bullets tore through the fuselage.

The SAS men were thrown about, even in their belts; but they were trained for such emergencies.

'Out and attack,' Gracey shouted, as the doors opened.

The men leapt from the aircraft, immediately spreading out, smothering the airport buildings and more especially the control tower with bullets . . . but as they did so, the tower exploded.

Sophie saw the concrete wall of the pierheads looming in front of her; she was some fifteen feet below the surface, moving easily, but still very aware of the turbulence just over her head. This was to the good, as it made her presence impossible to discern from above the water.

Immediately before her, Shane's flippers moved to and fro as he approached the harbour entrance. This was the first tricky bit, as the water between the pierheads was almost calm; but still there was no alarm from above them – that they could hear, anyway. Keeping on the bottom now, they moved across the sandy bed and towards the hydrofoil berth, slipping beneath it and into the mass of piles holding up the

RoRo dock. Here Shane jerked his thumb, and they broke the surface, in some ten feet of water.

From their position they could see the Cambridge Dock across the next arm of the harbour. The eastern berth was vacant – it was very seldom used except as an embarking or disembarking position – but beyond it, on the west side, they could see the yacht, sitting on the bottom, her superstructure rising above the warehouses on the dock itself.

'OK,' Shane said. 'Now, you carry the bag and stay close by me. We may have to break surface again, but hopefully that won't be until we're actually beneath the yacht and out of sight of anyone on deck. Right?'

'Right,' she said. 'What the . . . ?'

There was a frightening explosion of sound from the Cambridge Dock. From their position they couldn't make out what was happening, but in addition to shouts and screams there came the deeper boom of a heavy-calibre weapon.

'Christalmighty!' Shane said. 'Someone's attacking the yacht.'

'But . . .' Sophie stared in horror as, through the piles, she saw a body suddenly splash into the water between the yacht and the dock, followed immediately by another. 'That's James!'

She threw herself forward, swimming on the surface between the piles.

'Hey,' Shane said. 'Come back here. Hey . . .'

But she was gone, dipping below the surface as she reached the relatively open water between the two docks.

'Fucking women,' Shane muttered. She was going to get herself killed. While he . . . He put the bag back on his shoulder. He'd have to do the job by himself.

Sophie swam across the open water and into the second set of piles, only realising how shallow it was when her knees struck sand. She could only think, James! Falling from the dock. He had to have been hit. Oh, James . . .

Her head rose above the water, and she looked left and

227

right, saw nothing save a floating body close to the yacht's hull. Heart pounding, she waded towards it, hampered now by her flippers.

'Sophie!'

She turned sharply, saw James clinging to one of the pillars.

'My God! James! Are you hurt?'

She splashed towards him.

'I've twisted my ankle, I think. Nothing more.' He held her in his arms, squeezing water from her wetsuit as she was doing from his shirt.

'But what happened?'

'That lunatic Harding tried to take on the ship. God knows what's happened to them up there. I fell when the gangway collapsed. I think Tom Lowndes has had it. That's his body over there.'

Sophie shuddered.

'Where's Shane?' James asked.

'Behind me.' Sophie looked over her shoulder, but couldn't see him. 'He *was* behind me. James, what are we going to do?'

'Get out of here for a start. Back towards the deeper water.'

'But Shane . . .'

They were checked by another deep explosion from above them.

'What are they using?' Sophie gasped.

'Some kind of mini-cannon. Hell. Come on.'

He grasped her arm, and was checked again, this time by a pistol shot; the bullet smashed into the concrete pile above his head. This was immediately followed by another.

'You stop there,' Salim shouted.

James and Sophie turned, to see the two men wading towards them; both carried pistols.

'Shit,' Sophie muttered.

The men came closer, and Salim levelled his gun at James.

'No!' Sophie screamed, throwing her arms round him.

Yazid made a remark in Arabic, and Salim lowered his gun.

'Where is your suit?' he demanded.

'He's hasn't got one,' Sophie said, desperately. 'He fell off the dock. He wasn't in the water with me.'

Again the men exchanged remarks in Arabic. Then Salim gestured with his gun. 'You go,' he said, pointing at the bow of the yacht.

Sophie glanced at James.

'I don't think we have any choice,' James muttered.

From above their heads there came two more explosions, and more shouts.

Sophie and James waded to the bow of the yacht, their captors immediately behind them. On the port side they saw a rope ladder hanging down from the deck, some twenty feet above their heads.

'You go up,' Salim said.

Sophie stooped to reach below the surface, and he levelled his gun.

'I'm taking off my flippers,' she said. 'I can't climb the ladder in them.'

He lowered the weapon again, and Sophie cast a hasty glance along the length of the hull. But the ladder was well forward, and she could not see more than halfway – which was just as well, she supposed: if she couldn't see Shane, then nor could the two Arabs, who didn't even know he was there.

Supposing he *was* there, and hadn't just abandoned the whole thing.

She tugged off her flippers and climbed the swaying ladder; heads peered down on her from the deck, and when she swung her leg over the rail she found herself in the midst of several crewmen. She had no idea what to say, or what expression to assume, so she turned away from them, both to look down at James, climbing behind her, slowly because of his injured ankle, and then across the inner harbour at St Peter Port.

The rain had stopped, and there was some blue sky, although the wind remained strong and gusting. There were a lot of people over there, gathered against the shops on the far side of the esplanade, or in a large group on the pier above the visitors' marina. They were staring, and shouting at each other, but they were making no move towards the yacht. How could they? she asked herself, when they were unarmed, and when . . . she smelt smoke, and gaped at the warehouses and cafés on the Cambridge Dock as James joined her and their captors pushed them round to the starboard side of the ship. These buildings were on fire, where they had not been torn apart by the shells from the bazooka. There was no sign of life, but there were three bodies sprawled on the dock itself.

'Oh, my God,' she muttered.

'Your friend Harding,' James said.

Not my friend, she wanted to reply. But there was no means of telling if Harding was one of the bodies.

'Up,' Salim said.

Sophie climbed the ladder to the bridge, again checking in consternation as she saw the burned-out destruction in the wheelhouse.

'Oh, the ship is still seaworthy,' Jeannette said, having returned from below. 'Captain Honeylee will have to use old-fashioned navigational methods, such as his sextant, that is all. So, you are the little bitch who has been causing us so much trouble.'

Sophie found she was shivering, and hated herself for it; it wasn't fear so much as sheer cold, as the breeze cut into her soaking wetsuit.

'And Mr Candish,' Jeannette went on. 'You really have been a nuisance.'

'Do you really think you are going to get away with this?' James asked.

'Of course. There.'

Jeannette pointed, and they saw the first bus returning; it was just rounding the memorial, and instead of using the one-way system was coming up the southern arm of the White Rock. People had been shouting at it, but the driver of the bus had ignored them. Now it stopped, and a score of armed men got out, pushing before them their prisoners. Sophie gulped as she made out the Bailiff and Lady Martel, and Sir James and Lady Earnestly, followed by the Chief of Police. All were still in dressing gowns over their nightclothes, and wore slippers; they looked both dishevelled and exhausted by their ordeal.

'Our way out,' Jeannette said. 'We will leave on the next tide. Do you know, I think we will take you with us as well, to amuse me. But first, there are one or two things I wish you to tell me.' She smiled at Sophie.

Al-Rakim and his people crammed themselves into the hire car and drove out of the airport at full speed. Behind them the terminal buildings blazed merrily. People were running out of their houses on the Forest Road to see what was happening; none paid any attention to the speeding hire car, although the traffic controllers were running along the road shouting warnings.

'Where are we going?' someone gasped.

'We are going to the yacht,' al-Rakim said, and gave a grim smile. 'There we fight to the last, eh?'

Gracey's men instinctively went to ground when they saw the airport buildings exploding, sprawling on the grass and tarmac with their weapons levelled.

'Hold your fire,' the Colonel said, and levelled his binoculars. As far as he could make out through the smoke and flames, only a couple of hundred yards away, there was no one alive in there; but the mission had gone catastrophically wrong . . . because of that message Sheikh Hassan had managed to send.

Sheikh Hassan! He looked over his shoulder, at the 727

sitting motionless on the grass verge beside the taxi-way. He couldn't see the co-pilot.

'Shit!' he muttered. 'Captain Lewis.'

'Sir!'

'Hold your position here for a moment.' He got up and ran back to the aircraft. The steps had not been lowered, and he had to swing himself up into the cabin, which was empty. He ran forward to the flight deck. Mallon lay back in his seat, his head a mass of blood. The co-pilot lay on his face, blood trickling away from the stab wound in his chest; and the radio operator, the only other member of the skeleton crew, was slumped in his chair, at least unconscious from a savage blow to the head.

'Shit!' Gracey commented. It had just not occurred to him that such a mild-mannered man as the sheikh was capable of such violence – he had forgotten that the man was a dedicated terrorist – but equally it had not occurred to him that the two men he had left on the aircraft would not be able to deal with him. And where the hell had he got that knife?

He stood in the doorway and looked out over the airport. The runway was situated on a hill, and to the north the land fell away; the fence on that side was actually out of sight from his position. The sheikh was obviously somewhere over there, but it was impossible to be certain where; and once he got over the fence, he would very rapidly be in a built-up area.

He blew his whistle, and a sergeant got up and came back to him.

'The fucking sheikh has got away,' Gracey told him. 'He's on foot, at the moment, but he may be armed with a knife. Take ten men and go after him. We want him alive, mind. But we want him.'

'Yes, sir.' The sergeant hurried off.

Gracey returned inside the aircraft, moved the radio operator's body – he was definitely dead, from the head wound; Rakim's bullets had not reached this far back – and called Heathrow. 'Is the PM still there?'

'No, Colonel, the Prime Minister is on his way back to Downing Street.'

'Then who *is* there?'

'I am here, Colonel Gracey,' the Home Secretary said. 'Is everything under control?'

'No, sir. Nothing is under control. The terrorists got word we were coming, sir. They have blown the airport terminus and withdrawn.'

'Great God Almighty! Withdrawn where?'

'I imagine to the harbour and the yacht. There is nowhere else they can go.'

'But that means . . .'

'Yes,' Gracey said. 'They will almost certainly now begin their programme of executions and demolitions.'

'Shit!' the Home Secretary said.

'I have also to report, sir, that Sheikh Hassan has escaped.'

'Oh, my God,' the Home Secretary groaned. 'Keep going, Colonel. How much more bad news do you have?'

'That's it, at the moment. I anticipate being able to recapture the sheikh, very shortly. But as regards the overall situation, I'm afraid it is now a case of going in, as hard and as fast as we can.'

'But . . . collateral damage . . .'

'We will avoid it where we can, sir; but it needs to be done. May I suggest that the Navy vessels north of Alderney are instructed to make for St Peter Port Harbour as quickly as possible. They should enter the harbour and storm the yacht – if we have not already done so.'

'Yes,' the Home Secretary said. 'Yes. Do you need additional ground support?'

'No, sir. I have sufficient men for the job.'

'Well, what about aircraft? We could send over a Harrier, which could destroy that yacht with a single bomb.'

'And the hostages?'

'You think they're on board?'

'If they are not, they will be very shortly.'

'But if they're going to be executed anyway . . .'

'I think, if we act promptly enough, we may be able to save some of their lives, anyway,' Gracey said. 'I must go now, sir.'

'Well,' the Home Secretary said, uncertainly. 'Good luck.'

Gracey jumped down from the aircraft and ran back to his men.

'Is it true the sheikh has escaped?' Lewis asked

'We'll get him back, or pick him up when he tries to reach the yacht. Let's go. We need to be at the harbour in ten minutes.'

'How do we get there?'

Gracey pointed. At the back of the airport there was a hire car garage. 'We requisition.'

'Will there be anyone there on a Sunday morning with the airport closed?'

'Like I said,' Gracey told him. 'We requisition.'

'Now,' Jeannette said, 'tell me what you were trying to do, underwater.'

'We were trying to get on board,' Sophie said.

'Oh, really? With what in mind?'

'I'm not going to tell you that,' Sophie said.

The two women gazed at each other.

'Do you really think you can defy me?' Jeannette asked.

'Try me,' Sophie told her.

Jeannette smiled. 'I shall do that.' She turned to James. 'Do you know what she was trying to do?'

James licked his lips. 'Sophie . . .'

'He doesn't know,' Sophie said. 'We didn't tell him.'

'We? So there was someone else,' Jeannette remarked. 'Well, no matter. Put her in that chair,' she told Salim.

James stepped forward, and was brought up by Jeannette's pistol. 'I have no reason not to kill you,' she said.

'Please don't do anything stupid, James,' Sophie said.

She made no effort to resist Salim as he pushed her into the steering chair.

'Now take off the wetsuit top,' Jeannette commanded.

'I can do it,' Sophie said, and tugged the top down to her waist. She wore only the borrowed bathing suit underneath.

'Now, tie her to the chair,' Jeannette commanded.

'Sophie,' James begged.

'Please, James.' She managed a quick glance at her watch. It was ten to twelve. Only twenty minutes!

Salim had produced a length of line from a locker and this he now passed several times round her waist before securing it behind the chair. This pinned her arms to her sides.

'Now,' Jeannette said. 'Yusuf, give me that soldering iron.'

Sophie drew a deep breath.

Honeylee came in from the wing. 'Al-Rakim is back.' He blinked at Sophie.

Jeannette turned to watch al-Rakim's hire car pull on to the dock. As she did so, one of the mobiles buzzed. Salim answered it. 'It is the watch house. They have spotted a man in the water by the hydrofoil dock. Do you wish him shot?'

'Ah,' Jeannette said. 'Your accomplice, no doubt, Miss Gallagher. No, do not shoot him. Tell them to make him surrender and bring him up here. Perhaps he will be more co-operative.' She smiled at Sophie. 'But I am still going to burn your tits, you little bitch.'

Sophie's shoulders sagged. If only she could see her watch. There was a clock on the control panel, but that had stopped in the electrical outage following the Very pistol onslaught.

But anyway, she suddenly remembered, she didn't even know if Shane had actually planted his charge.

Rakim hurried up the ladders. As he did so, several more cars raced on to the dock, discharging the remaining twenty-odd of the terrorists. The watching crowd seemed to sway back and forth, but they still lacked any leadership, any understanding that there was anything they could do.

'What happened to the sheikh?' Jeannette demanded. 'Did the plane crash?'

'No. They got it down. There must be a couple of hundred SAS men on board. I do not know what happened to the sheikh. I blew the buildings and left. But I imagine they'll be down here just as fast as they can. I think we have had it.'

'We have not had it,' Jeannette said. 'We still have the ship, and we still have the hostages. I have had them brought aboard for just this situation. Those people will not dare to attack us. Our terms are the same. Once Sheikh Hassan has been delivered to us, we will simply sail away.'

Al-Rakim swallowed, but there was no arguing with this woman's determination. 'What time can we leave?'

'Not for another five hours, apparently,' Jeannette said. 'We will just have to be patient. Salim, fetch the Bailiff and the Governor up. Leave their women for the time being.'

Salim hurried down the ladders.

'Captain,' Jeannette said, 'prepare your gun. Yusuf, leave that radio and organise the men. They are to keep out of sight but be prepared to repel any rush at the ship.

Al-Rakim looked inside the wheelhouse. 'What the shit happened?'

'We were attacked by Very pistols, would you believe? But everything is under control. The lunatics who have done this have been eliminated.'

Al-Rakim was looking at Sophie. 'Miss Gallagher,' he said. 'Why did you come here?' He almost sounded sorry for her.

'That is what I am hoping she is about to tell us,' Jeannette said. She picked up the soldering iron, made sure it was glowing hot. Again James tried to move, but Yazid was standing against his back, a pistol thrust into his ribs.

Sophie drew another deep breath.

'Pull down the bathing suit top, al-Rakim,' Jeannette said.

236

Al-Rakim obeyed. 'Why do you not tell her what she wishes to know?' he asked. 'She will really hurt you, you know.'

'Get stuffed,' Sophie told him.

He stepped away from her, and Jeannette came forward. Sophie could not stop staring at the glowing tip of the soldering iron. She knew she was going to scream and scream and scream.

'I think, the left one first,' Jeannette said, and was distracted by noise from the deck.

'Oh, find out what it is now,' she snapped.

'We have the man from the water,' Abdullah shouted.

'Oh, very good. Bring him up.'

A moment later Shane was pushed into the wheelhouse.

'What the hell . . . ?' he demanded, gazing at Sophie, then at the soldering iron.

'Your little friend has not exactly been co-operating,' Jeannette said. 'You could save her a lot of pain, and some disfigurement, were you to tell me what you two were up to.'

'Ah,' Shane said. 'Well . . .' He had discarded his bag somewhere in the harbour, and there was no way of telling, any more than with Sophie, that he had had anything to do with explosives.

They heard the blaring of horns, and several cars emerged from the bottom of St Julian's Avenue. The crowd on the front had been growing with every moment; now it surged forward as British army uniforms were recognised, and then back again as the cars showed no intention of stopping.

'Shit!' Honeylee growled. 'We are up the creek.'

'No, we are not,' Jeannette told him. 'Fetch the hostages, and a loudhailer.'

The cars stopped at the entrance to the White Rock, and men leapt out, deploying as they did so, seeking any available shelter, automatic weapons thrust forward.

The Bailiff and the Lieutenant Governor were thrust up

237

the steps to the bridge, their hands cuffed behind their backs.

'Out there,' Jeannette pointed, and the two men were pushed on to the bridge wing. A huge sigh went round the watchers on the dock and the esplanade.

Jeannette raised her loudspeaker. 'You know who these gentlemen are,' she shouted at the crouching soldiers. 'If you attempt to storm this ship, they will die, before your eyes. And then their wives. We have other prisoners as well. Also, all our explosive charges are set and can be detonated from this ship. In the meantime, we are still awaiting the delivery of Sheikh Hassan. Deliver the sheikh, do not attempt to attack us, and we will leave on this afternoon's tide. The hostages will be set free the moment we feel it is safe. They will not be harmed unless we are attacked.'

'Bloody cheek. What do you reckon?' Lewis said. 'I think I could drop her from here.' He was a superb marksman.

'Then the hostages will be killed,' Gracey said, 'and Guernsey will be blown apart; I need to call London.' He used his mobile, got the Home Secretary and explained the situation.

'This looks like a stand-off,' the Home Secretary said.

'We can't just let them get away,' Gracey protested.

'For the time being, it looks as if we have to. Have we got the sheikh?'

'Not yet. But we can certainly stop him getting to the ship.'

'And the hostages?'

'It's my estimation that the terrorists are now thinking more of their own skins than the sheikh's. They need the hostages to get out and get away.'

'I hope to God you're right, Gracey; but do nothing unless in your estimation success can be guaranteed, and their demolition charges neutralised. Keep in touch.'

Gracey switched off.

'Do we go in?' Lewis asked, enthusiastically.

Gracey sighed. 'No we do not. We wait.'

Hartwell himself had been flown out to his ships by heli-
copter; he hadn't seen real action since the Gulf, and he
wanted to be in at the death. He stood on the bridge of HMS
Blackwall Tunnel beside a somewhat overawed lieutenant
commander and watched the Little Russel opening before
them.

'Tide?' he asked.

'Just turned. We won't be able to get into where the yacht
is lying.'

'If we can make the outer pier we'll put men shore,' the
Admiral said. 'Have them issued with rifles and bayonets.
And I want one too.'

The lieutenant commander gulped. 'Yes, sir.'

A signals rating appeared at the back of the bridge.
'Message from London, sir.'

'Yes?' Hartwell said.

'Abort your operation and stand by for shadowing, sir.'

'What? Great God in Heaven! Who sent that?'

'The Minister of Defence, sir.'

Hartwell glared at him, then at the lieutenant commander.
Then his shoulders sagged. 'There's been a foul-up. Very
good, Commander. Reduce speed and tell the squadron to
do the same. We'll wait here.'

He went to the radio room to make some calls.

'Well,' Jeannette said, returning into the wheelhouse, leaving
the two Guernsey officials on the bridge wing guarded
by two of her people. 'That seems to take care of that.
Now, you, young man, tell me what you were trying to do
underwater.'

'Not trying, lady,' Shane said. 'I did it. The best thing you
can do is surrender now, while you can.'

'Surrender,' Jeannette said contemptuously. 'We did not
come here to surrender. Do you not know that from my

239

stateroom I can detonate every one of the charges we have laid? I can destroy this entire island. Now tell me what you have done.'

Shane shrugged and looked at his watch. 'On your head be it, lady. Try counting backwards from ten,' he suggested.

Jeannette stared at him, then pointed at Honeylee. 'Get men over the side. Get . . .'

There was a huge explosion. The yacht seemed to jump out of the water before settling again, while from below there came the sound of breaking timbers and a chorus of shouts and shrieks of fear.

'Wowee!' Shane shouted.

'My ship!' Honeylee had almost been knocked over by the movement, while al-Rakim had actually fallen to his hands and knees.

'Bastards!' Jeannette had also lost her balance; now she levelled her pistol. But the blast had also distracted her protectors, and before anyone else could move James came to life. Sophie had been absolutely right when she had said he was still suffering from the after-effects of the drugs pumped into his system. The whole day had had an unreal, nightmarish quality; but being blown off the dock had at least got his brain working, and now he had been forced to watch his girlfriend tortured . . . well, nearly. He gave a roar, clasped both hands together and swung them as hard as he could into the side of Jeannette's head. She gave a little shriek of her own and crashed to the deck, the bullet smashing into the after bulkhead.

Shane was also in action, swinging his arms left and right to scatter the men immediately surrounding him, and in the same movement snatching one of the Minimi rifles from their hands. This he now also swung, catching Honeylee across the head and sending him to the deck.

James had dashed outside to where the two guards were also just recovering, and staring over the side rather than at the hostages. James hit one on the jaw, so hard that the sailor

240

staggered back and struck the rail with such force that he went right over, dropping his rifle as he did so. The second man brought up his weapon, and James shoulder-charged him, sending him also against the rail. He regained his balance, but as he again tried to level his rifle the Lieutenant Governor kicked him in the leg, as hard as he could. He gave a howl and fell to his knees.

'If you knew for how long I have wanted to do that,' the Governor said. 'Can you get these things off us?'

'Not till I find the key,' James said, and waved to the men on the shore, at the same time firing his rifle into the air. 'Come and get us!' he bawled.

The SAS gave a cheer, and rose as one man.

The sailor was just recovering, and James hit him again, laying him out. 'Stay here,' he told the two men. 'I'll get back to you.'

In the wheelhouse, Jeannette was slowly getting to her feet. Honeylee appeared paralysed, completely overcome by the destruction of his yacht. Al-Rakim was still on the deck; Salim had backed against the bulkhead, covered by Shane's rifle.

'Untie the lady,' Shane told him.

Salim obeyed, and Sophie replaced the straps of her bathing suit – she was sweating and shaking – then looked past Shane at the ladder, up which three men were coming, led by Dr Hamath. 'Look out,' she shouted.

Shane turned, and was struck by a bullet fired from the doctor's pistol. He half-turned and cannoned against the bulkhead, which became splattered with blood.

Jeannette used the opportunity to grab her own pistol, turned to face Sophie, who was helpless, as there was no weapon nearby, and was distracted by James, returning from the wing. She fired at him and he fell.

'James!' Sophie screamed, and hurled herself at him. Vaguely she heard the smack of another bullet striking the bulkhead above her head; then she was holding his head.

241

'Damn!' he said.

At least he was alive, but like Shane, who had now fallen to the deck, he was bleeding. Sophie turned to see who was behind her, but both Jeannette and Hamath had disappeared down the ladders. She was consumed with anger, caused both by her treatment and by her two partners having been hit, when it had seemed virtually all over. She didn't know how badly either of them had been wounded, but she did know there was nothing she could so about them, save avenge them.

And stop Jeannette exploding the charges! Because that was obviously where she had gone.

She heard movement behind her, and turned her head to see Salim coming forward; but Shane had retained his rifle, even when slumped against the door, and he shot the mate at close range. Salim collapsed in a huddle.

'Bastard,' Shane muttered. He was close to fainting, but now he turned the rifle on al-Rakim, who gave a shout and hurled himself at the ladder, virtually falling down it to the next deck.

Sophie felt sick, at the sight of Salim's body, but she grabbed her wetsuit top and pressed it against the wound in James's abdomen. 'Please,' she shouted at the Lieutenant Governor, who had come inside, 'help them.'

'I would if my hands were free.'

'Oh . . .' She scrabbled over the floor, found a rifle, got up, holding the weapon in both hands.

'Just what are you doing?' the Governor asked.

'I'll be back,' Sophie told him, and ran to the top of the ladder.

'Stop right there, you little bitch.'

Honeylee had regained his feet and was standing on the deck behind the wheelhouse, brandishing a revolver. Sophie swung round and squeezed the trigger of the Minimi. She had no intention of hitting him – wanted to scare him off. The force of the explosion knocked her backwards, and she had to drop the rifle and grab the rail with both hands to prevent herself falling down the ladder. While she stared at the captain, lying on his back, his chest dissolved into a mass of blood.

'Oh, my God,' she whispered. She, Sophie Gallagher, had just shot a man. No matter that he had had it coming. She had still just taken a life.

'Good shooting,' the Lieutenant Governor said.

There was a whang and a crash, and Sophie realised someone was shooting at *her*.

The Lieutenant Governor ducked. The Bailiff, also still handcuffed, flattened himself against the bulkhead.

Sophie grabbed the rifle again and fired, again with no clear idea of whom she was shooting at.

'Get away!' someone shouted in English, and she stared at the SAS men leaping over the bulwarks, while the terrorists fled every which way.

Sophie scrambled to her feet, and slid down the ladder, still holding the rifle.

Captain Lewis was at the foot. 'Drop that weapon,' he snapped, levelling his revolver.

'I'm on your side,' Sophie told him. 'Look, there are wounded men up there. Get help.'

Lewis looked her up and down, then shouted, 'Medics!'

Several men hurried past them to gain the ladder. Sophie took advantage of their appearance, and Lewis's distraction, to duck past him, and get through the nearest bulkhead door.

'Come back!' he shouted. 'You'll be killed.'

Sophie took great breaths as she discovered she was in a small galley. This was empty, but there was a lot of noise from below her. She ran to the aft door, threw it open, and someone fired at her. She gasped and fell to her knees, while returning fire. The noise of the shots echoed round the ship, and Sophie got up and went through the door into the saloon. This was now empty, and relatively undamaged, apart from some bullet holes in the bulkheads.

Behind her she could hear the SAS men; but in front of her was another door, and she remembered that this led downwards. She ran to it, and was again shouted at from behind her. Lewis had followed her with a dozen of his men. The rest were securing the decks and disarming those of the terrorists who had had the time to surrender.

Sophie opened the inner door, looked down the staircase . . . and at a man looking up. His face was familiar, and in the same instance she had a vision of Sister Morgan falling to the floor of the hospital in a pool of blood.

Harb grinned at her, and raised his rifle. But Sophie fired first, realising that this time she knew what she meant to do. And didn't make it. Her hands were trembling and the bullet took Harb in the shoulder, spinning him round and sending him in a heap down the last few steps.

'Holy Jesus Christ!' Lewis exclaimed. 'Where did you learn to shoot like that?'

'I didn't,' Sophie told him, and went down the stairs.

'OK,' he panted behind her. 'You've done wonders. Now get out and let us professionals take over.'

'There's something I need to do,' she said, and jumped over Harb's groaning body.

'Medics!' Lewis was shouting.

Sophie faced the corridor to the staterooms. Beneath her she could hear timbers groaning and the gurgle of incoming water; the yacht was simply settling around the huge hole in its hull, into which the rising tide was pouring. Indeed, water was flooding up the next ladder from the engine room; but it had not yet reached the stateroom deck, and Jeannette had still to be in there . . . with her box of tricks.

Sophie ran along the corridor, listened to shouts and thumpings on some of the doors, where the women were confined. But she had no time for them now. Then she was faced by two other women, emerging from a further door. They gaped at her, screamed as she waved her rifle, and ducked back into shelter. She reached the door at the end of the corridor. This was locked. Sophie stepped back. She had seen locks shot out in many movies, but had no idea of where exactly she should aim.

'Wait!' Lewis was at her shoulder, and now he had Gracey with him, as well as several of their men.

Lewis levelled his revolver, and fired twice. Wood and metal slivers flew up around them, but the door was open.

They stepped inside, for a moment taken aback by the lavish furnishings. Facing them were al-Rakim and Hamath, and behind them, Jeannette. She held her control box in her hands.

'Goodbye, Guernsey,' she snarled.

'And you,' al-Rakim said, raising his pistol.

There was a vast explosion of sound. Sophie squeezed the trigger on her Minimi and kept squeezing; there were still some twenty bullets left in the magazine. They smashed across the room, shattering everything in their path. Al-Rakim fell to one side, Hamath to the other. Jeannette had ducked behind the ornate bed. Now she stood up again, still holding the control box. But before she could flick the switch, Lewis fired again; his bullet struck the box, shattering it, and continued on its way into Jeannette's body.

She fell backwards against the bulkhead, then slid down it to the deck. Her terrier emerged from beneath the bed to lick her face.

'By heck,' Jack Harding said, emerging from his hiding place behind the destroyed warehouse. 'So we did it after all.'

'We?' Sophie asked coldly, as she was escorted from the ship by the two officers.

'Jack started the whole thing,' Harry Lewis said. 'He's a bally hero.'

'He undertook unauthorised action and got three people killed,' Gracey said.

'Well, a chap had to do what he could,' Harding protested. 'Three? Thank God it was only three. I thought I saw four go down.'

Gracey nodded. 'One of them, James Candish, survived.'

Harding swallowed. 'I tripped,' he said. 'I tripped, or I would have been one of the dead.'

'Well, Mr Harding,' Gracey said, 'fortune always does favour the brave. Doesn't it?'

'That man makes me want to spit,' Sophie said, as she climbed the ladder to the bridge, where the medics were looking after Shane and James.

'The truth of what happened will out,' Gracey assured her. 'It always does. But you, little lady . . .'

'I'm all right,' Sophie said.

She wasn't, she knew. She was still shaking. She found it difficult to believe that only forty-eight hours ago she had been contemplating nothing more important than going to the airport to pick up a group of tourists. She knew she had gone berserk in the stateroom. The images of Sister Morgan and PC Dickinson had kept dancing before her eyes, as had the knowledge that friends like Captain Harrison and Derek Doofield had been gunned down without mercy. Now they were confused with other images: Harb's expression immediately before she had shot him; al-Rakim's face, as he had lain dead beside the doctor; and Jeannette, being mourned by her dog. At least Honeylee's body had been removed. But James . . .

He was sitting up, swathed in bandages.

'Oh, James!' She knelt beside him.

'It's back to the hospital, I'm afraid.'

Helen had been allowed on board, and she was kneeling beside a similarly bandaged Shane. 'I'll look after him,' she promised.

'Who actually fixed the charges that blew up the ship?' Gracey asked, busily releasing the Lieutenant Governor and the Bailiff.

'He did,' Sophie said.

'I think we'll have to get him some kind of medal,' Sir James said. 'And you, Miss Gallagher.'

'And one for markmanship,' Lewis suggested.

'I don't ever want to see or touch a gun again, as long as I live,' Sophie said.

Ambulances had arrived, and Shane and James were placed on stretchers to be carried down. By now, the shooting over, the crowd had flooded forward to line the dock and the street and watch the wounded and dead being carried out. Sophie and Helen stayed with the SAS officers; they would go up to the hospital later on.

Jack Harding was escorted away by cheering supporters.

'Don't say it,' Gracey recommended. 'Ah, who have we here? Where did you find him, Sergeant?'

'Lurking about a housing estate about a mile from the airport.'

Sheikh Hassan, as always, looked perfectly spruce, if a little hot. He gazed at the yacht, sitting on the bottom, while the tide rose about her – her once immaculate decks and superstructure spattered with bullet holes, her wheelhouse still a blackened wreck.

'Such a beautiful ship. My brother will be most unhappy.'

'One of these fine days we're hoping to make him more unhappy yet,' Gracey told him, and listened to the chirp of sirens as Rear Admiral Hartwell's little squadron entered the harbour. 'You'll have a berth on one of those, going back.'

'I would like to see Jeannette.'

Gracey nodded. 'I think that can be arranged; but you won't like what you see. Take him on board, Sergeant.'

Hassan was led away.

'You mean,' Sophie said, 'that that inoffensive little man was responsible for all this?'

'That inoffensive little man is a cold-blooded murderer,' Gracey told her. 'But I don't think he's going to be blowing up anyone else for a very long time. Now, ladies, we must go and locate all those charges that didn't go off, and defuse them. Miss Gallagher, we wouldn't have won without you and your friends. We'll be in touch.'

'I think,' Helen said. 'We could both do with a drink before I go back on duty.'

'That's a brilliant idea,' said Peter Smith, emerging from the crowd. 'I'll buy, and you can give me the scoop of my life.'